NEGLECTED CONSEQUENCES

BY

L. ANN

NEGLECTED CONSEQUENCES

Copyright © 2023 by L. Ann.

All rights reserved.

No part of this book may be used or reproduced in any manner whatsoever without written permission except in the case of brief quotations embodied in critical articles or reviews.

This book is a work of fiction. Names, characters, businesses, organisations, places, events and incidents either are the product of the author's imagination or are used fictitiously. Any resemblance to actual persons, living or dead, events, or locales is entirely coincidental.

Cover design by A.T. Cover Designs

Interior Formatting by Crow Fiction Designs

Edited by Margot Mostert

First Edition: February 2023

ISBN9798372801172

L.Ann Online -

www.lannauthor.com

Dedication

This book is mostly Claire Marta's fault.

To all Forgotten Legacy's followers.

Thank you for coming on this journey with me and for loving my broken rock stars as much as I do.

This one is for you.

If you're a crier, make sure you have tissues to hand.

Warning

Neglected Consequences is not what you could term a "normal" romance story.

Please be aware that this book deals with issues of childhood abuse, adult trauma and PTSD. Please go into it with care.

You absolutely need to have read the other books in the Forgotten Legacy series ,otherwise Neglected Consequences will not make sense. This is NOT a standalone book.

PLAY LIST

What Lovers Do - Maroon 5

Natural - Imagine Dragons

Nightmares - Palaye Royale

Cut Me Up - Friday Pilots Club

Off My Mind - Joe P

999 To The Devil - Call Me Karizma

Outrun Myself - Jack Kays

Monsters - All Time Low

Self Sabotage - Waterparks

Issues - Boy Epic

You're Not Alone - The Broken View

Fork In The Road - Goody Grace

Broken - Palaye Royale

Always Do - The Kid Laroi

The Foundations of Decay - My Chemical Romance

Bad Place - Hunna

Battle Scars - Mod Sun

Mad World - Palaye Royale

All The Small Things - Blink 182

Brother - Gerard Way

Empty - Let Down

Hollow - Belle MT

Hurt - Updog

Why Worry - Set It Off

Sharks - Imagine Dragons

Morbid Mind - Jack Kays
Runaway - Mod Sun
The Devil Doesn't Bargain - Alec Benjamin
Blood - Call Me Karizma
Don't Let The Light Go Out - Panic! At The Disco
I'm Still Here - Boy Epic
What Did I Do? - Hayd
Maybe - Machine Gun Kelly
Sweet Heroine - Yungblud
Where were you? - Girlfriends
Memories - Yungblud
Paranoid - Palaye Royale
I Don't Care - Friday Pilots Club
Have Faith In Me - A Day To Remember
Bois Lie - Avril Lavigne
Play With Fire - Sam Tinnesz
Pretend - Nothing/Nowhere
Chasing Cars - Snow Patrol
Screamager - Therapy?
Level of Concern - Twenty-One Pilots
Better Now - Etham
Ain't No Rest For The Wicked - Cage The Elephant
Teenagers - My Chemical Romance
Original Me - Yungblud & Dan Reynolds
The Hype - Twenty-One Pilots
Sex & Candy - Marcy Playground

Heroin - Badflower

Loverboy - You Me At Six

This Is Gospel - Panic! At The Disco

No More - Huddy

I'm Not Okay (I Promise) - My Chemical Romance

House of Memories - Panic! At The Disco

Memories - Maroon 5

Forgive - Trevor Hall

Animal - Badflower

WHAT LOVERS DO - MAROON 5

Gabe

Remy moved ahead of me, out of the car and across the drive to the main door of the house.

"You know you didn't have to come in with me, right?" I said. "I'm more than capable of carrying my suitcase."

My bodyguard cast a look at me that spoke volumes. "Do you think you're hiding how much pain you're in right now?"

"I don't know what you're talking about. I'm fine."

I *wasn't*. My leg was killing me—agony licked like fire along my thigh and hip. And why? Because I overdid it during the final gig in the US leg of the tour last night. Overconfidence at the speed of my recovery from the accident nine months ago drove me to ignore the signs of *impending doom*, and I backflipped off the stage. The pain when I landed almost made me pass out. Key word being *almost*. I pushed through it and finished the set without a single dropped note or outward sign of the agony I was in. The second we finished the encore, I claimed exhaustion and slunk back to the hotel room, hoping no one noticed the slight limp or the way I was favoring my leg.

I thought I got away with it—none of the band mentioned it, not even Seth and his sharp awareness of everything about me. After an unsurprising sleepless night, we boarded the flight back to L.A., and I added overwhelming exhaustion to the pain. All I wanted to do was crawl into my bed and not move for a month. I wanted to sleep, but Harper wasn't due to come home for another two days. She'd left partway through the last week of the tour to travel to Chicago and meet some people who were interested in donating to the foundation we were building. Without her beside me, sleep wasn't so easy to come by. Insomnia was a constant companion, regardless of my newly health-conscious lifestyle. I still went days without, even with Harper nearby, but when I *did* sleep with her beside me, I slept well.

Remy unlocked the front door, disrupting my musings, and he stepped inside, placing my suitcase against the wall. "Do you need anything else?"

"No, I'm good. Thanks, man." I walked past, patting his shoulder as I went. "Now go *home*."

"As soon as I do a quick walk around and make sure there are no monsters lying in wait for you."

"*Remy!*"

He chuckled and stepped back through the door. "Don't forget to set the alarm," he instructed and I nodded, covering my mouth as I yawned and leaned against the doorframe and watched him go.

Once the car lights disappeared down the drive, I straightened and moved deeper into the house, savoring the silence and stillness. I'd spent the last three months living on a tour bus, surrounded by the band, noise, and activity almost twenty-four-seven, with occasional snatched moments of privacy with Harper. Coming home to the calm of my personal space was like a balm to my tired soul. The only thing that would make it perfect would be when my lavender-haired soulmate returned.

I rubbed my thigh absently and headed to the bedroom. A shower to freshen up after the flight, and then bed. The door to the bedroom was open, and I was searching for the light switch when I heard it. A faint soft sigh.

I frowned.

Was someone in here?

The last time I found someone in my bedroom without invitation, I'd been held at knifepoint and a crazy fan tried to get me to make a baby with her.

With cautious movements, I plucked my cell from my pocket and searched out the flashlight app, tapped the icon and let the light flood the room. The concern of finding some crazy stalker in my bed eased when I spotted bright lavender hair spilling across one pillow.

Harper.

She must have come home early. On silent feet, I padded across the carpet and looked down at the sleeping woman sprawled across the center of the bed. My heart thudded, loud in my ears, the way it always did when I saw her, and I caught myself before my hand touched her cheek.

Shower, I told myself firmly. She wouldn't appreciate me crawling into bed with the stink of nine hours travel on me. I forced myself to turn away from the temptation waiting for me beneath the sheets and exited the bedroom.

I didn't stay under the spray of the shower for long, taking just enough time to wash away the smell and dust from travel, but it was still too long for my leg. But I felt more like myself, apart from my thigh, which was throbbing, when I stepped out of the bathroom, a towel wrapped around my hips. Tired, sore, but mostly human. I definitely *smelled* better. Returning to the bedroom, I dropped the towel and eased beneath the sheets, careful not to wake Harper.

The second I lay down, she murmured something, and I froze. She rolled to face me, and came to rest against my side.

"Oh!" Her gasp was loud in the silence of the room. "Why are you so cold?" Her voice was a sleepy drawl, and I wasn't certain she was awake.

"Took a shower. Sorry. Go back to sleep." I shifted slightly so I could wrap an arm around her waist and pulled her closer to me.

Her hand slid over my chest, and her face nuzzled into the crook of my neck. "I'm glad you're home." The words ended in a quiet yawn, and seconds later, her breathing eased out again.

I chuckled softly, turned my head, and buried my face in her hair. The scent of cotton candy swept over me, and the residual bit of tension holding me tense seeped away from my body.

I was home.

My eyes closed, and I let sleep pull me under.

***

Consciousness returned slowly, bringing with it a slice of heaven I thanked the universe daily for giving back to me. I lay still, losing myself in the feel of Harper's tongue licking its way over the tattoos covering my chest, down my ribs and lower, until her warm breath fanned over my hip.

"I know you're awake." Her voice was an amused whisper. "Your breathing changed." She ran her tongue along my dick—which had clearly woken up long before the rest of me.

My fingers clenched into the sheets, gripping the cotton so I didn't reach for her head and take control. I fucking *loved* it when Harper decided she wanted me, when *she* started something instead of waiting for me to make the first move. But I knew if I displayed any sign that I wanted to call the shots, she'd let me. It wasn't that she was particularly submissive. She just wasn't forward with her own desires ... not the way I was.

Her fingers curled around my dick and gave one slow pump. I groaned. She laughed, repeated the action, and ignored the way my hips jerked involuntarily in an attempt to get her to speed up.

"Gabe?"

"Hmm?" Words were outside of my skill set currently.

She gave my dick a gentle squeeze, then flicked her tongue

over the tip. "Was there ever a time you thought we would never get back together?"

I forced myself to lift my head from the pillow and peered down my body to where she was lying between my legs.

"Why do you ask?"

"I don't know. I was thinking about it when I woke up. How if I'd left work early or not been on a shift that night, you might have been seen and left before I got there."

I thought back to the night she came back into my life. "Maybe," I admitted. "For a little while, anyway."

She ran her tongue down the length of my dick. "I love you."

"Always and forever, Frosty."

Her lips parted, and she sucked me into her mouth. My head fell back against the pillows. *"Fuuuck!"*

She chuckled around my dick, and the vibration caused my eyes to roll back. Her mouth was how I imagined heaven would. My nerves tightened, the blood rushing through my veins like molten lava, heating every inch of my skin. I wrapped a hand in her hair and gave a gentle tug.

"Come up here."

She crawled up my body, her legs settling on either side of my hips, and smiled down at me. My fingers caught the hem of her t-shirt, and I laughed quietly.

"As much as I enjoy seeing you in Forgotten Legacy merch, I love what it's hiding more. Lose the shirt, Frosty."

She didn't even hesitate, pulling it over her head, then

tossing it aside. I twisted and pinned her beneath me before it hit the carpet. Her legs lifted, wrapped around my waist, and I didn't even hesitate. I reached between us, gripped my dick and buried it inside her. She was slick with arousal, and I slid in easily. Bracing myself on one hand, I used the other to run my knuckles down her cheek. Her eyes met mine, and I held her gaze as I rolled my hips, driving myself deeper into her body.

"I think if you'd stayed away and not come back for Siobhan's birthday party, it might have taken longer for us to get to the same place," I said. My lips skated over her throat, along her shoulder, as I thrust slowly in and out. "But, eventually, we'd have ended up in the same room." I found her nipple and licked a circle around it. "You're my other half, my *soulmate*. That can't be ignored. We'd have found a way."

"Do you really believe that?" Her fingers ran down my spine, her nails dug into my ass, and she urged me closer, *deeper*.

"With every fiber of my being, Frosty," I whispered. "A world doesn't exist where we wouldn't end up together."

***

I must have slept again, because when I next woke up, the room was dark and Harper's side of the bed was empty and cold. I rolled over onto my stomach, not quite ready to let go of sleep, and closed my eyes. Only to open them again when I heard a voice that *wasn't* Harper's talking outside the bedroom.

Stretching out an arm, I groped on the nightstand for my cell and squinted at the display. Fuck. Eleven in the morning. I'd slept for a solid six hours, not including the brief interlude when Harper woke me up. I dropped my cell onto the mattress and sat up, swung my legs out and stood. I tested my weight on my leg, and when it didn't give out, I took a cautious step forward.

So far, so good.

There was a pair of gray sweatpants draped over a chair in one corner of the room, so I pulled them on and then walked out. The house we'd bought was one-story. It had been an unspoken agreement when we started looking for somewhere to replace the penthouse I owned. Beyond the door, there was a short hallway, with two bedrooms, not including the one we'd chosen for ours, leading off it. It broke off in two directions just beyond the bathroom. One side led to my studio, the other to the main part of the house, where there was a living room, kitchen, and dining room.

Seth was standing at the junction of the hallway, speaking to someone on his cell. I walked past him and found Harper in the kitchen, leaning against the breakfast bar, looking tempting with her lavender hair in a messy ponytail, and dressed in my old Nirvana t-shirt. It barely covered her ass so I moved up behind her, ran my palm up her thigh, and pressed my dick against her.

"Morning, gorgeous," I dropped a kiss against the curve of her neck. "Why is your ass on show?" I slid my fingers beneath the top and over her stomach so I could cup one breast and squeeze.

"It's not. I'm wearing shorts."

"No bra, though." I pinched her nipple.

"Don't do that when we have company." She slipped out of my arms.

"It's only Seth."

"*Only* Seth?" The man in question queried, pocketing his cell as he entered the room. "I thought I was your ride-or-die?"

"Ahhh." I moved across the kitchen to meet him, hooked an arm around his neck, and pulled him into a hug. "But you won't let me ride you, Hawkins." I kissed his cheek. He pushed me away.

"No press here to see your antics, asshole."

I shrugged, laughed, and walked over to the coffee machine. "I *enjoy* kissing you. It's one of the highlights of my day." I studied the options, pushed a button and watched the machine do its thing. "Why are you here, anyway?"

"Karl's been trying to get hold of you. He said you weren't answering your cell, so I came to make sure you weren't dead or something."

"It was definitely *something*." I took the mug from the machine and lifted it to my lips, smirking at Harper who, predictably, was bright red. "What does he want?"

"Didn't say. Just that he needed you to go to NFG as soon as I could get you there."

"Why didn't he call Remy?"

"I didn't ask. I'm just playing errand boy. So go and get some clothes on. I have shit to do today."

I took another mouthful of coffee, dragged a hand through my hair, and yawned. "I'm tired. I wanted to stay home today. I'll call him. Surely it'll keep until Monday."

"You'll get your fucking ass down to my car and do as you're told. I'm supposed to be taking Riley out for lunch, not babysitting you."

"Well," I pursed my lips. "*You* went from best friend to daddy in zero to sixty."

He glared at me. "What the fuck is wrong with you?"

"Nothing, my love." I batted my eyelashes at him. "I'll get dressed. We don't want you having an aneurysm." I set down the mug and walked out, blowing him a kiss as I passed.

Neglected Consequences

NATURAL - IMAGINE DRAGONS

Gabe

"Where's Carter?" I asked when we walked out of the house, and I found Seth's car parked at an angle in the driveway.

"Left him to hurry Riley up."

I snickered. "You didn't tell him you were coming here, did you?"

One side of Seth's mouth curled up. "Of course I didn't."

"So we're going out without adult supervision? That's exciting. How long has it been?"

"It'll be longer if you don't stop talking and get in the fucking car before Remy sees us."

"Wow, you *really* are in full-on daddy mode right now. Has Riley unlocked a new kink?"

He didn't respond to that, striding around the car and climbing into the driver's seat. I hopped in beside him, yawning. "When are you going to buy a new car?"

"I don't need one. This is fine."

"This is *my* old car, from nine years ago."

"And there's nothing wrong with it."

"Do you need money? I can loan you a dollar." I rested my head against the seat and closed my eyes. "Fuck, I'm tired. I hope whatever Karl wants doesn't take long." I cracked open one eye. "Do *you* know what he wants?"

"No. He said it was important he spoke to you today, though." He glanced at me as he pulled onto the main road. "Have you done anything stupid other than almost setting back your recovery when you backflipped off the stage?"

I grunted. "You saw that, huh?"

"Of course I did. The doctors said it could take up to a year to heal completely. Stop taking fucking risks."

"Sorry, *daddy*." I yawned again. "Can we stop somewhere and get coffee?"

"You remember that part where he wants you there as soon as possible?"

"Yeah, but *coffee,* Seth." I added a whine to my voice, which I knew would annoy the fuck out of him.

He blew out an irritated breath. "Fine."

"Thanks, *daddy*."

His glare was just as irritated as the sigh. "Will you stop saying that?"

"Why?"

"Someone ran an article last week about the age difference between me and Riley. They said it's because she must have daddy issues."

I snorted. "There's only ten years between you, not fifty. You're not old enough to be her dad." I straightened in my seat. "What did Riley say about it?"

Seth laughed. "It's Riley. She doesn't give a fuck."

"Then why are you complaining about it?"

"I just hoped the bullshit would settle down once she turned twenty-one."

"Don't worry about it. They'll find something more interesting to talk about soon, and then they'll forget all about your age difference." I grabbed the door handle. "Oh look, stop! Coffee shop!" I jabbed at the window. "Stop the car."

"Really?"

"Yes, really! The coffee at NFG is shit. Find somewhere to park. I'll run in and grab coffee …" I licked my lips. "And donuts. I'll be fast."

***

I'll be fast—famous last words. Neither of us had a bodyguard with us, and our ball cap superpowers clearly weren't powered up enough to disguise us well. Someone spotted us the instant we stepped foot inside the coffee shop.

Seth slanted an *'I told you so'* look when three girls overturned their chairs in their haste to reach us. I patted his shoulder, and stepped forward to meet them, accepting the pen and paper thrust in my face with an amiable smile, and kept my body between them and him.

"We can't stop, girls. We're on our way to the record label.

We just need to get coffee. Let me sign that for you first, though." I smiled, the charming rock star firmly in the ascendant, and posed for photographs.

Seth was a little more standoffish, but our fans accepted that. He would sign autographs and pose for the odd photograph, but there were no hugs, and definitely no kisses from him. He distanced himself from them before I did, and ordered our coffees. By the time they were ready, I'd satisfied our fans, and we were able to leave without further interruption.

"And *that* is why we should have gone straight to NFG," Seth said as he pulled back into the traffic.

"It's good press, sweetheart. Keeps the fans loyal." I took a sip of coffee and sighed happily. "All is well in the world, Seth."

His eye roll said everything.

***

"Get your ass in here," Karl bellowed the second we stepped off the elevator.

I traded glances with Seth and crossed the reception area to our manager's office.

"Not you, Seth. You stay out here." Karl pointed to one of the couches, wrapped a hand around my arm, and dragged me inside.

"Karl, what the fuck, man?" I pulled free, and slowed down, masking a wince at the sharp stab of pain that shot through my thigh.

"Close the door and sit down," he barked.

"Why are you yelling at me? I haven't done anything. I flew back from the last gig with the band and went straight home, I swear."

"I know *that*. Sit down!"

I pulled out a chair and sat down, eyeing him. "Is everything okay? You look a little ... *frazzled*."

"How did Seth seem to you?"

I twisted my head to find Seth through the glass walls.

"*Don't* look at him!" Karl snapped.

"Karl, what the fuck is wrong with you? Seth ... is Seth." I shrugged.

Our manager sighed and rounded his desk. "I need to show you something. Close the blinds."

I frowned, but did as he said. Karl could be highly strung, especially with the shit we'd put him through over the years, but this seemed like a whole new level. "What's going on? You're worrying me now."

"There's an article running in tomorrow's Inquisitor. Someone I know there gave me a heads up."

I turned to face our manager. "I swear, Karl, I haven't done anything."

He shook his head. "It's not about you. Come and sit down."

"If it's not about me, then why have you dragged me in here? It's *always* fucking me."

"Not this time." He pulled open a drawer and took out a sheet of paper. Looking down at it, he pursed his lips.

"Karl?" I wasn't joking. He really was worrying me. "How bad is it?"

"Bad." He handed the paper to me. "Sit down and read it."

I stared at him for a second longer, then dropped my eyes to read the article.

"Oh, fuck."

Neglected Consequences

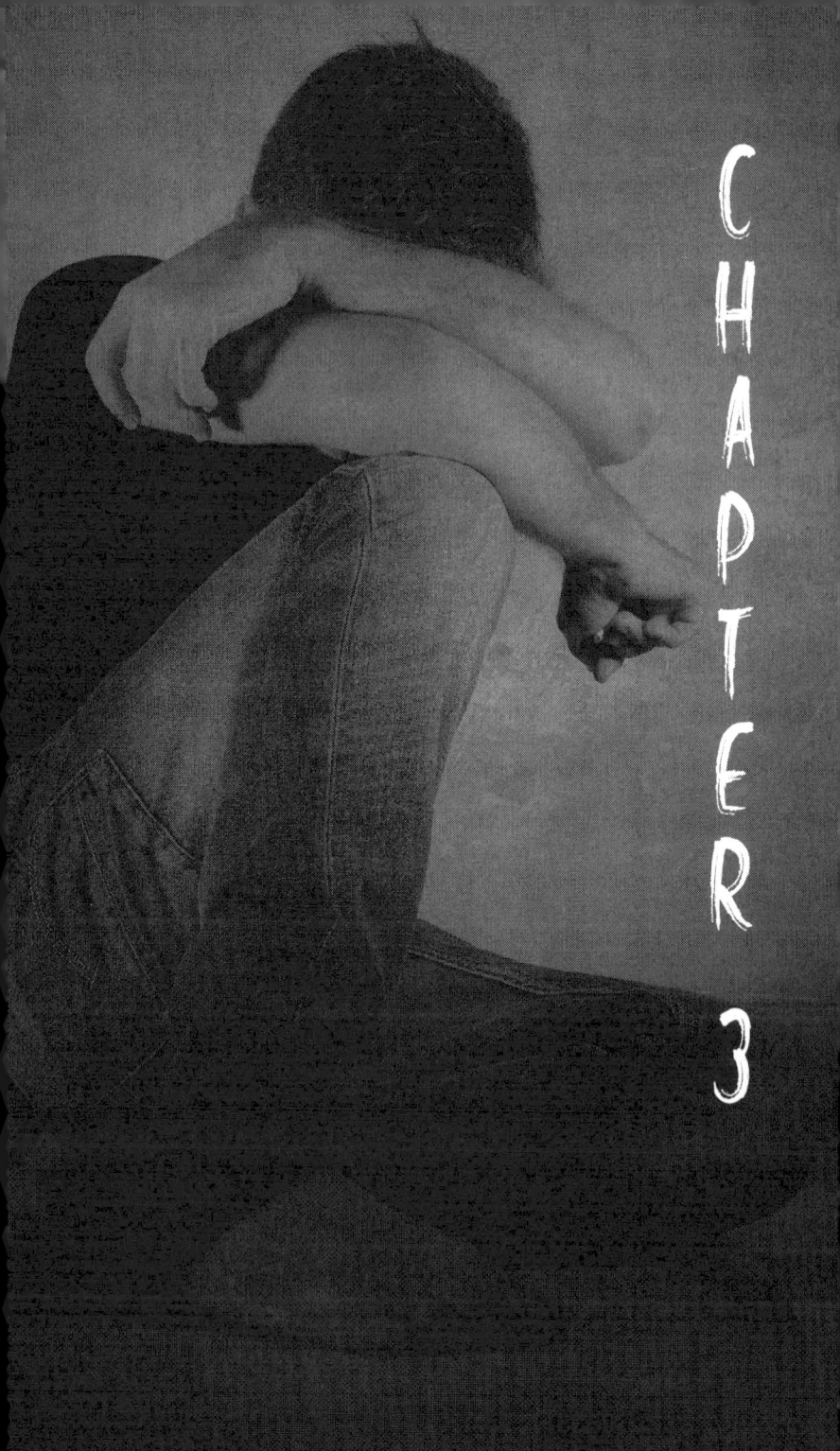

NIGHTMARES - PALAYE ROYALE

Seth

I checked the wall clock for the hundredth time. It was typical that the first chance I got to spend the afternoon with Riley since we started touring, without having to cut it short for something band-related in months and fucking Gabe gets summoned. Just once… *just once*… I'd have liked to go a couple of weeks without some drama or other happening around him. Was that too much to ask?

If it wasn't his antics when he was single, he was causing sensational headlines from being caught fucking Harper outside a stadium on the hood of a car, or crawling out from under a table at a restaurant licking his lips. Those were *normal* things though. Nothing that required a visit to NFG to explain. So what the fuck had he done this time? And how bad was it that Karl wanted to talk to him without me in the room?

Harper was going to lose her shit … *again*. How many times did he have to fuck up before he realized there was a limit to the amount of bullshit she'd swallow from his behavior?

I stood, seriously thinking about leaving Gabe to deal with his shit alone, when the elevator dinged and Carter and Remy stepped out. I sighed. *Busted.*

"Where's Riley?" I asked when she didn't follow them out.

Carter's head swung toward me, and something flickered across his face, gone before I could decipher it. "She's still at home."

"I thought I told you to hurry her along so we can make our reservation?"

"Is Gabe with Karl?" Remy asked before Carter could answer me.

"He's been in there for almost an hour. What did he do this time, Remy?"

Gabe's bodyguard looked at me. He had an almost-identical look on his face to Carter. "This isn't about him."

I frowned, nerves tightening and my stomach tensing. "Then why are we here?"

Remy's eyes lifted to look over my shoulder seconds before Gabe spoke my name.

"Seth." His voice was low and urgent. "Come in here."

I turned in a slow circle and found Gabe standing in the doorway of Karl's office, with Karl behind him.

"What's going on, Mercer?"

"Just come in here." The note in his voice raised the hairs on the back of my neck.

"Gabe—"

"For fuck's sake, Seth. Just fucking come in here, will you?

Do you have to fucking argue with me about it?"

For once, Karl didn't say a word about him snarling at me.

"This better be fucking good," I snapped and stalked into the room.

"Call me when you're done." Karl stepped out, closing the door gently behind him.

My frown deepened. "And where the fuck is *he* going?"

Gabe blew out a breath and rubbed a hand against the back of his neck. "He thought it might be better if it's just me and you."

I waited for him to explain. When he said nothing else, I scowled at him. "Well, spit it out."

"It's… You're going to want to sit down."

"What is it? Another baby claim? Someone coming out of the woodwork selling bullshit stories? Did you get married to a starlet last time we were in Las Vegas and forget it happened?"

A metallic click pulled my gaze down. Gabe's lighter was in his hand, his thumb flicking it open and closed. A chill slithered down my spine.

"Fuck, tell me you *didn't* get married to someone?" The irritation left my voice, leaving concern behind. "Gabe, what's going on?"

"You're kinda right about something coming out of the woodwork." He raked a hand through his hair. "Fuck, I don't know how to soften this, man. The Inquisitor is running some kind of exposé tomorrow. Karl has tried to muffle it, but…" He gave a helpless shrug. "He hasn't been able to."

"What *kind* of exposé?"

Gabe's eyes looked past me, and he swallowed. "Someone uncovered details about your past."

"My ... *past? What story?*"

"About your dad."

"My *dad?*" I'd only spoken to my dad this morning. "What details?"

"*Not* Jake. Your ... fuck." He rubbed a hand down his face. "Seth, someone has talked about your past with The Inquisitor. Whoever it is knows *everything*. It talks about how you were raised in a cult, which revolved around ..." He stared down at his lighter. "Well, you know what it revolved around.

"The Inquisitor managed to track down the names of all the kids that were taken out of the commune. It talks about Marcie and how she was groomed. The two children she gave birth to when she was just a child herself ..." He licked his lips. "You and Lexi, obviously. Then it details how she was sent away, but had been told you were both dead. Whoever they interviewed knew *everything*. They even gave the newspaper your biological dad's name, and claimed he was innocent and it had all been a horrible misunderstanding."

I stared at him. He was talking, but the words made no sense. It was just noise surrounding nine words—*someone has talked about your past with The Inquisitor.*

I was cold, yet I could feel sweat trickling down my spine. My stomach churned. My vision dimmed.

"Seth?" Gabe's voice came from far away.

Something touched my arm, and I swung out a hand, slapping it away.

"Seth? Talk to me. Say something."

I blinked, and glared at the face in front of me. Gabe, expression intense, came into focus.

"My... *father*?" My voice broke on the word, and I hated the fact that it was *fear* I could hear. "He's in prison."

Gabe shook his head, and his eyes closed briefly, then he uttered the words I'd been dreading hearing for the past twenty years. "They released him last week."

"Why wasn't I informed?" There was nothing in my voice. No anger, no fear. I marveled at how calm I sounded.

"I don't know. We can find out. Karl has Matthew Carmichael on it." Gabe mentioned NFG's lawyer.

"Have *you* seen the article?"

He twisted and snatched up a sheet of paper from Karl's desk. "Someone sent it to Karl this morning. It's not the entire thing, just part of it. He tried to stop it from running, but..." He gave another shrug. "He can't. They said they're leading with it tomorrow. Front page."

I made no move to take it from him. "What else does it say?"

The way Gabe's eyes jumped away told me he knew what I meant without me needing to go into detail. His reaction answered my question without him needing to speak. It said *everything*.

"Our records were sealed, and our names changed to protect

us." My voice was wooden.

"I *know*. But I guess the person who gave the interview knew all the details."

"They name who I am now?" I needed to warn Lexi. That stray thought was followed by the reminder that she was dead. That it was just me.

I swayed.

"Steady." Gabe wrapped an arm around my shoulders and forced me to move toward the couch set against one wall. "Let's sit down."

I dropped heavily to the couch running along one wall. Gabe walked away and returned a few seconds later with a glass half-full of an amber liquid. He held it out to me. The smell of whiskey hit my nose.

"Drink this."

I pushed it away, shaking my head.

"One won't hurt you. You're not an alcoholic. Drink the damn drink."

"I *don't* want it," I snapped, slapping it out of his hand. The liquid spread across the carpet. Karl was going to kill me. I lifted my gaze to meet Gabe's. "Where the fuck is he?"

"Who?"

"The man who fucked my mother and put two babies in her belly when she was still a fucking child."

"I don't know."

I pulled my cell out of my pocket and jabbed at the screen,

navigating my contact list. When I found Marcus DeMario's number, I hit call. It barely rang before he answered.

"I need you to find someone."

CHAPTER 4

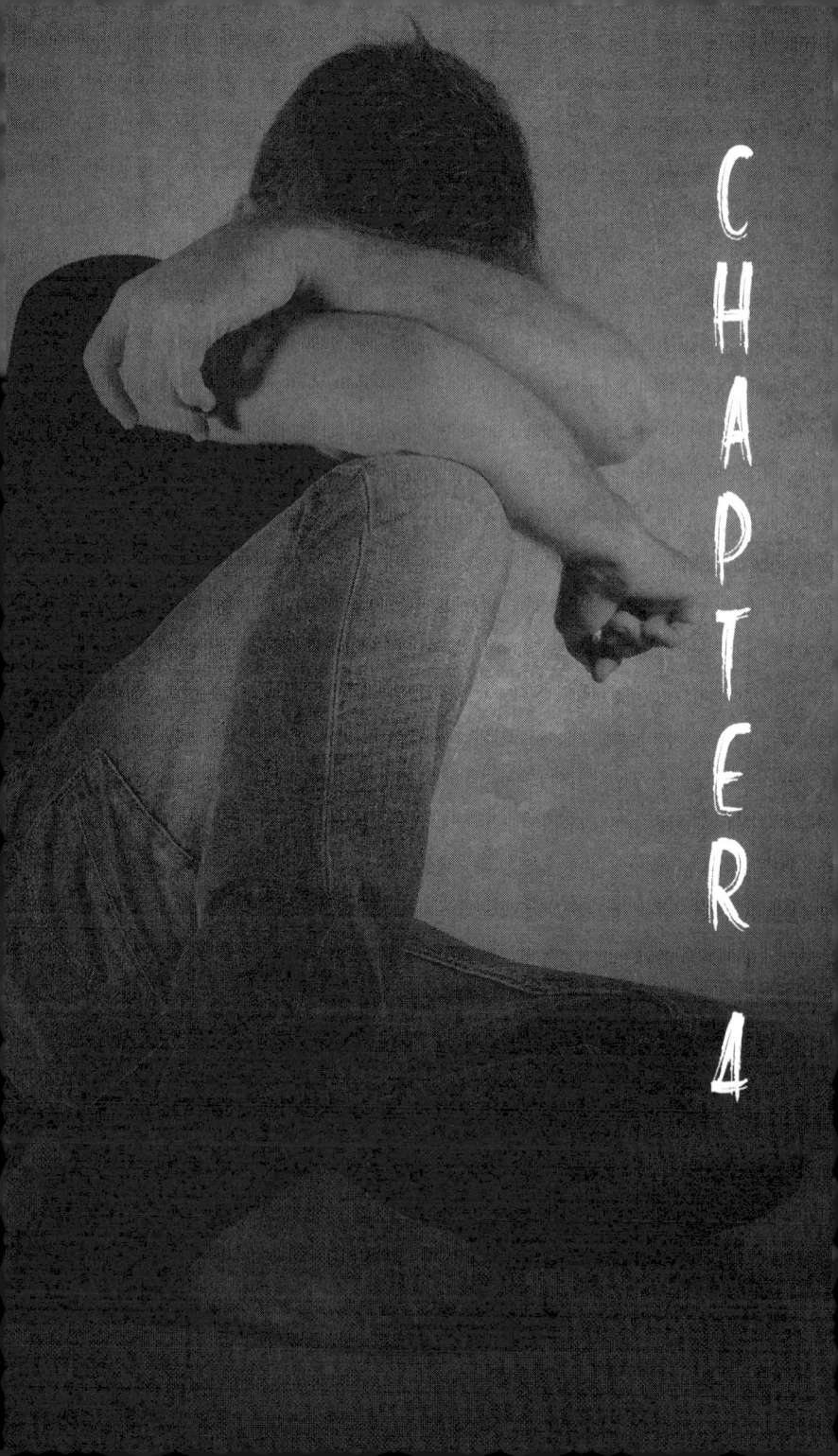

CUT ME UP - FRIDAY PILOTS CLUB

Seth

"Seth, don't." Gabe grabbed my cell out of my hand. We wrestled with it briefly, while Marcus shouted *hello* down the line.

Gabe won the battle and lifted it to his ear, planting one hand against my chest to stop me from reaching it. "Sorry, misdialed." He hung up.

"What the fuck?"

"You're not thinking straight. Give yourself a couple of hours at least to wrap your head around this."

"I *don't* have a couple of hours, do I? The entire fucking mess is going to be all over the world tomorrow. I need to act now." I held my hand out for my cell. "Give me my fucking phone back."

"Only if you don't call Marcus."

"Give me my fucking cell." I stood and advanced on him. He backed away, skirting around Karl's desk so it was between us.

"Not gonna happen. I'm doing this for you, Seth. The last thing you need is to see the fucking asshole."

"Come on, Seth. You're not thinking straight. You *know* why. What you need to do right now is *go home*, call your parents, warn them about what's about to happen."

"What *is* about to happen, Gabe? Just how much fucking detail has this article gone into?" I stalked around the desk. Gabe retreated, staying just out of reach. I didn't need him to tell me, but like an itch you couldn't ignore, I *wanted* him to detail it.

He pocketed my cell. "Let's just say the reporter did their research."

"Did their research." My voice was flat. "What the fuck does that mean, exactly?"

"They spoke to more people than just the one they initially interviewed. They even reached out to the prison your dad was incarcerated in."

"*He's not my fucking dad!*" My shout echoed around the room.

"No, I know. I'm sorry." Gabe held his hands up, and the placating move stirred my temper.

I lunged at him, lowering my head and hitting him in the stomach. We both went down in a tangle of limbs and rolled around the floor while I attempted to retrieve my cell.

"Fuck's sake, man!" The words ended with a grunt when I buried my fist into his side.

He retaliated by twisting around until he was on top of me and grabbed my wrists, pinning them above my head. "Will you fucking stop!"

I glared up at him. "Give me my cell."

"Not until you promise *not* to call Marcus."

"I'm not a fucking child." I tried to wrench my arms free.

"Then stop reacting like one." He put all his weight on the hands gripping my wrists, and held on.

We both stared in a silent battle of wills as we waited for the other to concede. I knew Gabe wouldn't give in. This would remain a standoff unless I played it a different way. I lowered my lids and nodded, relaxing my body. Gabe held on for half a minute longer, then slowly released his grip on my wrists. The moment he did, I bucked my hips, threw him off, and grabbed my cell from his back pocket before he could stop me. I jumped to my feet and stalked out of the office.

"Seth!" Gabe shouted from behind me. I ignored him and kept walking.

Carter pushed himself from the wall and caught up to me as I stormed toward the elevator, ignoring Karl calling my name.

"We need to get you back home before the frenzy starts." I glanced at my bodyguard but didn't reply. "Seth? Are you listening to me?"

"Where's Riley?"

"At the house."

"Does she know?"

"I don't know.

"Did *you* say anything?"

"No. It's not my place to tell her. I just told her I had to come and get you."

"But *you* know." It wasn't a question. The elevator doors slid open, and we stepped inside.

"My job is to keep you protected. *I* have to know what's going on with your life to do that efficiently."

I nodded. "I need security for my parents. I'm surprised no one has tried to contact them already."

"If I had to guess, I'd say they didn't because that would have taken away the element of surprise they're hoping to hit you with."

"Who leaked it to Karl?"

"That reporter friend of Gabe's." He hit the button for the underground parking lot. "I've brought in extra security for the house. There will be guards roaming the grounds to keep the paparazzi out. Karl has suggested we cancel any upcoming appearances until everything dies down, and you stay home and out of the public eye while we decide how to respond to the article tomorrow."

"What you're saying is I'm going to be a prisoner in my own home for the foreseeable future?"

"It's either that or face the media before you're ready."

I blew out a breath and stepped out of the elevator, taking my car keys from my pocket.

"I'll follow you home." Carter didn't even try to convince me to leave my car there and ride with him.

Nodding, I set off toward my car, climbed in and jammed the key into the ignition. I didn't check to see if Carter was ready before slamming my foot on the accelerator and speeding out of the parking lot.

Halfway to my house, I changed my mind and turned the wheel sharply so I could take a left, and drove to my parents' house. There was *no way* I was leaving them to find out about the upcoming shitshow by reading the article, and I wasn't telling them over the phone either. They deserved to hear from me face to face.

My dad's car was in the drive when I arrived. I parked at an angle and hopped out. The rumble of an engine informed me that Carter had kept up with me, and he brought his car to a stop beside mine. He climbed out and shot me a look, making his annoyance with my mid-drive change of plan clear. I shrugged and set off toward the front door.

"Mom? Dad?" I called their names and banged my fist against the door. It swung open less than a minute later to reveal my dad.

"Seth?" His smile faded when he saw my face. I guess I didn't look very happy. "Is everything okay?"

I shook my head. "Is Mom home?"

"She's out the back." He stepped back to let us in, and I strode through the house until I could exit out the back. I searched around until I found my mom kneeling before a rosebush.

Had it been any other day, I'd have smiled at the image. She wore a large-brimmed flowery hat to shield her face from the sun as she tended her roses.

"Mom." She looked up at my voice, breaking into a smile.

"Seth!" Dropping her gardening tools, she stood and hurried

over to me, arms wide to gather me into a hug. "I didn't know you were coming to visit today."

I lowered my face so she could kiss my cheek. "Is Riley with you?" She peered behind me for my girlfriend.

"No. She's at home. I came straight here from NFG. I need to talk to you and Dad."

Her smile fell away at the grim tone in my voice. "Are you and Riley okay?"

Fuck. I hadn't even considered that. My heart faltered. *Would we be okay after tomorrow?* I forced myself to smile.

"We're fine. That's not why I'm here. Can we go inside?"

Neglected Consequences

CHAPTER 5

OFF MY MIND - JOE P

Gabe

I didn't go after Seth. Carter would have his back, and anything I did or said right now would cause more issues than it solved. It was obvious that the news had blindsided him. Why wouldn't it?

He was angry, and I would be the perfect target for him, just like he was for me. We'd get into that later, once his mind was settled on the path he wanted to take. He'd been there for me when I needed someone to lash out at, so I'd make sure I was available to him once he was ready.

After the elevator closed on him, I slumped onto one of the seats in Karl's office. Our manager walked in seconds later.

"That went better than I expected. Did you manage to tell him everything?"

I lifted my gaze to meet his. "It could have been worse. He refused to read the article, but yeah, I made it clear what was coming."

"I'm surprised it's taken this long for the information to get out, I have to be honest. I expected it to happen when he first got together with Riley."

"I guess they were more focused on the age difference between them than anything else, and then everything else going on with the band took attention away from that story." I toyed with my lighter. "I know he went to see Dr. Santos a couple of times. But, according to Harper, Riley told her he quit after three sessions. She didn't say why."

"If he's not ready to talk about it, then he won't be comfortable. You know how it works, Gabe. It took *you* and Dex a while to figure it out."

I nodded. "I think there's something more, though. He's been with Riley for almost four years, but she still doesn't live with him full time."

"Not everyone moves at the same pace."

"Yeah, but *four years?*"

"Riley is only twenty-two. I can understand them waiting."

"I guess." But I knew about Seth's issues. I knew the things he suffered, the nightmares he had. And I was *sure* there was more behind him not asking Riley to move in with him than his girlfriend was admitting to. "He shouldn't be alone right now, though. The last thing he needs is to get stuck inside his own head."

"Speaking from experience?"

I laughed quietly. "Maybe. A little bit. I know what it's like, Karl. You get this little voice whispering inside your head, eating away at everything you are until only the negatives remain. It's not a pretty place to be."

Karl got a weird look on his face.

I frowned. "What?"

"Nothing."

"Bullshit. I don't believe you. Why are you looking at me that way?"

"I was just thinking about how far you've come. There was a time, not that long ago, when you would *never* have admitted to suffering from any kind of insecurity or anxiety."

I shrugged. "Guess I had to grow up eventually, huh?" I pushed to my feet. "Can I take a copy of the article? Seth refused to look at it, but once he's calmed down, he'll want to see it. I'll try to get him to do that today before the shit hits tomorrow. Is there anything we can do to stop it? Have you asked Matt?"

Karl nodded. "There's nothing we can do. There are no minors to protect anymore, so we can't use that angle. I don't know how they managed to get hold of the sealed documents. I think the original person who spoke to them was possibly another victim. Maybe they felt like it was closure for them, of a sort."

"But how did they link Seth Hawkins to Nathaniel Enshaw?"

"I'm not sure. We're looking into it."

I sighed. "Okay. Let me know if you find out. You know he's not going to leave it alone. He'll want to face the man who fathered him."

"What do you think he'll do?"

"I'm not sure. How would you feel coming face to face with the man who abused you for the first nine years of your life? At least *my* da only hit me."

"Only?"

"Compared with what happened to Seth, my childhood was unicorns and rainbows." I raked a hand through my hair. "I'm heading back home. I need to talk to Harper and then get the rest of the band together to talk. This is about Seth, but it's going to have an effect on all of us. We're supposed to hit the studio next week to start on the new album."

"We can postpone."

"We'll see what happens. We can't predict how people are going to react until it's out there."

Remy joined me when I left Karl's office.

"How bad is it?" he asked when we entered the elevator.

"Bad." There wasn't a lot to say. Seth's reaction was the result of being blindsided. Once he had time to think, to *digest* what was about to be out in the world for everyone to see, the small clash we'd had in the office would be nothing compared to what was coming.

I wasn't certain how much he'd shared with Riley, but she needed to be prepared. Seth would kill me for interfering, but I didn't see any other choice. I pulled out my cell and called Harper.

"Hey, Frosty."

"Hey. Are you in trouble?"

"No. I don't want to explain over the phone, but I'm coming home now. We need to go to Seth's place."

"Why? What's going on?"

"I'm on my way home now. It's ... gnarly. I'll see you soon."

"Okay. Did you want to go as soon as you're back?"

"Yeah."

"I'll get ready."

"Thanks, babe." I went to end the call, and hesitated. "Hey, Harper?"

"Yeah?"

"I love you."

I could hear the smile in her voice when she replied. "I love you, too."

***

"*Seth?*" Harper repeated for the third time. She looked down at the article, then over at the old news report I'd pulled up on my cell from when Seth was a kid. "Are you sure?"

"I'm sure. Do you remember when he joined our school? The school paired us together. The principal probably thought putting the two abused kids together made sense. Like attracts like. It took a while. A year, maybe? I think we were twelve. But eventually, he told me his history.

"We got stoned and drunk on cheap cider, lying out on the roof of his parents' place. We'd shoplifted the cider and were righting all the wrongs of the world while we stared at the stars. A girl had shown me her …" I stopped, shrugged, then continued. "It was the first time I'd seen a naked girl, and Seth made a comment about how he'd seen enough naked bodies to last a lifetime. He said if he didn't see another one for the rest of his life, he'd die happy."

Harper sighed. "His reaction to Riley's age makes so much more sense, knowing what happened. Does she know?"

"A little. I don't know how much he's told her. He still keeps her at arm's length in some ways. How often does she stay over at his place? I know she's not living there. She's still at her mom's."

"I asked her that a while ago. She said it was complicated. I wondered if they were having problems."

I paced the room. "I don't *think* they are. He goes through phases where ... Well, being around him can be difficult. I think he's trying to protect her from him during those episodes."

"What happens?" Harper propped her chin on her hand and watched me as I paced the room.

"Nightmares, lashing out, mood swings, the usual. I wondered if maybe he'd got a handle on it all. He stopped drinking around the same time I did."

"Maybe he did. But having this all out in the open isn't going to make it easy for him." She intercepted my path and pressed a hand against my chest. "Gabe, stand still. You're making me dizzy."

I looked down at her. "We need to go to Seth's. I have to get him to see what's in the article before it hits."

"We will, but you need to take a breath first. You're no good to him if you're on edge as well. Everyone knows how your moods bounce off each other. If you're calm, it will help him more."

I dropped my head to bury my face into her hair and looped my arms around her waist. Sucking in a deep breath, her scent of cotton candy surrounded me, eased the tension in my spine, and

I nodded against her hair. "You're right, but this … it's not good, Harper. He barely held it together when Lexi chose to exit."

"I know." Her arms wrapped around me. I stood there, letting her closeness do what it did best—soothe my soul—then straightened. "Okay, let's go."

CHAPTER 6

999 TO THE DEVIL - CALL ME KARIZMA

Riley

When Seth left, muttering about Gabe and whatever trouble he'd gotten himself into, I headed into the photography studio out in the back. The building used to be where Seth's sister lived, and it had taken a long time for him to come to terms with the fact that she wasn't coming back. After Forgotten Legacy hired me as their official band photographer, he'd spent weeks going through all her things, and once it was empty, turned it into a studio for me.

We made plans, talked about moving in together once I turned twenty, but the timing never seemed right, so I still lived at home with my mom. It wasn't that I didn't think Seth loved me. He did, and he made it clear, often, but sometimes I wondered if taking that ultimate step scared him. The last person to live with him he'd lost, and I knew he still struggled with it, so I didn't push. Once he was ready, we'd take another step in our relationship. Until then, I was prepared to wait.

I spent most of my days at his place and stayed over two or three nights a week. There wasn't a day where I didn't see him. As the band's official photographer, I often tagged along for interviews and appearances. On our downtime, we explored Los Angeles, finding hidden little places away from the tourist areas, and driving Carter crazy while he tried to work out ways to keep us safe.

"Riley? You out here?" Gabe's voice shattered the silence, and I straightened from flicking through the photographs I'd taken of the band at a photoshoot a few days ago. Closing the album, I walked to the main door and threw it open.

Gabe and Harper were walking around the pool and heading in my direction. I looked for Seth but didn't spot him. I didn't question how Gabe had let himself in. Both men had access to everything the other owned. It was something both me and Harper had to accept. They were close, closer than brothers, and I understood why so many of their fans were convinced there was more intimacy between them.

They had a closeness that was typically reserved for lovers, but I knew, as did Harper, that they never had been. They were bonded by history, by shared experiences. Brothers in every way except blood.

"Did Seth miss you?"

Gabe shook his head. "No. He left NFG before me. Isn't he here?"

"No." Now he was closer, I could see the faint stress lines around his eyes and the crinkle in his brow as he frowned at me.

"I thought he was with you."

"He picked me up for a meeting at NFG, then left with Carter. I thought he was coming home. Have you seen him in the last hour?"

"No." My heart rate picked up. There was something in Gabe's tone that raised the hairs on the back of my neck. "Is something wrong? Where is he?"

Gabe's lips were set in a thin line as he looked around. When he caught sight of his bodyguard coming through the doors of the house, he turned.

"Remy, call Carter and see where Seth went."

Remy nodded, and walked a little distance away to make the call. He was back a few minutes later. "He's at his parents' place. Carter said he'll be back soon." His attention swung to me, and he frowned. "Seth asked me to take you back home before he gets here."

"What? Why?"

Gabe's heavy sigh drew my eyes to him. "I was afraid of that." He rubbed a hand down his face. "How much has Seth told you about his past, Riley?"

"I know where he grew up..." I darted a quick look at Harper. "I know the things he had to do."

"Someone has told the press." He pulled a sheet of paper from his back pocket and held it out to me. "They're running the article tomorrow."

"No," I whispered. "*Why*? After all this time, why would they do that?"

"That's not all. Whoever they interviewed linked Seth Hawkins to Nathaniel Enshaw. One of the kids who got rescued, *and* they managed to track down his biological father and talk to him."

There was a heavy weight in the pit of my stomach, but Gabe wasn't finished.

"Seth discovered today that his father was released from prison recently, and whoever was interviewed for the article claims that he's a victim, too."

"That man was *not* a victim!"

"We know that, Ri. I guess Seth went to warn his parents about the incoming storm, and that's why he's trying to send you home. He wants you out of the line of fire when the shit hits."

But I knew that wasn't it. Seth wanted me out of the way because he thought people would read about his history, and then look at the age gap between us. They might think he was a product of his trauma and had groomed me into being with him. None of which was true. Seth had worked *hard* to overcome his past, and my age had kept us apart, not brought us together.

"I'm not leaving."

Gabe's nod was approving. "That's my girl. He's going to try and push everyone away. We can't let him do it. It's going to be instinctive for him to try, and things are going to get rocky, but we have to keep strong, Ri. Don't let him force you to leave."

I glared at Remy, who raised an eyebrow. "Are you going to try and force me to leave?"

"I don't work for Seth. I can't promise Carter won't, though.

His loyalty is to Seth."

"Does Karl know? Is that why he wanted to see you?"

"Yes, that's why he had Seth take me to NFG. Karl was the one who found out first. There's no way he could have delivered this news to Seth. It had to be me."

I gave a slow nod. That made sense. The two men understood each other; their bond and trust in each other reached levels beyond normal friendship.

"Give me a few minutes to read this?" I walked around the pool and perched on the edge of one of the loungers.

The printout was laid out the way they would print the article in the newspaper, or on the website, or however they planned on distributing it. Probably both, I thought, as I skimmed over it. Most of the details were similar to what had been written in the article Seth had showed me years ago.

But where that article made no reference to Seth Hawkins because, at the time, Seth had been a young boy, this one linked Nathaniel Enshaw, child victim, to Seth Hawkins, rock star guitarist of Forgotten Legacy. There were photographs of Seth as a child, with dark, wary eyes, bruised and scared, beside ones of the guitarist, lean, tattooed, and brooding. Side by side, there was no way of denying they were the same person.

The article talked about his sister Olivia, aka Lexi Hawkins, and how she'd committed suicide after years of struggling to come to terms with her childhood abuse. The description was clinical, cold, emotionless, and my heart broke again at the thought of

Seth seeing his sister's last moments shared in such a way.

I lifted my gaze. "Has he seen this?"

"Not yet. He refused to read it." Gabe sat opposite me, lighter in hand. Harper stood behind him, one hand resting on his shoulder, her thumb stroking lightly up and down his neck.

"Why are you here?" Seth strode through the doors.

Gabe stood. "I wanted to check if you were okay."

"Not you." His dark eyes flicked to the paper I held, then up to my face, and his features turned to stone as I watched. "Riley, go home."

"Seth—"

"No. *Go home.*" He reached forward and snatched the paper from my fingers, then spun away. "Carter, take her home."

Gabe sighed. "Give us a minute." He set off after Seth.

Neglected Consequences

CHAPTER 7

OUTRUN MYSELF - JACK KAYS

Seth

I tossed the sheet of paper detailing my entire childhood onto the table without looking at it and pulled open the refrigerator. I knew what I'd see as soon as I opened it. Bottles of fruit juice and water. I sucked my bottom lip into my mouth as I studied the contents.

"What the fuck are you doing?"

I straightened and turned to face my best friend. "Looking for something to drink."

"That's *not* what I mean. Why are you sending Riley away?"

I shrugged. He knew the answer to that. I didn't need to explain it to him.

"You haven't even read it. What did your parents say?"

"The usual. They're here for me, they'll be vigilant, they won't talk to anyone. If I need to talk, their door is open." I waved a hand. "Yadda yadda."

"Don't dismiss their concern. They don't deserve that."

"I'm not." He arched a brow. "Why are *you* here, anyway?"

"Because I wanted to make sure you were okay."

"Just fucking peachy." I swung back to face the refrigerator. "Take Riley home when you leave if Carter hasn't done it already." I took out a bottle of water, wishing it was something stronger, and walked out of the kitchen.

Predictably, Gabe followed me. I stopped in the hallway. "Read the room, Mercer. I need some time alone right now."

"Being alone is the last thing you need."

I sighed. "Gabe, I'm *fine*. We've weathered worse bullshit than this. I just need time to process it, okay? I have to make some calls. I need to speak to my mother and make sure the asshole hasn't tried to find her." *My mother.* My stomach twisted at the thought of speaking to her. "I can't do that with you all fussing over me like I'm a child," I continued, my voice level. "So *please*, take Riley, and get everyone out of here so I can concentrate on what I need to do."

I walked past him and up the stairs. Gabe would do one of two things. He'd either follow me and continue to push, or he'd *hear* what I was saying and do what I asked. When he didn't appear after a few minutes, I assumed he'd done the latter. I sat on the edge of the bed, sipped the water, and waited, listening.

My bedroom was at the front of the house, the window was open, and eventually I heard voices, followed by slamming doors, and then a car's engine firing to life. I stood and moved closer to the window and watched as it disappeared down my drive.

When Riley didn't show up after five minutes had passed, I felt confident that Gabe had succeeded in either making her go with him or Carter. I knew she'd be hurt. *I'd* hurt her by making her leave, but she'd feel even worse if she stuck around while I worked through this. I took out my cell and opened the messages app.

ME - I love you, Shutterbug. Just give me a few hours, okay?

Her response was immediate.

SHUTTERBUG - I'm worried, Seth. You shouldn't be alone.

ME - Trust me. I'll send Carter to pick you up later. We'll order takeout and watch classic horror movies. Make a plan.

The three dots showed up, disappeared, showed up again, and then her reply came through.

SHUTTERBUG - If I don't see Carter before five, I'm coming for you, Lucifer.

That made me smile.

ME - Promise?

SHUTTERBUG - Threat!!

I laughed.

ME - Noted.

Tossing my cell onto the bed, I crouched down and pulled out a small locked metal box from beneath it. It was thick with dust, evidence that I'd shoved it under there the day I moved in and rarely looked at it again. I set it on the floor and sat down, my back propped against the bed frame, and eyed it.

The key was on a hoop with all my others—house keys, car keys, studio key, and this ... the key to my past. Something I never thought I'd have to unlock after the last time I'd deposited something in it. I'd hoped that finding my mother and helping her would ease some of the guilt I felt.

Guilt. I laughed out loud. *Fucking guilt.*

Gabe thought he knew my history, and he did. *Most* of it. Riley thought she knew, but the truth was I'd told her even less than Gabe. The things they didn't know... Would it make them look at me differently? Would it make them hate me? *Pity* me? Be disgusted by me? All of the above?

I guess we'd all find out soon enough. It wasn't lost on me that the printout had ended mid-sentence and whatever else they were printing would be worse than what was already available. I patted my pockets, fished out my keys and then dragged the box toward me. My hand shook as I pushed the key into the lock, and I hesitated before turning it. The padlock clicked and opened, and I sat and stared at it.

If I opened the box ... I had to face everything that was inside it. I could no longer hide—from my past, from my experiences, from *myself*.

Could I do it?

Neglected Consequences

CHAPTER 8

MONSTERS – ALL TIME LOW

Seth
Age 9

Olivia shifted restlessly on the thin mattress beside me, snuggling closer. I dragged the thin sheet up to her chin and tucked it around her body, making sure she was completely covered. It was cold in the basement. The barred window had cracked a few months ago, and no one had bothered to fix it, so when it rained, it leaked down the walls and made everywhere damp.

My sister coughed, the sound rattling in her chest. She'd been sick for a couple of weeks, which made my father angry. He wanted her to look pretty, and it was hard to do that when her nose was red and sore from sneezing. But, at least if she was sick, they left her alone. Maybe she would die.

I should be wishing for that, but there was a selfish part of me that didn't want her to escape our life, didn't want her to leave me alone, so I didn't. I prayed for her to get better. Not that God gave a fuck about us. I wasn't even convinced such an entity existed, or maybe he did, and he enjoyed making people miserable.

Was this what normal life was like? From the whispers of the other kids who were here, I didn't think it was. Some of them talked about families who loved them. Parents who were looking for them. People who would be upset that they were missing. But me? I'd never known anything different. I'd been born here, and I would probably die here. I just couldn't do it before Olivia. I couldn't leave her alone to take all the punishments.

Olivia whimpered, her entire body shivering, and I dragged off my sheet and carefully placed it over her. She needed it more than me. I was strong. My father told me often enough.

Stop crying, Nathaniel. Show me what a good boy you are. How strong you are. You'll learn to enjoy this. Do what your father says. If you relax, it won't hurt as much.

A thud sounded above my head, and I looked toward the window, frowning. The sun wasn't up. Why were people moving around upstairs? They never rose before the sun. Unless … was it a party? If they were having a party, they might gather two or three of us to entertain them.

I hoped not. I was still sore from the last party; the bruises had yet to fade. I didn't think about the other cuts and bruises. If I didn't acknowledge them, then they weren't there.

"Nate?" Olivia's mumble drew my eyes down to her. She wasn't awake, her eyes still closed, but I must have disturbed her. I stroked a hand over her dark curls.

"Shhh. It's okay. Sleep, Liv." I kept up the motion until she settled again, then slowly crawled off the mattress and made my way to the stairs, stepping over the other sleeping bodies.

There were six of us in the basement, but only me and Liv were related. I'd seen others come and go. They'd arrive in the middle of the night, scared and crying, and be tossed down here with us. I'd lost count of how many had been carried out, cold and silent, months later, not strong enough to survive the games my father and his friends liked to play. The ones who did survive grew up, and older, at which point they'd either disappear or join the games as an adult ... and the cycle would continue.

There was another thud, heavy footsteps ... more than one set by the sound of it. And I tracked the direction of the noise with my eyes. I'd learned over the years what each part of the house sounded like. Self-preservation required that knowledge. If I knew someone was coming, I could make sure I was the first person they saw, which gave the others a reprieve. Especially if they only needed one toy to play with.

These footsteps were moving toward the door in the kitchen, which led down to us, so I sat on the bottom step. If they came through and saw me first, they'd take me and leave Liv behind. They never took us both together. For all of their depravities, they didn't like to play with siblings. Sure enough, the door at the top of the stairs swung open, hinge creaking, and light spilled through. I didn't move, didn't look around, and waited.

Voices spoke to each other, too low for me to pick up the

words or figure out if I recognized them, and then the top step creaked as someone stepped onto it. I counted the creaks as they walked down, and when they reached two away from where I sat, I stood and turned, holding out my hands. I kept my head lowered.

You didn't look at their faces. That was the rule. No eye contact unless they demanded it ... and sometimes they did. Usually the women. They liked looking at my face, stroking their fingers over my lips and cheeks. They said I was too pretty to hide.

Seconds passed. My arms ached from holding them out, waiting for the rope to be wrapped around them, so they could lead me upstairs. Why hadn't they done it already?

I risked a quick glance up, my eyes pausing on the boots standing on the step just above me. I frowned. They were black, scuffed, laced up, and covered in dirt. My father's friends wore sneakers or leather-soled shoes, shiny and expensive. Had he found some new friends?

"Put your arms down, son." I jumped at the gruff voice, and my heart sped up. A new voice. That meant new rules, new games, and new expectations. I had to learn what this one wanted and quickly. It was the only way to survive.

A hand touched my wrist.

Shit, he'd told me to drop my hands and I hadn't obeyed.

"Sorry, sir," I whispered and lowered my arms.

"What's your name?"

My name? Why did he want my name? The men never wanted to know what I was called. Only the women.

Oh, Nate, such a pretty boy. I'm going to teach you everything you need to make me happy. You want to make me happy, don't you, pretty boy?

I shut off those memories, clenching my jaw.

"Nate ... Nathaniel, sir."

"Nathaniel," he repeated. I nodded. "Hmm. I don't have a Nathaniel on the list."

List? Why was there a list?

"I should be, sir," I said. "I'm more experienced than the others. I learn fast. I can do whatever you want."

The man in front of me crouched, and calloused fingers touched my chin, lifting my head. "Look at me, son."

My eyes darted up to meet his, then away again.

Was this a trick? A test to see if I remembered the rules?

I had a quick glimpse of dark features, lips set in a grim line.

"It's okay. You don't need to be afraid."

Yeah, sure. Haven't heard that line before. I fought not to let my thoughts show on my face.

"How many of you are down here, son?"

"Six, sir." *Did he want all of us?* "But my sister is sick. She can't join the entertainment right now, sir. My father said so." I added the last line hurriedly, just in case he thought I was being defiant.

"Your sister? How many girls are there?"

"Two, sir. There used to be four but the other two got broken."

"Broken?"

I shrugged. That was how it had been explained to me. "They

were broken," I repeated. "So Father took them away."

"I see. Could you wake the others up for me?"

My frown deepened. "Everyone, sir? But my sister—"

"It's not for …" He cleared his throat. "What did you call it? Entertainment? We are here to help you, Nathaniel."

"I don't understand. It's my place to help you, sir. What do you want me to do?"

"You would be helping me a lot if you could wake the others and bring them upstairs. Can you do that for me, Nathaniel? We just want to talk to you."

Neglected Consequences

CHAPTER 9

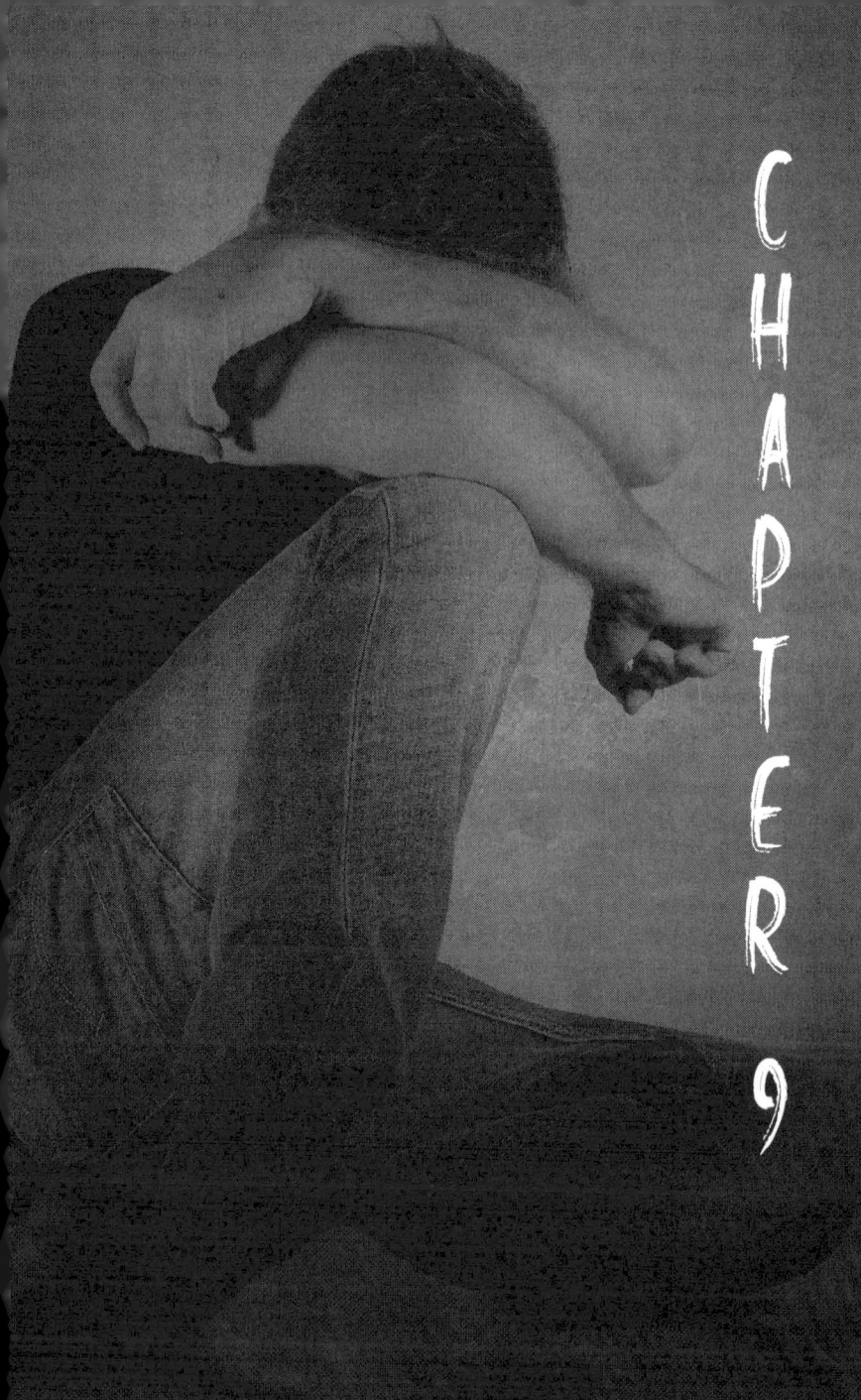

SELF SABOTAGE - WATERPARKS

Seth

I traced a finger over the faces in the photograph. Me, Lexi, Oscar, Peter, Susie, and Devon. Aside from the six of us, there had been another three kids, one girl and two boys, at the compound. They'd been older, kept separate, being *taught* how to become handlers for the younger kids. I never knew their names, only their sexual preferences.

The last time I'd seen them was the day we were taken from the compound. We'd traveled in separate cars to the police station and from there, had been sent out to different families. Only me and Lexi had been kept together, although they'd tried to separate us once. I walked the fifty miles to the house she was being fostered in, and we'd run away, only to be caught a day later. From that moment, they fostered us together. Sometimes I thought that Lexi would have been better off if I'd left her alone. Maybe she would still be alive if she hadn't had me there to remind her of our shared past every day.

I dropped the photograph onto my lap and leaned my head

back against the mattress, letting my eyes slide closed.

Which one of them had sold their story? How had they tracked it back to me? Did my father know who I was? Did he know where my mother was?

Marcie Enshaw—my biological mother.

I needed to call her. She'd spent two years in the facility I'd paid for and eventually been deemed well enough to leave. She was clean and healthy. As healthy as she could be, after years of abusing herself, anyway. I'd found a private closed residential care facility where she could have her own apartment. The fee included therapy visitations and an on-site nurse. I also set up a weekly allowance so she could at least *feel* normal.

But we didn't speak, didn't communicate. I tried at first. But it was too difficult for us both. Every time I faced her, it set her back in her recovery and sent me into a spiral of black moods and nightmares.

I hadn't wanted to find her. That had been Lexi's obsession. Her hunger to know if she had survived the same way we had. So I did it for her, in the hopes it would give her some peace, some *closure*. Only she chose to opt out of life before I could tell her I'd tracked the woman down, and left me to deal with everything alone.

You're not alone. You have Forgotten Legacy and Riley.

But how much longer would I have them for? When it all came out …

I shook my head and pushed to my feet. I needed a drink. Something stronger than water. There had to be alcohol in the house somewhere.

Leaving the box and its contents on the floor, I walked out of the bedroom and down to the kitchen. Wine would do. I was sure there'd be wine on the rack. Riley enjoyed a glass now and then. I pulled open the door to the wine cooler and... *aha*! There it was. A bottle of red.

I took it out, grabbed a glass and filled it up. My eyes found the printout on the kitchen table and I crossed over to pick it up. I drained half the glass, filled it back up, then sat down to read.

***

"Fuck's sake. Seth!"

Gabe's voice sounded weirdly muted as he called my name. I opened my mouth to tell him to stop shouting and sucked in a lungful of water, and consciousness returned with a vengeance.

"What the—" I coughed, spat out water, and opened my eyes. I was lying on the steps leading into my pool, the water lapping around my chin. I frowned, trying to make sense of the situation. *Why the fuck was I in the pool?*

"Jesus Christ, why is it always the fucking water with you?" Hands hooked under my arms and hauled me backward.

I didn't bother fighting and let him drag me out of the water. He dropped me once I was completely out of the pool, and I squinted up at him.

"What are you doing here?"

"Riley called me when you were a no-show for your date. How much have you had to drink?" He picked up an empty wine bottle, and tapped a second with his foot.

I shrugged.

"This was your grand master plan, huh? Send everyone away and get wasted? I thought you had calls to make. Did you do that before or after you got drunk?"

"Fuck off, Gabe."

"I should have fucking known you'd do this." He ignored me. "Why the fuck did I think you might actually deal with this like a *normal* fucking person?"

"I'm not a fucking *normal* person!" I shouted and shoved myself up to a seated position. Big mistake. The world spun. I closed my eyes, and battled against motion sickness. "I didn't ask you to come here. Go home."

"No. You could have fucking drowned."

"Maybe I should have."

Silence fell. I opened my eyes. Gabe was staring at me, gray eyes narrow.

"I'm going to put that statement down to you being fucking drunk." His voice was flat.

"Whatever helps you to sleep at night." I grabbed the side of the lounger closest to me and pulled myself upright. "God fucking forbid you feel bad about something. The world must remain rainbows and roses; otherwise, Gabe Mercer might feel sad."

His jaw clenched, eyes burning with anger. "You're such a fucking asshole when you're drunk. Get a shower and sober the fuck up."

My lip curled into a sneer. "You've turned into such a good little boy, haven't you? No drinking, no smoking, the perfect fucking boyfriend. Ticking all those boxes, huh, Gabe? Is your sex life as vanilla as your behavior these days? Harper finally got her way, I guess, and forced you back into the box."

My head snapped sideways with the force of his punch. I laughed. "Pussy. Is that all you've got? I'd have thought after being on the receiving end of so many punches from your dad, you'd have learned how to fucking hit properly."

His features blanked. "Fuck you, Hawkins."

"You'd like that, wouldn't you? Isn't it what you've always wanted?" I couldn't stop the words spewing from my lips. "Tell me, Gabe, is it me you imagine when Harper's sucking your dick? I bet I could give her some pointers on the best way to get you off."

Instead of the expected punch, he shook his head, turned and walked out.

"Is that a no?" I called after him. "I thought you were gay for me, Gabe? Here I am offering to give you what you want, and you're just fucking off? Would it have been more tempting if I'd already stripped off and been on my knees with my mouth open, waiting for your dick?"

The echo of the door slamming was his only response.

CHAPTER 10

ISSUES - BOY EPIC

Gabe

I sat in the back of the car, but didn't tell Remy to drive away. Part of me was waiting for Seth to come out of the house after me. The rest of me was fighting against the urge to go back in there and beat the shit out of him.

"What do you want to do?" Remy slid down the privacy glass and twisted to look at me.

There was a loaded question, if ever there was one. What I *wanted* to do was go three rounds with the drunken asshole I'd left inside. "Carter is going to have to keep an eye on him. I'm not sure Riley should be here. Not with the mood he's in, but he shouldn't be left alone."

"How bad do you think it'll be tomorrow?"

"I don't know. The article is pretty shitty, but nothing in it is a lie. I don't think anyone will give much of a fuck about it. It's Seth's reaction to it. He doesn't want people to know this shit about him."

"It was going to come out eventually. Things like this never stay buried."

I dropped my head against the back of the seat and pinched the bridge of my nose. There was a headache forming, beating against my temple. Was this what passing thirty was like? "I've asked the rest of the guys to meet me at the studio. Let's go there. Can you call Carter and make sure he checks on Seth?"

"He's already on the grounds, just out of sight. He'll be vigilant. What about Riley?"

"That's not my call. I can tell her what happened, but beyond that, it's her decision on what she wants to do." I found my cell, scrolled through to Riley's number and hit dial.

"How is he?" Her voice was strained.

"Drunk, angry, lashing out."

"I'll call a cab."

"Ri… He's not in a good place. I think you might want to give him some space."

"I'd rather see for myself. Your relationship is different from the one I have with him. Maybe he'll be okay with me."

"Maybe … just be wary, okay? Let Carter know when you arrive so he's nearby. He's a fucking nasty drunk. Call me if you need help."

"Thanks, Gabe." She ended the call, and I tossed the cell onto the seat beside me. "Let's go to the studio."

***

The rest of the band was already inside when I arrived. Luca was fooling around on his drum kit, while Dex was sprawled across the couch messing around with his cell. They both looked up when I walked in.

"How's Seth?" Dex swung his legs off the couch and sat up.

"Offered to suck my dick and teach Harper new tricks." I dropped down beside him and propped my feet on the table.

Dex snorted. "Oh man, that's not good."

I rolled my eyes. "You think?"

"How much of the article is true?" Luca came out from behind his drums and sat beside my feet on the coffee table.

"All of it. We can't sue for defamation. There's not a single lie in it. Well, aside from his asshole of a father being falsely imprisoned. That's bullshit." I yawned and rubbed a hand down my face. "We need to work out how we're going to deal with it when it goes public tomorrow. Do we release a statement? Stay silent? Wait for Seth to work through his shit?"

"What does Karl think?" Luca asked.

"He was waiting to see how Seth reacted. Which, obviously, was not well." There was a dull ache behind my eyes, so I closed them and took a deep breath. "I don't know. I really don't. What do you guys think we should do?"

"We could wait and see what the fallout is when the article is published," Dex said after a moment's thought. "See where public opinion falls. This might all disappear fast or it could build and escalate. It's hard to say. Do you have a copy of the article? I haven't seen it yet."

I took a folded sheet from my back pocket and handed it to him. When he finished reading it, he passed it to Luca, who gave it a cursory glance and threw it on the table. "What the fuck is wrong with people? Why can't they just leave things in the past where they belong?"

"My guess is someone needed money, so they sold their story. It has to be one of the other kids involved. Did they expect it to escalate? Maybe, maybe not. I don't know how they would have known Seth was one of the kids from the original news story."

"Oh, that's right. He had his name changed, didn't he? Wouldn't those details have been sealed?"

"Yeah, I thought it was." I sat up abruptly. "Lexi's suicide letter was addressed to Nate Enshaw, not Seth Hawkins."

"So? I doubt he tossed that in the trash," Dex said.

"No, but it had to be delivered to him. I think she gave it to a lawyer, with instructions to send it to Seth if she died. So *someone* out there knew there was a link between Nathaniel Enshaw and Seth Hawkins."

"Wouldn't that be against all the rules lawyers have to follow?"

"Unless it was a secretary or office worker." I sighed. "I don't know. It's a stretch, but that's the only thing I know of that connects Seth to Nate."

"There's another thing that links him," Luca said slowly.

I swung my head to face him. "What?"

"His mother."

"Fuck." I'd forgotten about her. Seth didn't see her or talk about her. *Would she have spoken to reporters?*

"Do you know where she lives?"

I shook my head.

"Could ask the reporter who their source is," Dex suggested.

"You know they won't share that information."

"No, but a few well-placed questions could get the answer without them intending to do it," Luca argued.

I nodded slowly. "That's true. Maybe Karl can get them to talk, somehow. I'll call him. He might even know where she lives."

"Riley will know," Dex said.

"She won't tell me without checking if it's okay with Seth first."

"Loyal girlfriends. What fuckery is this?" Dex chuckled. "Do you remember when it was just us against the world?"

"Do you miss being single?" Luca arched a brow.

"Fuck no. I just mean we have this huge support system in place now, and sometimes it's a little bit surreal to think about."

"I just wish every time things start to stabilize the universe wouldn't throw some new shit at us," I muttered.

Dex bumped me with his shoulder. "You wouldn't have anything to use as song lyrics if the world was cotton candy and rainbows. The drama keeps us edgy."

"That's one way to look at it." I pushed upright. "Okay, I'm out of here." I wanted to go home and wrap myself around Harper. I was feeling out of sorts, uncomfortable, on edge, and I didn't like it.

CHAPTER 11

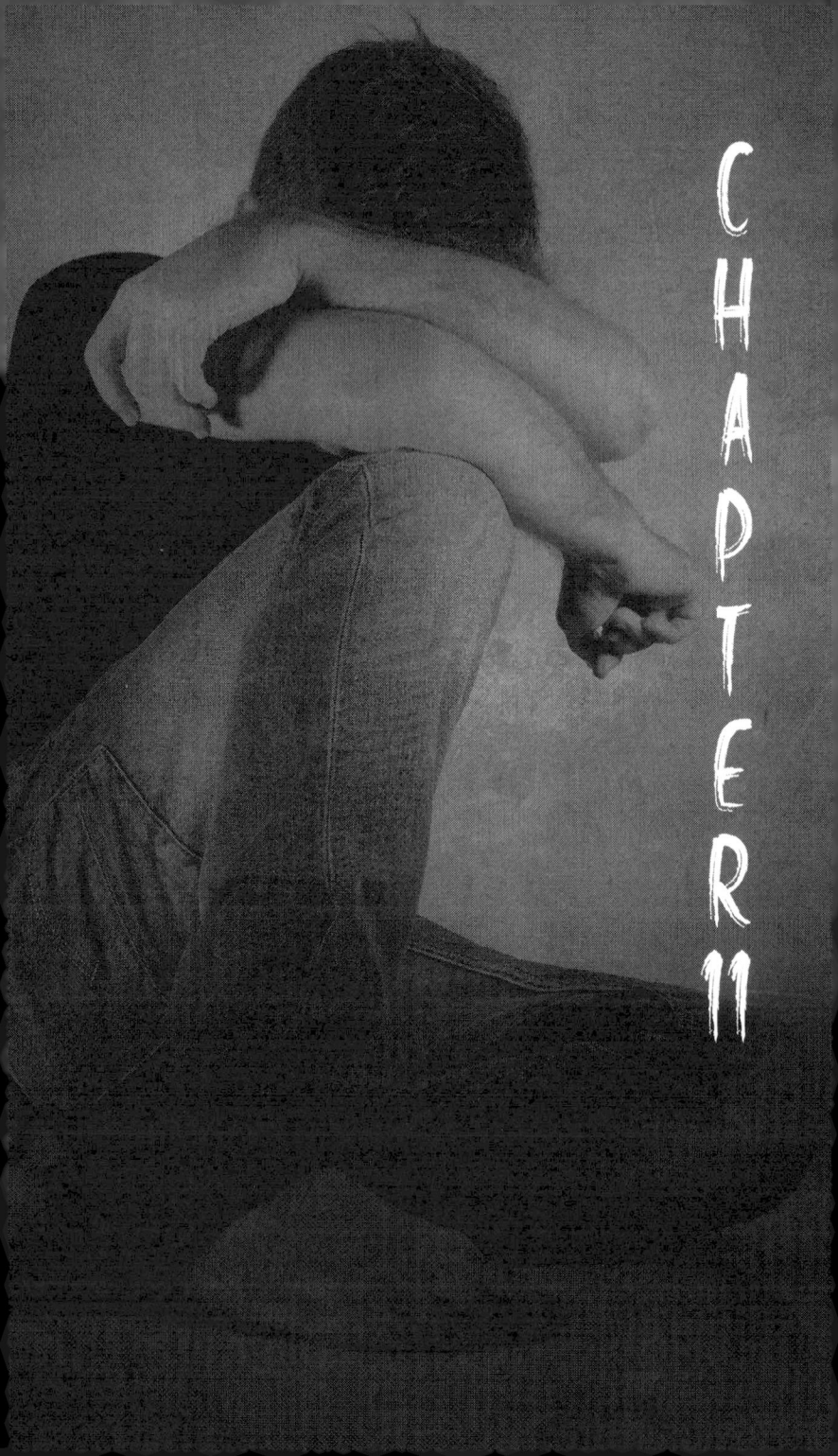

YOU'RE NOT ALONE - THE BROKEN VIEW

Seth

I'd made serious damage into the third or fourth bottle of wine—I'd lost count—when the familiar scent of lemons reached me seconds before Riley came into focus. Sprawled out on a sun lounger, bottle in hand and sunglasses covering my eyes, even though the sun had set, I watched as she came toward me.

She perched on the edge, near my feet, and looked at me. "I told you I'd come looking for you if you didn't come to collect me at five."

I lifted the bottle and touched the top against my forehead in a salute. "What time is it?"

"Nine." She reached for the bottle. "Can I take that?" I moved it out of her reach.

"Get your own. There's another four bottles in the kitchen."

Her sigh was soft. "How many have you emptied?"

"Who cares? Did you want to order takeout?" I levered myself up into a seated position and squinted at her. "What movie did you pick?"

"No, and none."

"Oh." I fell back against the lounger and lifted the bottle to my lips. "Let me know when you do. I could eat."

"How about a deal? You put down the bottle and take a shower, then I'll order us some food, and we can find a movie to watch."

"You sound just like Gabe," I grumbled. "Next you'll be asking to suck my dick." I peered at her, pursing my lips. "Actually, that sounds like a pretty good idea. I wouldn't say no." I waited, one eyebrow hiked in query. She didn't respond. I rubbed my jaw, winced when it hurt, and frowned. "Did someone hit me?"

"I don't know. I only just got here. Did you and Gabe fight?"

Her words sent a slither of unease through me. *Had we?* I vaguely remembered arguing with him. *Had he hit me?*

Riley took the bottle from me while I was distracted, and I reacted too late to stop her. "I'll give it back if you take a shower." She said, backing away toward the doors leading to the kitchen.

"I'll shower if you join me."

Her smile lit up her face. Christ, she was pretty. She deserved better than having my darkness taint her.

"That, I can do." She held out a hand. "Come on then, Lucifer."

It was only when I staggered to my feet that I realized how much I'd had to drink. The world spun. I lost my balance and would have fallen if Riley hadn't caught my arm and pulled it over her shoulders. She wrapped her arm around my waist.

"I don't remember the last time you were this drunk."

I dipped my head, breathing in her scent, and guilt washed over me. "I'm sorry. I just …" I shook my head, unable to explain.

"I know." Her voice was soft. "Let's get you inside."

***

The hot water on my skin and Riley's fingers in my hair as she massaged my scalp eased the tension that had held me in its grip since Gabe told me about the upcoming article. For the moment, locked inside the shower with the woman I loved, I could pretend my entire history wasn't going to spill out for the world to read in just a few short hours.

I focused on her touch, the way her fingers felt, how her lips pressed randomly against my shoulder and the back of my neck while she washed my hair. The role reversal wasn't lost on me. I was spiraling, and she knew it. We'd been here a time or two before, but not quite this bad. I'd had moments of darkness over the years we'd been together. Days where I couldn't tolerate being touched, or have anyone around me, and she'd quietly gone about her business, until I came back to myself.

Knowing she was there snapped me out of it faster. I stopped reaching for alcohol as a distraction from the ghosts that haunted me and started reaching for her, instead. I thought that meant things were getting better …

Her fingers trailed down my neck and found my shoulders, kneading gently, and I tipped my head forward to rest against the tiled wall. Riley didn't speak, didn't ask questions, just worked on the knots of tension bunching my shoulders together until I felt them loosen. Her palms slid down my back, thumbs massaging either side of my spine and my eyes closed, her touch chasing the darkness away, at least temporarily.

When her fingers reached my ass, I pushed away from the wall and turned. Cupping her face between my palms, I tipped her head up and kissed her. Her lips parted for my tongue, and I licked away the water beading on them before delving inside to taste her. Her arms rose, looped around my neck and the movement lifted her breasts, so they brushed against my chest. My lips left her so I could bite a path down her throat, as I backed her across the shower until her back hit the tiles.

"Why do you stay with me?" I licked a path down to one breast and sucked her nipple into my mouth.

"Because I love you."

I bit down. She gasped, her back arching.

"That's not a good reason for staying with someone if they're hurting you."

"You don't hurt me. You hurt yourself."

I kissed my way down her stomach, lowering myself to my knees in front of her. My lips found the devil tattoo on her hip. "I need you to go back to your mom's place tonight."

"What? No." Her refusal was predictable.

I leaned back and looked up at her. "Shutterbug, please do this for me. I don't want you here when that article drops."

"And that's *why* I should be here. I'm not going to leave you alone." Her fingers landed on the top of my head and threaded into my hair. "I *love* you, Seth. What kind of girlfriend would I be if I walked away when you're going through this?"

I wrapped my arms around her hips, and rested my head against her stomach. "I'm not going to be able to protect you from this, Riley. You don't understand. *No one* does. This article tomorrow? It's only the start. Once other outlets jump on it, it'll be everywhere. You won't be able to move without seeing someone somewhere reporting on it. Do you really want to be associated with that? It's going to be a media circus."

"You were a *child*, Seth. You can't be held responsible for what those people made you do."

"I know that ... up here." I unwound one arm so I could tap the side of my head. "But, after tomorrow, I'm no longer Seth Hawkins, guitarist in Forgotten Legacy. I'm Nathaniel Enshaw, abuse victim. They'll look at our relationship and question whether I am repeating the cycle."

The fingers in my hair tightened and she pulled my head back. "You did *not* groom me, Seth." There was a bite to her voice, fire in her eyes. "If anyone is at fault, it's me. *I* chased *you*. I didn't tell you my age. I *knew*, even without knowing *why*, that you would have an issue with it."

"But—"

"No!" She dropped to her knees in front of me and pressed her hands to my face. "You are not sending me away. We are going to weather this storm together."

CHAPTER 12

FORK IN THE ROAD - GOODY GRACE

Gabe

I couldn't sleep. Not unusual in the grand scheme of things, but it *felt* different. Harper had gone to bed hours ago, and I'd promised to follow her. I even started to. I showered, brushed my teeth, and got as far as the bedroom door before retreating back through the house and outside to sit beside the pool.

Seth's words echoed around my head. Not what he'd *said* particularly—I *knew* he was lashing out at the closest target. His behaviors were ingrained in my head the same way mine were in his. It was the tone in his voice, the utter despair overlaid with anger.

I shouldn't have walked out and left him. I shouldn't have let him push my buttons to the extent that he drove me away. I *knew* Seth, knew his triggers and his reactions and the way he responded to stress, and I *still* let him get under my skin with his fucked-up comments. I pushed up from the rattan chair and ook like glass. I contemplated jumping in. Maybe the water could wash away my own sins. Wash away the guilt of turning my back on my best friend when he was hurting.

"Gabe?" Warm hands smoothed over my shoulders, and the scent of cotton candy surrounded me. "Have you been to bed at all?"

I shook my head and covered her hands with mine.

"You're just wandering around out here naked?"

I glanced down. Huh, I was still naked after my shower. I hadn't even noticed. Her lips pressed against my back, between my shoulder blades.

"What time do the newspapers become available?"

"Five." I ran my tongue over my bottom lip. "I shouldn't have let him get under my skin."

"Seth's always been able to trigger your responses. He knows exactly what to say to get you to do what he wants."

"This was different." I turned to face the woman who'd held my heart since the day we met. "We've always fought. It's just a part of who we are, but this was different, Harper."

"Do you want to go over there?"

"Yes... but I can't." I blew out a breath. "I don't know what to do. This whole thing could snowball fast. His father is out of prison. His mother is... wherever she is. What if his father goes looking for her? Could *she* be the one who gave the press Seth's name?"

"Someone could talk to her, maybe, and find out."

"I've asked Karl if he has any idea where she lives. I think we need to know, at the very least, if his father has been in contact with her."

"Would he be allowed to do that?"

I laughed, the sound harsh in the quiet night. "He's been in prison for over twenty years, Frosty. You think he gives a fuck about what he's allowed to do?"

"I guess you're right. He wouldn't ... You don't think he'd try to talk to Seth, do you?"

I rubbed my forehead. A headache had been threatening all day, since Karl showed me the article. I could feel the tightness around my eyes. "I don't know. Carter has put more security on Seth's place, but no one knows what the guy looks like. For all we know, he could pretend to be a fucking journalist and hang around until Seth comes out."

"Do you think he'd do that?"

"I *don't know!*" I stopped, hearing the bite to my tone and took a deep breath. "I'm sorry. I just don't know," I repeated quietly.

"You should come inside and try to get some sleep. Seth won't be the only one targeted by the press in the morning. You're his closest friend. They're going to come for you, Dex, Luca, and his parents. We all should be prepared not to go out anywhere for the next few days. At least until the initial frenzy dies down."

She reached down for my hand and tugged me away from the pool. "Come to bed, Gabe." I let her draw me back into the house and along the hallway to our bedroom, but I didn't enter. I propped my shoulder against the doorframe and watched as she crossed the room.

The robe she'd worn to find me slipped from her shoulders and fell in a soft whisper of silk to the floor. She was naked beneath it, and I admired the way her hips swayed as she made her way toward the bed. My heart skipped a beat. We'd come so close to not having this, not being together. I'd almost lost her forever. And now I was on the verge of losing Seth. I needed them both. They were part of me. They were my anchors. Without *either* of them, I was incomplete.

"Gabe?" Her soft voice dragged me out of my thoughts, and I summoned a smile. "It'll work out. Let's get through tomorrow and then regroup." She held out one hand. "Come to bed."

I pushed away from the doorframe and closed the distance between us. Taking her hand, I pulled her into my arms.

"I love you, Harper."

She smiled up at me, her hands linking behind my neck. "Always and forever, Gabe."

***

"I have an address." Remy strode into the kitchen. "Carter sent it over to me."

"An address for what?" I set my coffee down onto the table.

"Marcie Enshaw."

"What ... how?" But even as I asked, I knew the answer. Carter would have taken Seth to the place he'd bought for her on the odd occasion he'd been to see his mother. If I'd been thinking clearly, I would have remembered that. Thankfully, Remy *had*. "Give me ten minutes to put some clothes on, and we'll go pay her a visit."

"That's not a good idea. The papps are crawling all over the road outside the house. If we leave, they're going to follow you."

"I don't care. I want to know if she's behind this, and if so, what the fuck was she thinking. She doesn't need money. Seth gives her an allowance."

"Maybe it's not enough. How long has it been since he checked in with her? Could she have gone back to her old ways?"

"I …" I sucked at my bottom lip. "Once an addict, always an addict, you mean? It's possible, I guess. We'll head over and find out."

"You should stay here and let me and Carter do that."

I shook my head before he finished speaking. "No. I'll go. She might be more inclined to talk to me."

Remy didn't look convinced. I didn't care. I was going to do this. I *had* to find out who had leaked the story. I couldn't protect Seth without all the information. So I'd face the papps outside, and go and find the woman who'd given birth to my friend and get the answers he would need, so he didn't have to.

I told Remy to wait for me and went to change out of my sweats and into jeans and a t-shirt. I was pulling on a pair of sneakers when Harper walked in.

"Where are you going?"

"Out with Remy. He's found Marcie Enshaw's address."

"Is that wise?" She knew without me saying a word that I was going to see her. "Have you spoken to Seth?"

"He's not answering his cell." I tried to call him as soon as the sun rose. He hadn't picked up, nor replied to any of the texts I followed the call up with.

"Maybe you should wait until you've spoken to him."

I shook my head. "What if there's more to come out? We need to know."

Neglected Consequences

CHAPTER 13

BROKEN – PALAVE ROYALE

Riley

"No!" Seth's shout tore me out of sleep with a jolt. My eyes snapped open just in time to see him launch himself out of bed and drop to his knees on the carpet.

"Seth?" I leaned up on one elbow. He ignored me. "Lucifer?"

"I'm sorry. I'll do better."

I frowned. His voice was so low I wasn't sure I heard correctly. "Do better at what?"

"Whatever you want." He rose to his feet, and before I could react, he was on top of me. "Do you want me to make you feel good? I can do that." His fingers stroked over my arms, traced over my nipples and then hooked into the thin straps of my top.

"Seth, stop." I caught his wrists as he dragged the straps down my arms.

"Stop?" He frowned, then his features cleared …yet his expression looked off. I couldn't say why, but something wasn't right. "Oh, I understand." He slid down the bed. "You heard about what I can do with my tongue. Is that what you want? My tongue on you?" His mouth touched the thin slither of skin on show between the hem of my top and the waistband of the shorts I was wearing. "Tell me what you want me to do."

"Seth, please ..." I touched the top of his head. "What are you doing?"

"Seth? My name is Nathaniel." He ran a palm up my thigh. "But I can be Seth for you, if that's what you want."

He was asleep. Not only that, he was dreaming about being Nathaniel and ... My heart stuttered. Was he reenacting the things they'd made him do? I bit my lip. I didn't know what to do. I'm sure I read somewhere about not waking someone if they were sleepwalking. Did this count?

His fingers were creeping beneath my shorts. I pushed on his shoulders. He ignored me, lips kissing my stomach, my hip. His fingertips brushed over my pussy. I swallowed, my body reacting to his touch, but my mind screamed at me that this wasn't right. "Stop." My voice was firm.

He froze. "I'm sorry. Did I do something wrong?" His voice was small, almost childlike, and full of so much terror. "Please ... tell me what I should do. Let me make you happy."

I pressed my lips together, blinking away the tears which sprung to my eyes, sucked in a deep breath and cleared my throat. "N-Nathaniel, come and lie beside me. I ... I don't want you to ... to do that right now." I stumbled over the words while I prayed I was doing the right thing and not about to make everything worse.

He crawled up my body, and for a second, I thought he was going to ignore me. His dark eyes stared down at me, and then he shifted sideways and settled beside me.

"That's good," I whispered, fighting to stop my voice from shaking. I reached out to stroke a hand over his hair, pushing a stray lock of hair from his face. It was longer than usual, flopping down into his eyes instead of the short style he usually maintained. "I'd really like you to close your eyes. Could you do that for me?"

"Are you going to hurt me?" The question was toneless, and my heart broke.

"No, I just think it'd be nice to lie here for a while ... don't you?" I stroked over the angles of his face, along his jaw, his lips, along the aristocratic nose. My thumb ran over his eyebrows, touching the small hoop piercing with the little devil hanging from it. "Close your eyes, Nathaniel." I couldn't bear to see the blankness in his gaze, the *emptiness*.

He did as I asked, thick black lashes lowering. "Sleep now," I whispered. I carried on stroking over his skin, keeping my touch light, as gentle as possible, until his breathing evened out, and only then did I let the tears I'd been holding back fall. I cried for the man I loved, the boy he'd been, the tragic childhood he had suffered, and the mess it had left him in.

How he had the strength to continue to function, and to *love* the way he did, amazed me. I sniffed, and twisted to find the box of tissues beside the bed, and wiped my face. When I turned back, it was to find Seth's eyes open and focused on me.

I stared at him. Was it Seth or Nathaniel?

"Why are you crying?" His finger caught a stray tear, and he scowled down at it.

"Seth?" My voice was cautious.

His eyes lifted to meet mine. "Were you expecting someone else?"

I'd never been so relieved to hear the dry sarcasm in his voice, and I threw myself at him, wrapping my arms around his waist and knocking him onto his back. His hands came to rest on my spine, pulling me close.

"What's going on?"

I shook my head, pressing kisses to his throat. "Nothing. Just a bad dream."

Fingers found my chin, tipped my head up and away from his throat. "I can help with that."

He rolled, came down above me, and covered my mouth with his. I fell into the kiss. Maybe I shouldn't have, but the sheer relief of having Seth back instead of the lost little boy I'd had a glimpse of made me desperate to anchor myself in reality. And the reality of Seth's mouth on mine, of his hands slipping beneath my top to find and cup my breasts, chased away the living nightmare of earlier.

Maybe subconsciously, he felt a similar sense of relief. His movements seemed urgent as he dragged my t-shirt up my body and over my head, and he lowered his head to kiss a path down to my breast. When his tongue licked over my nipple, I froze, his words of a few minutes earlier coming back to me.

Seth, attuned to my every mood, looked up at me. "Riley?" His voice was soft.

I shook my head. "Wait. Give me a second." I couldn't get the lost expression he'd worn out of my head, the despair in his voice when he'd asked me what I wanted, how he could make me happy. I thought about how when he saw my tears, he immediately associated helping me feel better with making me orgasm. It wasn't the first time, I realized. *Every single time* I was upset about something—an argument with my mom, frustration over my day, *anything*—his instinct was to kiss, to touch, to drive me to orgasm ... yet, if I really thought about it, none of those times included having full sex, or me pleasuring him.

Oh god, had I been continuing the cycle he'd learned as a child?

I bit my lip and wriggled out from beneath him, so I could sit up. He didn't stop me, rolling onto his side and propping his head up on one hand.

"What's wrong?"

"I love you, Seth." I sat on the side of the bed, my back to him.

"Then why are you all the way over there?" Fingers trailed down my spine. "Shutterbug?"

I twisted, caught his shoulders and pushed him down onto the mattress. He didn't resist, falling back against the pillows while I climbed over him so I could straddle his waist. His hands curved over my hips.

"I like where this is going." A small smile tipped his lips up.

"If I hadn't come here tonight, what would you have done?"

"Fallen into a wine coma, and woke up tomorrow dehydrated, hungover, and very irritable." His thumb stroked over the waistband of my shorts. "Take these off."

"Do you remember waking up?" I ignored his demand.

"To find you crying? It was only a couple of minutes ago. Of course I do. What kind of bad dream was it?"

Neglected Consequences

CHAPTER 14

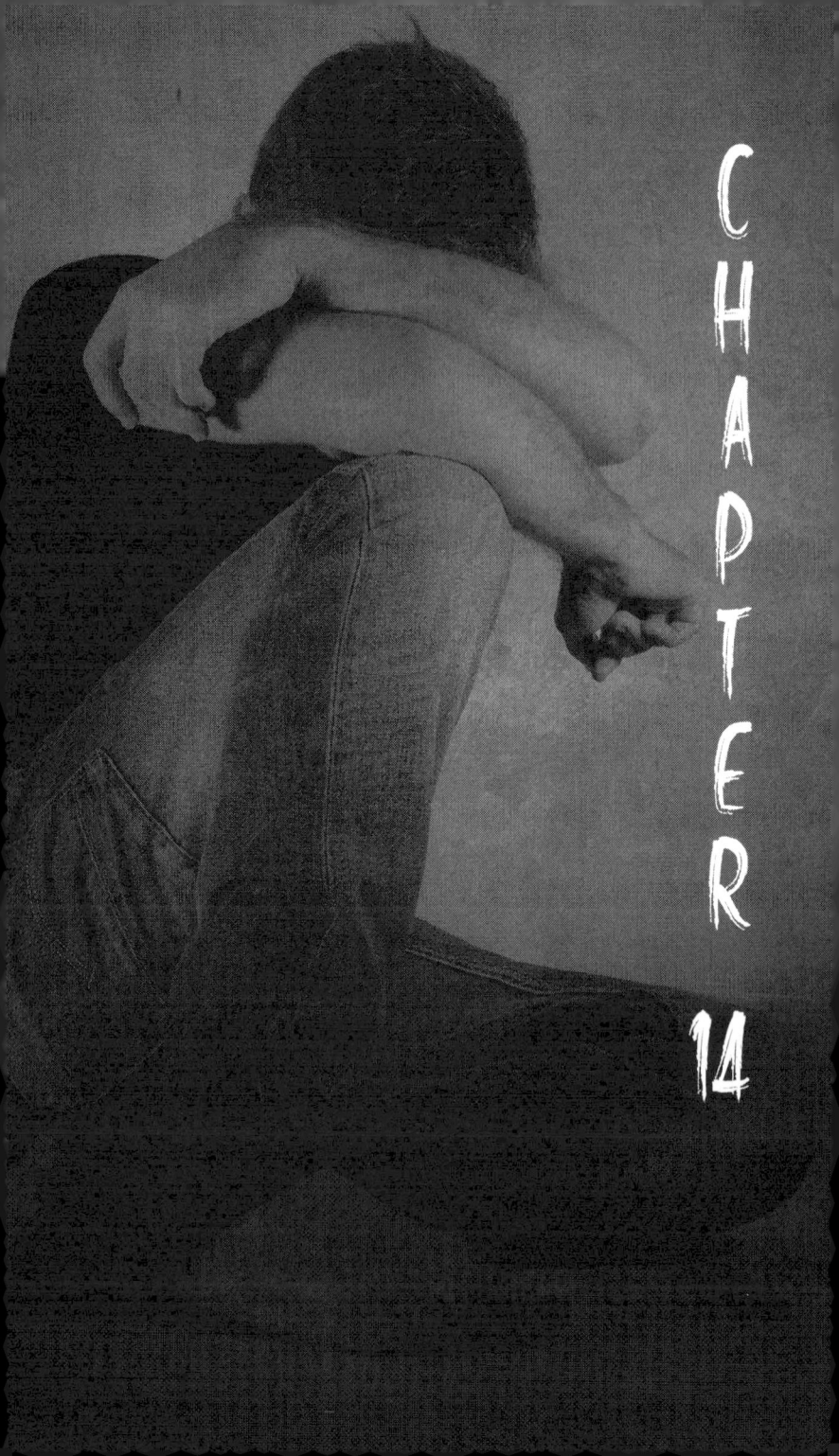

ALWAYS DO - THE KID LAROI

Seth

I kept my voice light, but I *knew* why she was crying. I *knew* it wasn't from a dream she'd had. I *knew* what I'd done moments before. I'd been in a weird half-awake/half-asleep state, roused out of a dream about my past. That, combined with the alcohol I'd consumed, had kept me in the dream when I opened my eyes.

I stroked a finger down her cheek when the silence lengthened. "Ri, it's okay."

"Is it?" A tear escaped and tracked down her cheek.

"Hey." I cupped her face, brushing the tear away with my thumb. "Don't cry for me, Riley."

"But—"

"No." I pulled her head down to mine and kissed her. She resisted, her hands hitting my shoulders and pushing away.

"Stop doing that."

"Doing what?" I reached for her again.

"Trying to make me feel better." She locked her arms

stopping me from sitting up.

"You don't want me to make you feel good?"

"No! Yes! Of course I do. You *always* make me feel good." She stopped, sighed, then lowered her head so she could press small kisses along my shoulder. "I just mean ... let *me* make *you* feel good for a change."

Her lips burned a path down my chest, flicked at the bar piercing my nipple, and continued down, her destination clear. My eyes slid closed, when she pushed one hand beneath the waistband of my sweats and curled her fingers around my dick.

"Tell me what you like, Seth." Her breath was warm against my hip.

I tensed, her words sending a twinge of uneasiness through me. Words I associated with my past. Words I'd said almost daily throughout my childhood. She kissed my stomach, licked over the tattoos which wrapped around my body, and dragged down my sweats. I didn't stop her as I fought against the memories threatening to ruin the moment.

This wasn't the same. We were both adults. Both willing.

I didn't realize I was gripping the sheets until Riley raised her head and said my name. I opened my eyes, and found her looking up at me, expression concerned.

"It's okay. I'm okay."

"You don't have to pretend with me." Her words were soft, and I groaned at the realization that so was my dick. Soft and unresponsive in her hand. The woman I loved had her hands on me, and I wasn't even fucking hard.

"I'm sorry. It's not—"

"Don't apologize." She bit her lip, staring up at me, then seemed to come to some kind of decision. She moved around on the bed until she could lie beside me. "Can we try something?"

"What kind of something?"

"Close your eyes." I threw her a frown, but did as she asked. Her fingers were still stroking my dick, light caresses up and down. "Do you want me to stop touching you?"

"No." The mattress bounced and my eyes popped open. "What are you doing?" *Why the fuck did I sound worried ... scared, even?*

"Close your eyes, Seth." Her voice was soft and her lips, when they brushed over my hip, were warm. "What is your favorite thing for me to do?"

"I like watching you come for me."

She kissed down my thigh. "That wasn't what I meant. What is your favorite thing for me to do to *you*? Is it this?" She gave a slow stroke of my dick. "This?" Her tongue replaced her fingers and she licked along my length. I hardened. She laughed quietly. "You like that, then."

I didn't answer.

"Seth?" She swirled her tongue around the head of my dick. "If you could ask me to do anything, what would it be?"

"Whatever you want." I resisted the urge to guide her back down onto my dick.

She shook her head. "No, I want to know what *you* want. Just one thing. Tell me *one* thing."

"Your mouth on my dick."

"Like this?" Her lips slid over the tip, and the sensation of being engulfed in warm wetness sparked my nerves to life.

"Fuck. Yes." I wanted to tangle my hand into her hair and control the speed she was sucking me. I wanted to open my eyes, but she'd said not to ...

My eyes snapped open.

Wait ... I could do all of those things. Why did I think I couldn't? I wasn't submissive. I didn't get off on being controlled, being commanded. Why was I following instructions?

The dream ... *nightmare* ... finally relinquished me from its grip, and the tightness in my chest eased.

I lifted my head to look down my body so I could watch as her head bobbed up and down. She licked at me, sucked, lapped at me, until I couldn't stop myself from reaching for her. I wound a hand into her hair and dragged her head up until only the head of my dick balanced on her lips. Her eyes lifted, caught me staring at her, and she smiled.

"Take what you want, Seth," she whispered ... and I did.

I forced her head down, her lips parting to swallow my dick, until I hit the back of her throat and she gagged. I held her there, savoring the way it felt. Her tongue slid along me, the wet heat of her mouth surrounded me, and I felt every move she made, every swallow as I controlled the way she moved, the depths she took me, with my hand in her hair.

She didn't stop me, didn't resist, and my hips jerked up, thrusting into her mouth, until my nerves stretched and tightened, my blood sang, and I threw my head back to fight against the orgasm building beneath my skin.

Her fingers stroked over me, along my thighs, between my legs to cup my balls so she could squeeze, stroke, and caress me. I gritted my teeth, my movements becoming uncoordinated as I lost the battle to stay in control. My dick throbbed, pulsed, and I spilled into her mouth, a guttural growl tearing from my throat. She didn't pull away, her lips sealed around my dick as I came… It lasted for minutes, hours, a *lifetime* … and she was there for all of it, swallowing down every drop as I jerked and shuddered beneath her.

I was boneless, weak, dazed. I couldn't move, couldn't even open my eyes, and I lay there, panting, chest heaving, heart racing as I struggled to realign my senses.

Fingers touched my arm, my jaw, my lips and I forced my lids to part. My head was like a heavy weight and I rolled it to the side and Riley's face filled my vision. Her lips glistened, and her tongue slid over them, licking away the last traces of my cum, and the action stirred my dick back to wakefulness. Her smile widened, and she traced over the tattoos covering my ribs with one finger.

"Come here." My voice came out low and gravelly.

She shook her head.

"I want to eat you."

Another headshake. I narrowed my eyes. "You said I should take what I want, Shutterbug." I moved, rolled, and pinned her beneath me. "And I want *you*."

Neglected Consequences

CHAPTER 15

THE FOUNDATIONS OF DECAY - MY CHEMICAL ROMANCE

Gabe

"This is the place." Remy pulled up outside the gated community. He twisted in the seat to look at me. "Are you sure you want to do this?"

"Have you checked the internet and television this morning? *Everyone* is talking about Seth. If his mother *was* behind this, we need to silence her before she says anything else."

"And how do you propose doing that?"

"Maybe she wants more money, a better house, a lifetime supply of heroin—*something*. Everyone has a price."

"You know someone who can supply drugs?"

I tapped my chest. "Rock star, Remy. Drugs are within reach all the fucking time."

After a second, Remy nodded, and rolled down his window to speak to the security standing near the gate. "We're here to see Marcie Enshaw."

"Is she expecting you?"

"No, but tell her that her son's friend, Gabe, is here."

"One moment." He disappeared inside the small booth and I could see him through the window, talking on a phone. He came back out less than a minute later. "Go through. Drive to the end of the road, then turn right. Her condo is number thirty-four, in block five. She's waiting for you."

Remy nodded, waited for the gates to open, then drove through.

"What is this place?" I leaned forward in my seat, looking out at three-story buildings. Each one was painted in bright colors, with balconies. Grassed areas surrounded by white picket fences separated each building. The way it was laid out gave the entire area an almost surreal too-perfect appearance.

"It's a private care facility, which gives its patients a feeling of independence. They have their own homes and money to spend. There's even a grocery store on the site. But they can't leave without company, and there is on-site nursing staff as well. It's a pretty clever set-up, to be honest," Remy explained. "Of course, it's only available to people with a certain level of income."

We reached the end of the road, and he turned to the right. I counted along until we reached block five.

"Guess we're here."

"And you are one hundred percent committed to doing this?"

"I get it, Remy. You don't think it's a good idea."

"I just think you should have spoken to Seth first."

"I would have if he hadn't decided to go down the 'fuck you and the horse you rode in on' route instead. All I'm going to do is talk to her, see if she spoke to anyone. For all we know, it's nothing to do with her." But my gut told me it had *everything* to do with her.

Remy opened his door and climbed out. I joined him on the sidewalk, and we both looked at the apartment building. The entrance door swung open before either of us could move, and a small dark-haired woman walked out.

I could immediately see the resemblance to Seth. From what he'd told me, she was only in her early forties, but she looked older. Seth thought she'd been around ten when she gave birth to him and twelve when she had Lexi.

They had the same dark hair, but as she drew closer, I saw her face shape was softer and their eyes were different. Seth's were dark, almost black at times. Marcie's were a light brown. I held out my hand.

"Hi. My name's Gabe. I'm a friend of Seth's."

She smiled. "I know who you are, sweetie. Come inside." Her voice was hoarse, raspy, but her smile was warm.

I glanced at Remy uneasily. She seemed pleasant enough, but something was off about her. Nothing I could pinpoint, but the back of my neck prickled, and my fingers curled around the lighter in my pocket.

"Is Seth coming to visit? I haven't seen him in a while. He called a couple of months ago, though. My sweet boy."

"I'm sorry, he's not."

"Come in. Come in." She caught my sleeve and tugged me forward. "You're very pretty. I can see why Seth likes you."

I stopped, sure I'd misheard. "I'm sorry?"

"He's very pretty, too. I can just imagine the two of you together. You would look very beautiful."

"I don't ... you mean photographs? Has he showed you photographs of the band?"

"No, sweetie, he hasn't. But I've seen them. On the internet and on the television. You complement each other wonderfully."

"I ... uh ..." I cleared my throat, uncomfortable with the way she was talking. "Have you seen the news today?" I asked as I walked into the condo Seth paid for her to live in. The space was light, airy.

"Yes. Isn't it wonderful? It must be so much better for Nate now everything is out in the open. No need to hide anymore."

"You think it's a good thing?" My gaze followed her as she moved around the room.

"Would you like something to drink? Soda? Tea? I do like a cup of tea, don't you? With honey, to make it sweet."

"No, thank you." My mind screamed at me. Something was wrong, off. I gripped my lighter tighter and looked around to check where Remy was. He stood in the doorway, a frown drawing his brows together as he scanned the room. He caught my eye and gave a discreet nod toward the door set on the opposite wall, and he lifted one finger.

"Hey, Marcie ... I can call you that, right?" I injected a warm note into my voice, wrapped myself in my public rock star persona. "Did I interrupt you?"

"Of course not, sweetie." She smiled again, and I finally realized what I was seeing.

Her eyes were glassy, unfocused. Her smile was overly-bright, almost comical in the way her mouth stretched open. I took note of the way she paced the room, her fingers plucked at the skin of the opposite arm, and I took a slow step backward toward Remy.

My gut was screaming at me to get out, to leave. My heart was telling me I needed to do this for Seth.

The door opposite swung open and in my heightened state of awareness, it seemed to happen in slow motion—a tall man, hair just as dark as Marcie's, stepped through.

I stopped breathing.

CHAPTER 16

BAD PLACE - HUNNA
Seth

I left Riley asleep in bed and crept out of the bedroom. I didn't know what magic the woman possessed, but I felt good... better than I should. Not perfect, but good enough to feel able to face the day without reaching for alcohol.

Carter was in my kitchen when I entered, my bare feet barely making a sound on the stone floor. He turned, mug of coffee in hand, and cast his gaze over me.

"You look tired." He held out the coffee.

"Thanks." I took it. "I'm okay. How does it look?"

"Two news vans, and the usual suspects. I wouldn't make any plans to go anywhere today."

I set down my mug onto the table. "I have to. Can you get me out of here without being seen? I need to speak to Marcie."

"You could call her."

"I want to see her. I think this might have been her. I want to see her face when I ask."

"You could *video* call her."

I shook my head. "I should have done it yesterday, but …" I waved a hand. "It didn't quite pan out how I planned."

"No shit." He glanced toward the door. "If you're insisting on doing this, we could take a different car. If you ducked down in the back seat, we might be able to get out without you being seen. I can't promise we won't be followed. There may even be reporters at the community when you get there."

"I'm willing to take the risk."

"Okay. When do you want to go?"

"Let me shower first. I'll wake Riley and let her know."

"I think you should bring her along. It might make things easier."

I considered it. "Maybe. I'll ask her."

"Ask me what?" Hands curved over my shoulders and lips kissed their way up my throat.

I angled my head, giving her easier access to my neck, and lifted my hands to link with hers. "I thought you'd sleep for longer."

"I missed you." She rounded the chair and climbed onto my lap, hooking one hand around my neck, and stealing my coffee with the other. I looped my arm around her waist to steady her balance while she sipped my drink.

"I'll be out with the car." Carter left the pair of us alone, closing the kitchen door quietly behind him.

"About last night—"

"Is that what happens on the nights I don't stay over?" She spoke over me. "You have bad dreams?"

"Sometimes. Not usually as bad as last night."

"You remember it, then? I wasn't sure."

"Something like that." I touched her cheek and guided her face round so I could meet her eyes. "I wanted to thank you."

"Thank me? For what?"

"For staying? For doing what you did?" I gave a self-conscious laugh when she frowned. "I don't know, Riley ... for being there for me."

"Seth, I *love* you. Why wouldn't I do those things?"

How could I explain? The only ... *only* ... person who'd ever been unconditional in their support of me was Gabe. And even though I'd been in a relationship with Riley for four years, in the back of my mind, I *still* questioned whether she'd walk away if she saw the reality of who I was.

Her palm curved over my jaw, and she shifted on my lap so she was facing me. "I'm not going anywhere. You showed me your past four years ago. Maybe not all of it, but *enough* for me to put the pieces together. This article they're publishing today doesn't change anything between us, Lucifer. You're always going to be my dark, beautiful angel, and I love you."

I turned my face and kissed her palm. "I have to go and see Marcie."

"Is that what you were talking about with Carter?"

I nodded. "Would you come with me?"

Carter was right. Having her with me would make things easier. I thought, when he suggested it he meant dealing with the situation, but that wasn't it. Riley's presence would make it easier for *me* to face *her*—my mother.

"Of course I will." There was no hesitation in her voice.

***

We opted to go in Carter's SUV, with its blacked-out windows, and ducked down on the back seat as he drove out of the gates, which separated my house from the world. Riley held my hand as he inched forward through all the reporters gathered outside. Shouts to Carter asking if I was in the car, in the house, whether I'd be making a statement came to us clearly. Carter ignored them, and eventually we broke free and he hit the gas and sped away.

We straightened on the seats once we were sure we weren't being followed, and I dropped my head against the back with a sigh. Riley didn't speak, her fingers tracing over my palm, the back of my hand, my wrist, and the touch eased the tension in my shoulders.

We made the journey to the gated community I'd paid to house my mother in silence and, after a quick murmured conversation with the security guard, we were allowed through. When we pulled up outside the block of condos my mother lived inside, there was another car, similar to ours, parked there.

"Isn't that Remy's car?" Riley said from beside me.

I straightened. "What? Why would Remy be here?" But I knew the answer to that. Remy was here because *Gabe* was. And sure enough, as we climbed out of the car, Gabe was coming out of the door, Remy close behind him.

"What are you doing here?" I bit out.

Gabe stopped on the path, blocking my way. "Don't go in there." He ignored my question.

"I said, what are you doing here?" My anger with him being there was irrational. I knew that somewhere inside, but I couldn't stop it from taking over.

"I knew you'd want to find out if *she* was behind the article. I came here so *you* didn't have to."

"Without talking to me first?"

"You didn't *want* to listen, remember?" He didn't react to the aggression in my tone. "Look, man, I get it. I understand how much this is fucking you up."

"You have no fucking idea!" I started past him. He grabbed my arm.

"Seth, listen to me. *Don't* go in there."

I shook him off. "Stop fucking interfering."

He stepped in front of me. "You think I'm going to stand by and watch while you go through this? You had my back when I lost Harper. Why the fuck do you think I'm not going to do the same for you?"

"I didn't ask you to."

"I didn't ask you to keep Harper from me when I was in hospital, but you did it, anyway, because you wanted to protect me."

"It's not the fucking same, Gabe!" I shouted.

"No, you're right. It's not. This is worse." He glanced at Riley. "He needs to turn around and go home."

"Don't fucking talk like I'm not even here. I'm here to see my mother. *My* mother, Gabe, not yours."

"Is this where you throw down the fact that I don't have a mother because she didn't care enough about me to keep on living? You're losing your touch, Hawkins." His voice was light, but I knew my unspoken barb had hit home, because his hand was in his pocket and I was certain it would be clutching his lighter.

"Stop making everything about you, Mercer. The world doesn't revolve around you and your fucking problems."

"Good to see you've finally grown a backbone, son."

Time stopped.

Neglected Consequences

CHAPTER 17

BATTLE SCARS - MOD SUN

Gabe

"Gabe." Remy's voice was a low growl behind me, but I didn't want to risk breaking eye contact with the man walking across the floor toward me.

He stopped two feet from me, and cold black eyes swept over me from head to toe and back up again. "I didn't get Nate's obsession with you when I saw you on television, but I see it now. You have a brokenness around you that would have attracted him when you were children."

His smile was Seth's, and the fine hairs on my arms rose. I took a step back, instincts honed from childhood recognized the danger. My instincts screamed that this man wasn't safe to be around, in more ways than Seth had ever detailed.

"Why are you here?" I marveled at how stable my voice was when inside I was fucking shaking. There was a darkness surrounding him. One I knew all too well.

"To reconnect with the mother of my children, of course." He held out a hand and snapped his fingers. Marcie scurried over to him. The look of utter adoration on her face as she gazed up at him turned my stomach.

"Aren't there any limitations on your release?" How the fuck did I sound so calm, when all I wanted to do was get the fuck out of there? "Why did they even let you out?"

"I was the perfect inmate. Never a problem. No trouble. Completely rehabilitated." He smiled at me again.

I wanted to tell him to *stop* fucking smiling. It was Seth's smile. *Seth's* eyes. Seth's features on an older face.

I wanted to throw up. "How did you know where she was?"

"I don't understand the question. I've *always* known where Marcie was. Haven't I, my love?" He looked down at the woman leaning against his side.

Bile rose up in my throat when she patted his chest and returned his smile, her eyes empty of anything but complete submission to the man beside her. "My Raphael has always watched over me." She looked at me. "He wants us to be a family again. Me, him, Nate, and Olivia."

"His name is *Seth*."

"That's the name he hides behind. His name is Nathaniel." The man took another step toward me.

"Stay where you are." Remy moved between us. "You don't come any closer. Gabe, go outside."

I ignored him. "Are you behind the interview? Did you set it up?"

"Me? Of course not. That was all Marcie. Nathaniel needed to be reminded about who he was, who he belongs to. It's time he stopped pretending."

"Pretending *what*? That he wasn't fucking abused by the people who should have protected him?"

He laughed. "*Abused?* Is *that* what he told you? I assure you, Nathaniel was a more than willing and enthusiastic participant in our entertainment... once he stopped sniveling, anyway."

"He was a fucking child." I snarled, and started forward.

"Enough!" Remy's hand slammed against my chest and shoved me back a step. "He's goading you. *Outside. Now!*"

I spun on my heel and stalked out, just in time to see Seth climb out of a car.

Fuck.

***

"Good to see you've finally grown a backbone, son."

Seth's face drained of color at the soft words. Riley gasped beside him and her eyes darted from Seth to the man and back again. I knew what she was seeing—the exact same thing I had. Two men of different ages with features so similar it was impossible to deny their connection.

"You were such a weak child, always sniveling and crying. Your sister was the strong one. She knew how to bend people to her will. So much potential lost. I had plans for Olivia. Where is she?"

Remy kept his body between us as the older man passed me and strolled toward Seth. My eyes didn't leave my friend.

"Riley, go back to the car." Seth's voice was quiet.

"*All* of you get in the cars," Remy said.

"Raphael," Marcie called, her voice high and girly. "Hasn't our son grown up to be so beautiful?"

Seth's eyes jerked away from Raphael and landed on his mother. His fingers curled and he launched himself at the older man. I lunged into movement before I even registered the thought, throwing myself in front of Seth and grabbing his arms, forcing him backward.

"No. Don't give him the satisfaction."

"Get the fuck off me." He fought against my hold.

"No, I can't let you do it, Seth."

"Back the *fuck* off!"

His wild swing connected with my temple. I staggered sideways, head ringing from the blow, gave myself a shake and went for him again. I was a second too late. He threw a punch at Raphael, who dodged it and grabbed Seth's wrist.

"Silly boy. Did you learn *nothing?*" He twisted Seth's arm up, hauling him closer, and bent his head closer. "Respect your parents, Nathaniel. You remember the punishment for disobedience, don't you?"

And then Carter and Remy were there. Carter hauled Seth away, while Remy forced Raphael away from us. "Community security is on their way," Remy told him. "Leave now."

"I have permission from Marcie to be here."

"Marcie is here under *Seth's* orders. *She* doesn't get to give permission."

The two men stared at each other. Remy's lip curled up, the

slightest hint of his teeth visible, and Raphael's smile faltered.

"Fine. If that's how this needs to be, I'll leave." His head swung around, gaze pausing on me. His smile returned, but he didn't say a word as he strode down the path to a car parked further along the road.

"Raphael!" Marcie cried out and Remy caught her as she attempted to run after him.

"Back inside, Ms. Enshaw."

At the sound of her voice, Seth pulled out of Carter's grip, but instead of going toward his mother, he spun and came toward me.

"Why the fuck did you stop me?"

"Because you were doing exactly what he wanted you to do."

"Not that. This could have ended years ago, but you fucking stopped me." He shoved at my shoulders. "You should have let me go."

At his words, memories hit me and I knew what he was talking about.

"You wouldn't let *me* go. Why the fuck would I let you?"

"So it was revenge? Because I stopped you from ending the pain all those times, you returned the fucking favor? That's what this is?" Okay, so Forgotten Legacy's Devil was coming out to play.

"What the fuck are you talking about?" I refused to rise to the bait. There were times to fight. This wasn't one of them.

"I could have been with Lexi now. You stopped me."

And just like that, exhaustion overwhelmed me. I sighed.

"Fine, you're right. That's what it was, Seth. I stopped you from killing yourself because I was being fucking petty."

Neglected Consequences

CHAPTER 18

MAD WORLD - PALAYE ROYALE

Gabe
AGE 11

"Gabriel, this is Nathaniel Enshaw. I want you to show him around the school today."

"My name is Seth." His voice was softer than I expected it to be.

"Oh! I'm sorry. In my records, you're listed as—"

"My name is *Seth*." He cut the school counselor off.

"Alright, Seth. I'm sorry. Do you have everything you need?" The angry-looking boy hefted the black rucksack. "Good. We've put you on the same schedule as Gabriel for now, while you find your feet."

He glared at me, then away.

"Okay, Gabriel, I'm going to leave Seth with you and check in at the end of the day. Get moving, boys, or you'll be late for class."

I shoved to my feet and walked out of the office.

"M-math is th-this way."

"What did you mean like attracts like?" He repeated the

words I'd said to him when I sat beside him in the hallway outside the principal's office.

I reached for his arm as we walked along the hallway. He evaded my grip, so I lifted *my* arm and pointed at the scar across my wrist.

"You m-made the same m-mistake I did." I ran my nail across my arm. "C-cutting horizontally instead of v-vertically."

"Yeah?"

"Yeah. See, c-cutting horizontally only n-nicks the vein. V-vertically o-opens it up and m-means you're m-more likely to b-bleed out before s-someone gets t-to you."

"Given it some thought, huh?"

I laughed. "Little b-bit." I stopped outside a door. "M-maths is in h-here." I didn't go inside. "They're a sp-special bunch."

"Special, how?"

I rubbed the back of my neck. "Y-you'll s-see." I pushed open the door.

The noise from inside washed over us. Kids laughing, shouting, and calling out to each other. I stepped through and attention immediately found me.

"Hey, st-st-stutter boy. Who's your boyfriend?"

I ignored the question and continued on my path across the room to the two empty desks in the far corner. A shadow fell across me, and a hand curled into my shirt. I sighed quietly. James Mallory—most popular kid in my year and personal pain in my ass. For some reason, he'd made it his primary focus this semester to try and bully me. *Try* because, usually, I just ignored him.

But today was different.

Today I'd already been my da's target. Today I wasn't in the mood to turn away.

I lifted my head, met his eyes, and smirked. "F-fuck you." I buried my fist into his stomach. He doubled over, eyes widening and breath leaving his lungs in an explosive, garlic-tinged gust of air.

There was a beat of silence, and then the class erupted.

"The little fucker gut-punched him."

"What the fuck?"

"Kill him, James!"

James was too winded to respond. I glanced around and spotted his two friends, Sean Cordyn and Philip Nestor, moving toward me.

Go big or go home, right?

I swung my bag off my shoulder and hit James in the face with it, knocking him down, and swung to face his friends. "C-come on …" The words faded as Seth slamming Sean's nose into his knee filled my vision.

I didn't have a chance to ask what he was doing before Philip was on me, pummelling me to the ground. His foot caught my ribs, and I rolled away seconds before his next kick connected with the side of my head. Before I could regain my feet, his body slammed into mine, and Seth's boot made impact with his mouth. Blood sprayed over me and Philip slumped, a heavy weight on top of me.

A hand appeared. "Who needs this kind of math?" Seth hauled me to my feet just as the teacher walked in.

"What the hell is going on in here?" he roared.

Everyone fell silent. I waited.

"Someone get Philip to the nurse. James, are you okay? Someone explain to me what happened!"

Seth looked at me. I shrugged. It didn't matter what I said. I knew how this was going to play out.

"Mercer attacked James, sir."

And *there* it was.

Mr. Martin's gaze landed on me. "Is that true, Gabriel?"

I shrugged.

"Tell me your version."

I didn't reply.

His attention turned to Seth. "You're the new boy. Seth, was it?" He waited for Seth's nod. "Do *you* want to tell me what happened?"

"The fucker went for Gabe, so he defended himself."

"Language, Seth." He pursed his lips. "Why don't the pair of you go down to the library? Gabe, you know what you're supposed to be working on, right?"

I gave another shrug.

"Okay, then take Seth and catch him up. Bring your work to me before lunch."

"But, sir, the new kid knocked out two of Philip's teeth," Sean protested. "And Mercer went for James first."

"You boys seem to think I'm blind to the way you behave. You might have other teachers fooled, but not me. Sit your ass down. Another incident like this and I'll have the three of you on report."

"You can't do that. *They* assaulted *us*."

"I'm pretty confident there was provocation. Philip will be fine. James should learn to keep his mouth shut." He turned back to us. "Go on. Get out of here."

I walked out of the classroom, Seth on my heels.

"You sh-shouldn't have h-helped me." We were halfway down the hallway before I spoke.

"It was three against one."

"It al-always is."

"Not anymore."

I frowned at him. "You h-have n-no reason to h-help me."

"Like attracts like, you said. Did you mean it?"

I nodded.

"Then there's your reason."

CHAPTER 19

ALL THE SMALL THINGS - BLINK 182

Seth

AGE 11

I don't know what it was about the gray-eyed dark-haired boy I'd been paired with. He was smaller than me, skinnier, and every time he moved, I could see bruises poking out beneath his shirt's collar or cuffs. Maybe he was right, and *like* did attract *like*.

But whatever he was dealing with, it wasn't beating him down and I liked that about him. He was a fighter. *I* was a fighter. Maybe together we could survive. Something about him attracted me. Not in an 'I want to fuck you' kinda way but I felt a connection to him, like two magnets seeking each other out.

The rest of the school day was uneventful. Different school, same shit. I figured out the hierarchy in the classes. Who were the popular kids—not Gabe, that was for certain. Who were the teachers' favorites—for the most part, also *not* Gabe. The math teacher seemed to have a soft spot for him, but the rest viewed him the same way our classmates did.

Odd. Outsider. Troublemaker.

He was all of those things. He embraced the role, but I recognized it for the act it was because it was the same one I used to distract from the truth, and hide from questions.

"Sm-smoke?" Gabe offered me a cigarette and I took it, bending my head to light it from the zippo that appeared in his hand.

We sat on the wall outside school. I was waiting for my new foster parents to collect me. I wasn't sure why Gabe was there.

"Don't you have a home to go to?"

He threw me a smile around the cigarette hanging from his mouth. "My d-da won't n-notice I'm n-not there."

"Did he give you those?" I pointed at the bruises on his arms.

"Yep. W-what did yours give y-you?"

"Emotional trauma." I laughed. "Or so I'm told."

"We sh-should drink t-to that."

"We should." I hopped down off the wall when the car holding my new foster parents pulled up. "This is my ride. Will you be okay?"

"I'm w-waiting for s-someone." He waved a hand. "In fact, h-here she c-comes."

I turned to see a young blonde girl coming toward us.

"Sister?"

He shook his head. "N-neighbor." He tossed the cigarette to the ground and stamped on it. "H-hey, F-frosty." The girl reached us and immediately rose on her toes to plaster a kiss to Gabe's cheek.

"You waited for me!"

"S-said I would. H-how was your f-first d-day?"

"Okay." She threw me a questioning look. "Who's your friend?"

"Seth. Th-this is Harper." He introduced the girl to me.

"I heard you got into a fight today." She wound her arm around Gabe's waist. "It's the first day back, Gabe. Couldn't you get through *one* day?"

He laughed, dropped an arm around her shoulder and squeezed. "Y-you kn-know me. C-can't resist tr-trouble." He winked at me. "See you t-tomorrow."

I watched as they walked away, arms around each other, the sound of the girl chattering about her day fading as the distance between us increased.

"Seth?" My new foster dad's voice called out. "You ready to go?"

I stooped, picked up my bag, and climbed into the back of the car. Lexi was already there. Her smile was wide and happy.

"How did your first day go? Mine was amazing. I met some girls. They said I should try for the cheer squad."

"Why? We'll be gone in a few months."

Her smile faded. "Don't be like that, Nate."

"Stop calling me that."

"Fine. *Seth*."

"How was your day, son?" Jake Hawkins, foster dad number four in the past two years, asked from the front of the car.

"I'm not your son." That killed the conversation immediately, but I could see him casting looks at me through the rear-view mirror as he drove back to the house that had been our new home for the past three weeks.

My lip curled as it came into view. Picture perfect. Front lawn with gnomes, white picket fence, and pastel curtains covering the windows. It was everything a child could have wanted, but there was no point in getting attached. We'd be moved on soon enough, when they realized they couldn't handle me.

***

Gabe wasn't at school the next day. I waited for him until the bell rang for the first lesson. When he still hadn't turned up by lunchtime I hunted down the girl he'd been with the night before.

"Where's Gabe?"

She looked up from her sandwich. "He said he didn't feel well." There was no sign of the smile that had covered her face the last time I'd seen her. Her eyes were red, shiny with tears, and there were dark circles beneath them.

"Are you okay?"

She set down the sandwich. "Seth, right?" I nodded. She stared at me, chewing on her bottom lip. "Look, he'll kill me if I say anything, but maybe you should go and see him." She pulled out a pad and scribbled an address on it. "I'm worried about him." She handed it to me.

I checked the address and calculated how long it would take me to get there and back. It wasn't far from the school, so I should be able to make it there and back before lunch break was over.

Harper's tear-streaked face was in my thoughts as I walked along the road. Something had upset her, but what? Was it something to do with Gabe? She was young, around Lexi's age, I guessed. Had someone hurt her?

I pushed open the door to Gabe's building and climbed the stairs to his floor. When I reached his door, I banged on it. It cracked open a few inches less than thirty seconds later.

"Wh-what are you doing here?" Gabe whispered through the gap.

"Why aren't you in class?"

"H-had something else t-to do."

"Like what?" I pushed the door, sending him back a step and walked inside.

"You d-don't just f-force your way into s-someone's home, Seth." His voice was tired, but he didn't stop me from entering.

"Are you home alone?" I looked around curiously. Beer bottles covered the kitchen sides, but it was the neat pile of white tablets and bottles of cheap cider that caught my eye. "What's that?"

"N-none of your b-business." His eyes darted from mine and I *knew* what he was doing.

"Did you already take any?"

He shook his head. "I'm n-not g-going to d-do it."

"Then why are they there?"

Silently, he peeled up his t-shirt, revealing a huge yellow bruise covering the left side of his body.

"Harper would k-kill me if I ch-checked out on h-her." His laugh was wry. "But sometimes, I j-just…" He huffed out a breath and turned away.

"Is your dad home?"

He shook his head again.

"How much cider do you have?"

"Th-three bottles."

"Grab it and let's get out of here. Dump the pills. What are they, anyway?" I walked across the room and picked one up. Standard over-the-counter painkillers. "I thought you were practicing your knife skills?"

He laughed. "T-too m-messy."

We took the cider, and headed out to the wooded area nearby, tucked ourselves away, out of the view of passers-by, and opened one of the bottles. Neither of us spoke, passing the bottle back and forth until it was half-empty. Gabe settled back in the grass, and threw an arm over his eyes.

I flopped down beside him. "It's quiet here. I like it."

"There's a n-new skatepark down the b-block. I think people f-forget this is here."

"Do you come here a lot?"

He rolled his head sideways and grinned at me. "Is th-that a pickup l-line?"

I scowled.

He laughed. "R-relax, Seth."

Silence fell again. The sun was warm on my skin, and I closed my eyes. I was half-dozing when Gabe next spoke.

"I k-keep a razor blade under my m-mattress. The only th-thing stopping me from using it is H-Harper. Why are y-you still h-here?"

"My sister."

CHAPTER 20

BROTHER - GERARD WAY

Gabe

"I can't get through to him." I'd said that three times since walking back into the house, but Harper didn't point it out. "It's like he's completely shut down to reason."

She set down a mug of coffee in front of me. "Maybe he has. Seth's always been pretty private about what his life was like before him and Lexi came to L.A. Having it spread out for the world to see can't be easy. You understand that. You felt the same way about your dad." She stroked a hand through my hair, tugged my head back and kissed me. "Give him some time, Gabe. Pushing him right now isn't working."

She was right. I *knew* she was, but I didn't want to hear it. I didn't want to think about not having Seth at the end of a call whenever I wanted to talk. Was that selfish? Sure, but we'd been in each other's lives for twenty years. If we didn't see each other, we *spoke* to each other every day without fail the entire time, and now … what? I was supposed to just act like it was okay to not do that? There hadn't been a day since we were paired up in school when we were eleven years old that we didn't have each other's backs. And now I was supposed to sit there and watch him self-destruct?

I stood and grabbed my jacket from the back of the chair.

"Gabe." Harper planted her hand against my chest. "You need to leave him alone."

"He didn't leave me alone when I was fucking up."

"It's not the same." Her hand slid up and curved over my jaw. "I know you want to be there for him, but right now you'll do more damage. Give him space. Let Riley take over for now."

"But—"

"If you go out there, the paparazzi will make a fuss. They're watching us as well as Seth. You know the second they see you, they'll go crazy. Remy has already caught three of them trying to scale the walls. He's brought in more security to patrol the grounds."

I sighed. "Okay, fine."

"Why don't you go down to your studio? Play some music, sing, *write*. I've got a couple of calls to make for the foundation, and then I'll come and join you."

"What you mean is I'm distracting you and you can't concentrate." I summoned a smile and lowered my head to kiss her before releasing her and heading out of the room. "Okay, Frosty."

"Gabe?" Her voice was soft when she called my name as I reached the door. I turned back. "I love you. *Seth* loves you. This will all work out."

***

Two hours of messing around in my studio and I had to concede that Harper knew me way better than I knew myself. The tension holding me taut had relaxed as I fell into the routine of writing lyrics and fooling around with my piano.

My fingers stroked over the keys and picked out the tune to 'Cigarette Daydreams' by Cage The Elephant. My voice filled the room, absently singing the lyrics without really thinking about it while I thought about Seth and the situation he was in. A noise, the sound of a door opening, turned my head as I reached the chorus.

Harper stood, framed in the doorway. I held her gaze, fingers finding the right keys automatically. Her smile was soft, head tilted slightly as she watched me. When I let my fingers slip from the keys, she came deeper into the room and stopped behind me. Her hands landed on my shoulders, and I leaned back to rest my head against her stomach.

"Feel better?"

"Sure." I didn't, but I'd give her what she needed to hear.

Her fingers stroked up my neck, over my jaw, and I let my eyes close. "Karl called. He wants to see you tomorrow. He said to tell you it's not something overly important, so not to worry about it."

"I'll call him back." I straightened. The fingers on my jaw tightened, pulling me back.

"Gabe, *tomorrow*. You don't have to do everything immediately. It's late, and you need to eat. I ordered Chinese."

At her words my stomach rumbled. *When had I last eaten? This morning? Yesterday?* With everything going on, I couldn't remember. I spun on the piano stool and caught her hand so I could pull her to stand between my legs. I pressed my forehead against her stomach and looped my arms around her waist. Her fingers threaded through my hair.

I could stay like this for an eternity, just us with nothing around to disturb the peace, but I knew it was an empty wish. There would *always* be something that required attention. I didn't begrudge it, not really. It was the life I'd chosen, *fought* for, but sometimes I wished I wasn't famous, wasn't known the world over. I wished I could just live a normal life with Harper in some quiet town, in a house, two-point-five kids, a pet, and a white picket fence.

I sighed and pushed upright, gave myself a mental shake and dragged out a smile from deep inside.

"Come on, Frosty. Feed me. I need the energy boost."

"Don't do that."

I frowned. "Do what?"

"Put on your public rock star face when we're alone. You don't have to pretend to be okay."

I had no reply to that, so I held out my hand. She linked her fingers with mine and we headed out of the studio and down the hallway to the kitchen, where she'd already laid out the food. My stomach woke up again the second the smells hit me, and she laughed. I dragged out a chair and sat down.

"Did Karl give any clue what he wants?" I asked while I loaded my plate up with food.

She shook her head. "Just said he wants to go over a few things with you, and not to worry about it."

"I still feel like I should call him."

"No. He was quite adamant about you *not* speaking to him until tomorrow. I think he wants the evening to himself. Maybe he's with Riley's mom. Poor guy is probably as stressed as you are over Seth. I'm sure the NFG office is fielding a lot of calls from the media right now."

I gave a slow nod. I hadn't thought about that. My focus had been purely on Seth and how everything was affecting him.

"Gabe."

I blinked, realized I'd been lost in my own thoughts and reached across the table to take Harper's hand. "I'm okay."

It was a lie. We both knew it, but as long as I kept saying it, we could pretend it was the truth.

CHAPTER 21

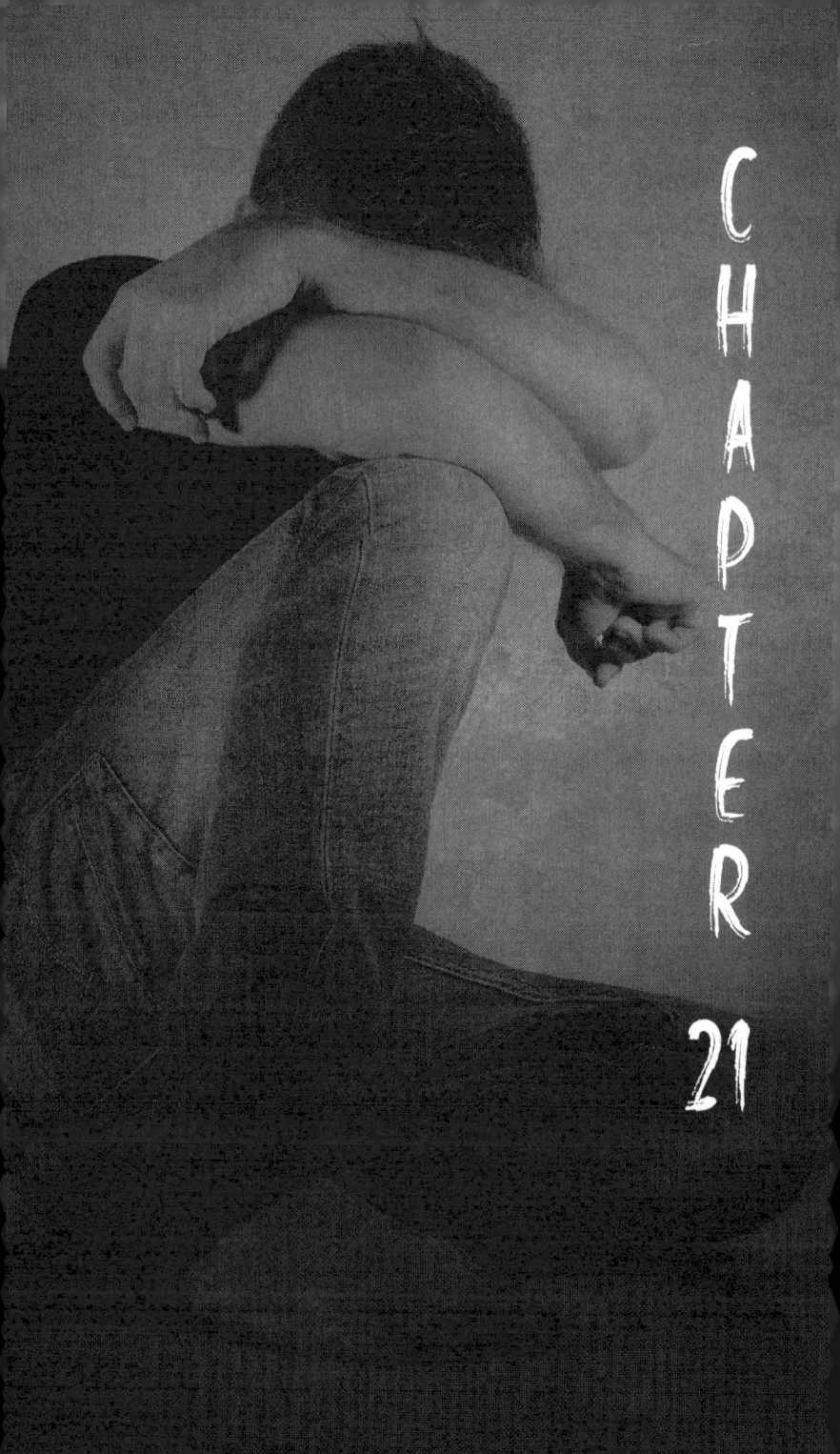

EMPTY - LET DOWN

Seth

Three days.

Seventy-two hours.

Four-thousand-three-hundred and twenty minutes since my world had imploded. Since the man who had donated enough sperm to conceive me and my sister had reappeared, behaving as though he had *every right* to be there. As though he hadn't done the things he'd done. Forced *me* to do things I didn't want to think about.

My cell lit up with an incoming call. I let it go to voicemail. That brought the number up to four calls in the past hour. All from Gabe. All ignored. I didn't want to talk to him. *Couldn't* talk to him, not without anger and disgust unfurling in my stomach. Anger with him. Disgust with myself. Neither emotion was rational. I *knew* that. But I didn't care.

After the confrontation with Raphael, I'd changed my mind about letting Riley stay with me to ride through the media frenzy. I told her I needed her to go back to her mom's and give me space. She'd argued, of course. But after hours of going around in circles, she'd finally given in and left me alone.

I'd upset her. It was all over her face. She thought the night she'd witnessed my regression to Nathaniel meant I was ready to be more open with her. It had, at that moment. It didn't now. With *his* return, it meant I had to be more careful. I didn't want him near Riley, and I needed to keep her far away from whatever was about to go down. To keep her safe, it meant I had to keep her away from me.

I opened a bottle of beer, tossed the cap onto the pile in front of me and took a long swallow. A number flashed up on my cell's screen. Dex. I connected the call and hit the loudspeaker.

"What?"

"So you *are* ignoring Gabe."

"What if I am?"

"Little bit childish, but whatever. I'm just checking to make sure you're still in the land of the living. Riley is at the bookstore with Everleigh and Siobhan. She's worried about you. Says you haven't seen her in a couple of days."

"That's right."

"Who exactly are you punishing right now, Seth? You, Gabe, or Riley?"

"No one."

"Bullshit. The media storm has already died down, and you're still holed up in your house, hiding from the world. Hate to break it to you, but your childhood trauma only made an impact on the people around you. The press don't care anymore. They're ready for the next story."

"Is that where you come in?"

"Me?"

"Gonna have a public overdose and give them a fresh taste of drama?" I lifted the bottle to my mouth and took another mouthful.

"Gabe's right. You're a mean drunk."

"I'm not drunk."

"Sure."

"What do you want, Dex? Did you draw the short straw?"

"No short straw needed. I wanted to check in with you, that's all."

"Well, you've done that. Now fuck off." I ended the call, drained the bottle, and opened another.

Standing, I rounded the lounger and walked across the grass to the self-contained apartment on the other side of the pool. Lexi had lived here for two years before killing herself. Now it was Riley's photography studio. Not that she was working in there right now. She was at her mom's. Far away from me and the poison working its slow way through my veins.

The scrape of a foot against stone sounded behind me and I spun, stumbled, and almost fell into the pool.

"Lexi?" The shimmering form of my sister took shape before me.

"What are you doing, Nate?" Cold fingers touched my cheek and I shivered. "This isn't your path."

"I miss you."

"You shouldn't. I'm always here. That guilt weighing you down? That's me. It's time to let it go. Let *me* go."

"I can't."

"You can. You're holding onto me for no reason."

"No reason? It's *my* fault. Everything is *my* fault, Lex. He's right. I wasn't forced to do all those things. I *chose* to do them."

"It wasn't your choice. Deciding to do something to save someone else the pain isn't a choice, Nate. It's survival. That doesn't mean you were willing."

"If I wasn't willing, I wouldn't have been so good at it. They wouldn't have always asked for me."

"That's not why you were good at it, Nate." Her figure receded and grew faint.

"Don't go. I need you here."

But she left, and took my last bit of fight with her. I grabbed another bottle of beer and lifted it to my mouth. I tipped my head back to drain it, and stepped forward. My foot hit … nothing … and I lost my balance. The bottle hit the water first, then I sank to the bottom of the pool.

"Seth!" A different voice, full of fear, called my name from what seemed like miles away.

"Lex?" I shouted my sister's name, choked, and my eyes snapped open as my head went under the water again.

Neglected Consequences

CHAPTER 22

HOLLOW - BELLE MT

Riley

"Get him out before he drowns!" I screamed at Carter, who threw me a look that spoke volumes since he was already in the water and dragging Seth out of the pool.

As soon as Carter had him on the ground, I dropped to my knees beside him.

"Seth? Baby, open your eyes." I shook him. He didn't move.

"Call 911." Carter gripped Seth's head, tilted it back and pressed his fingers to his throat. "Riley!" he barked and I jerked away, grabbing my cell. While I dialed emergency services, Carter pinched Seth's nose and lowered his head to breathe into his mouth.

"Hello. Hi ... I think ... I need an ambulance." My eyes were glued to Seth, and I had no idea what the person on the other end of the line was saying. "He was in the pool. I think he's swallowed water. He's not breathing."

And then Seth's head twisted to the side. He coughed, spluttered, and vomited water. I dropped the phone.

"Seth? Seth. Oh my god. Seth!" I caught his face between my hands, and vaguely heard Carter speaking, maybe to the person still on the call I'd discarded.

Seth's eyelashes fluttered, and he opened his eyes. "Lex?" His voice was low, rough.

"No. It's me. Riley."

"Ri?" The confusion in his tone was clear. He blinked, frowned, and then his expression cleared. "Shutterbug." His head dropped back against the tiles, eyes sliding closed.

"No. Seth, open your eyes. Look at me."

"I'm tired, Ri."

"I know. I *know*, baby, but please. I need you to stay awake." I pulled on his arm. "Sit up."

His eyes opened again, this time to pin me on the receiving end of a glare from *The Devil*. I recognized *that* look. I'd seen it a lot during the time he was trying to come to terms with my age and believed I'd purposely kept it from him.

"That glare doesn't work anymore, Lucifer. You don't scare me. Sit up." I worked my way beneath his arm and hauled him up. He was soaked through and, although it wasn't cold, he needed to get out of the wet clothes before he got sick on top of everything else.

"I've canceled the ambulance, but I think we need to get you checked over. You're lucky we arrived when we did." Carter held out my cell.

"I'm fine." Seth pulled away from me and staggered to his feet. "Why are you here? I told you to stay away."

"We've had this conversation already. Your mom and dad are worried sick about you. You haven't answered calls from anyone for days. Carter had to *break in*. What were you *thinking?*" I shoved at his chest, my own concern for him becoming anger when he scowled at me. "Don't you *care* what you're doing to everyone?"

"What am I doing? Was it you with your history all over the news for three days? I don't think it was. Why the fuck is everyone else upset?"

"You think you're the only person with a messed-up past?"

"Says the girl with the trust fund and two parents who love her."

"I'm not talking about *me*. What about Gabe? Dex's childhood wasn't pretty, either. And Luca lost his *twin brother!* You're pushing away the people who understand what you're going through. Who can help you."

His dark eyes speared me, and then his lip curled up. His smile was cold. "Do you know how I learned to do all those things with my tongue that you like, Riley?" He advanced on me, eyes glinting with malice. "Long hours of practicing on women four times my age. Being beaten when I didn't make them come in the allocated time. How about next time you're sucking my dick, I give you pointers on how to make me come faster? Want to know *how* I know *those* tricks? Do you think Gabe, Dex, and Luca learned how to fuck the same way I did?"

"Seth—" I backed away.

"Want me to tell you all the ways I've been fucked over the years, Riley?" His voice lowered, turned soft. "All the things I keep back from you because I know how fucked up I am? How I *shouldn't* want to do those things because I *know* I was trained to want them. Or maybe I should just show you how it feels to be kept on the edge until *I'm* ready for you to come? Or would you like to hear about how *I* was taught to come on command? Do you want to know how they did that? Would you like to know the trigger words to make that happen? Would you want that much control over me? Or maybe you already know them. Did I tell you about them while I was sleeping?" He cocked an eyebrow. "Or were they written about in the news articles? Do I have any secrets left?"

His voice was diamond hard, face carved from stone. The cold, brutal, sharp-tongued Devil he'd been nicknamed by Forgotten Legacy fans was firmly in the ascendant.

"Are you curious about my past, Riley? Do you wonder what I dream about? Do you want to know who *Nathaniel* is? Do you want me to *show* you? Would you even want me if you knew all the things I've done? Or would I be too dirty for you?"

My back hit the wall of my studio, and his hands slapped to the stone either side of my head. His head lowered, close to my ear, and his voice dropped. "Do you prefer the glamorous rock star? Or would you really like to experience The *Devil*?" He laughed, the sound sharper than glass. "No, the truth is you want to fix me ... like everyone fucking does. Because, god fucking knows, I'm broken, Riley. I'm beyond fucking repair. Don't you get that? You can't fucking fix me. *Stop. Fucking. Trying.*"

"Stop it!" I pushed against his chest.

He didn't move, didn't even sway back a little. "Stop what? Stop bursting the cute little daydream you have us wrapped in? Don't want the dark reality to ruin it?"

"Seth." Carter put a hand on his shoulder. "You need to back off."

"Do I?" Voice flat, he swung to face his bodyguard. "Last I checked, *I* employed *you*, not the other way around."

While he was distracted, I ducked under his arm and stepped out of reach. My movement caught his attention, and he turned back to look at me.

"Running away, Shutterbug?" That eyebrow shot up again, and a smirk twisted his lips. "Guess you don't like what you're hearing."

"You forget I was *with* you, Seth. You took me to the house you grew up in. I *saw* where you lived."

Something flickered behind his eyes, then they hardened again. "You saw the sanitized version."

"I saw *you*."

His head canted. "Did you now?" The words were soft. "And what did you see?"

Instead of answering him, I looked at Carter. "Can you leave us alone?"

"I don't think—"

Seth's laughter cut him off, sharp and bitter. "Do you *really* think I'm a danger to her? That I would *ever* touch her with intent to hurt?"

The other man glanced between us, clearly unhappy with the idea of leaving.

"I promise. It's fine." I assured him.

He hesitated for a second longer, then nodded. "I'll be inside."

Neglected Consequences

CHAPTER 23

HURT - UPDOG

Seth

Riley's eyes didn't move away from mine, but I could see the tension in her stance, the strain in her face as she held herself stiff. She wanted to leave, wanted to look away, but didn't want me to see it. But I *could*. I could see every single thought running through her head. Every emotion played across her face. She'd never been able to hide how she felt from me.

I jerked my chin toward the door of her studio. "Open the door."

"Why?"

"So we can go inside."

Her spine stiffened, and she threw her shoulders back, clearly attempting to make herself look taller, and less afraid of what I was going to do. "No."

"No?" My eyebrow hiked.

"Whatever you're going to do or say, I won't have you tainting how I feel about the studio."

"Tainting." I repeated the word slowly, tasting it. "Interesting word choice. Is that what you think I'm doing?"

"It's what *you* think you're doing."

I stepped toward her, anger boiling through my veins at the way she could see right through me. "Maybe I *want* to *taint* everything."

She tipped her head up, but didn't back away from me. I moved closer.

"No, you don't. You already think you taint everything. You want someone to prove that you don't."

I laughed. "That would be an impossible wish."

"Would it?"

I was close to her, close enough to feel the heat from her body, to see the flecks of gold in the green of her eyes, to see the faint smattering of freckles across her nose. "You asked me the other night if I sent you away because of the dreams, but that's not the reason. Do you want to know why I won't let you stay here?"

"Tell me." Her chin lifted, her lips pressing together to hide the tremor in them.

"Because I want to do things," I whispered. I lifted a hand and ran my finger down the length of her throat. "Things that would send you running from me. Have you ever wondered why I stopped sleeping with groupies for all those years? Why the women I fucked never came back for seconds? The real reason they call me *The Devil?*"

"I try not to think about the women before me." Her voice was steady, and she *still* refused to drop her gaze from mine.

My finger moved up along her jaw, stroked over her cheek, and I ignored the way touching her ignited a fire under my skin. I brushed my thumb over her bottom lip, then gripped her jaw and forced her head back. My other hand wrapped around her throat.

I lowered my head until my mouth was close to hers. Her lips parted, and mine twisted. "You need to do as you're told, Riley, and stay the fuck away from me. I should never have let you convince me we could work. You're too young, too sweet, too *clean* for the likes of me."

"Maybe your darkness is exactly what I need." Her voice was low, *urgent*.

I could feel the warmth of her breath against my cheek, and see the way her pupils were swallowing the green of her irises. Her tongue slipped out, licked over her bottom lip, touched mine, and the stab of lust that shot through me almost broke my resolve. I fought against the desire to cover her mouth with mine and tightened my grip on her throat to push her back against the wall. I was committed to this course, this *path*, and I would see it through to the end. To do that, I needed Riley away from me. I needed *everyone* to leave me the fuck alone.

Her hand came up to clutch at my wrist. I squeezed a little more, and her breath caught, eyes widening.

"When we were at the compound, we learned fast that if you showed weakness, you became prey. A target for those with a taste for fear. Lexi and I came up with a word. A code, if you will, to let each other know that we weren't okay ... without actually saying so. If I'd been involved in a particularly rough session with some of Raphael's friends, when it hurt too much to sit or be touched, I'd say *Nightingale*. She understood while no one else around us would. It meant I was in trouble, and I needed help."

Why the fuck was I telling her this? Just send her away.

"What kind of trouble?" The words were breathless, and I blinked down at her. My hold on her throat had loosened, and my thumb stroked small circles just below her jaw.

"The kind of trouble where you might bleed to death, where your body has been torn to shreds or beaten so hard you've broken a rib or think you might be bleeding internally. She'd beg for supplies to patch me up." I shook my head. "It doesn't matter. The point is …" There wasn't any point. There was no fucking reason to share any of that with her. "The point is I want you to leave." I dropped my hand and turned away.

"Are you breaking up with me?"

I closed my eyes, the tremor in her voice twisting my gut. "If I say yes, will you go?"

"I don't understand." The tremor turned into a sob. "The article doesn't say anything I didn't already know."

"It's not the fucking article, Riley!" I lost the battle to stay calm and spun back to face her. "I don't give a fuck about the article. It's *him*. He's back. If it was just the article, I could ride it out. Yes, it's fucking uncomfortable knowing everyone will look at me and see a victim, but I could deal with that. But *he's* here … in my fucking city, with my fucking *mother* … and she's looking at him like he's some kind of fucking god."

I strode back to her and pressed my palms to her face. Her

eyes shone with tears, and I bowed my head, unable to stop the words from flowing. "I love you, Riley. I *do*, but right now I need you away from me. I need some time to process everything. I'm not breaking up with you, but I need some space to breathe." I succumbed to the temptation pulling at me then, and kissed her. Her lips parted beneath mine, and I let myself take one last taste of her before drawing away. "You have to give me some time to deal with this *my way*," I whispered against her mouth, brushing away the tear sliding down her cheek with my thumb. "Can you do that?"

"What if I don't want to?"

My stomach twisted. "Then the answer has to be yes, I'm breaking up with you."

CHAPTER 24

WHY WORRY - SET IT OFF

Gabe

"Close the door." My heart sank at the words, but I did as Karl asked and closed the door, sealing us both inside his office. "Sit down."

I pulled out the seat opposite him and dropped onto it. I didn't think I could take any more bad news, and his tone of voice told me we weren't about to celebrate a happy event.

"There's supposed to be a photoshoot tomorrow. Seth's been in touch and said he won't be there."

There was a heavy weight in my stomach. "Why?" I already knew what the answer would be.

"He wants to take a break."

"A break … from what?" I hadn't spoken to him for three days. He was ghosting me. He hadn't blocked my number yet, but I was sure it was coming.

"From the band." Karl drummed the top of his desk with the tip of his pen. "He suggested you audition guitarists to finish the album."

I jumped to my feet. "*No!* What the fuck?" For once, Karl

didn't yell at me to sit down and shut up. He leaned back in his chair and waited while I paced the room, one hand in my pocket and wrapped around my lighter. "He's overreacting. This is fucking stupid."

"Is it?"

"Of course it is. Has he even checked social media? Everyone is supporting him. I've never seen such a huge outpouring of love for him before."

"I doubt he's checked. Right now, all his focus is on the feelings he's going through that this coming out has generated. He's asked for time and space to work things out."

"Then we put the album on hold. I'm not fucking recording with some random guitarist."

"Maybe you should speak to Dex and Luca before making a decision. They have a say in what happens as well."

I glared at him. He was right. Of course he was, but I didn't want to fucking hear that. I wanted everyone to be as angry as I was.

"There's something else. Just a heads up, really. But after the baby thing the other year, I want to make sure we're all aware of it. Some kid has been trying to contact you."

"A kid?" Christ, I hoped it wasn't another fucking pregnancy claim. I rubbed my temple and flopped back onto the chair. "And what's *she* claiming?"

"*He,* and he wants to meet you. He's been very persistent. He first reached out a couple of months ago and asked if there was a way to contact you directly. He was told, like everyone, any fan mail could be sent to the offices. He sent a couple of letters, dated two months ago, but they only landed on my desk this morning." He pulled open a drawer, pulled out two white envelopes and tossed them across to me. "He says his mom knew your dad."

"Poor woman. What does that have to do with me?"

"Open the envelope."

I blew out an irritated breath. "Do you have to be so fucking secretive all the time?" I ripped one of the envelopes open and pulled out the folded sheet of paper. "What's this going to be? Fan mail? My mom wants to suck your dick? Or maybe *he* wants to suck my dick." I unfolded it.

Gabe,
You don't know me.

I snorted. No shit, Sherlock.

But my mom knew your dad a while ago. I'd really like to meet with you and talk.
Tate

I frowned. "So what? This kid thinks he gets access to me because his mom knew my dad? Why are you even showing me this?"

"Read the second one."

I threw the first one back onto the desk and picked up the second. The writing was the same as the first, a mix of capital and lowercase letters. It looked like a ransom note.

Gabe,

I guess I didn't give you enough information in my first letter. Sorry, I was still surprised myself. I should have taken a bit of time to digest the news first.

When I said my mom knew your dad, I mean they had a relationship. Although, I think my mom is trying to make it sound less seedy than it was.

I glanced up at Karl. "Is this going where I think it's going?"

"Keep reading."

Anyway, the result of that relationship was me. I think we might be related. Could we meet? I have photographs of my mom with your dad. I forgot to add my cell number last time, so I've put it below.

Tate

My lip curled. "Seriously? Like we don't have enough to deal with right now. Can't you just get the PR department to sort him out? He's obviously fucking delusional. I'm not even sure my da could get it up and perform. He was fucking drunk twenty-four seven."

"I wanted to make sure that's the way you want it dealt with. After Meredith and then the way you decided to handle the pregnancy thing the other year, I didn't want to go ahead and make a plan."

I could hear what he wasn't saying. *I wanted to make sure I didn't waste my time dealing with this only for you to fuck it up later in some way.*

"Do whatever you need to do. Some kid looking for his fifteen minutes of fame isn't my top priority right now."

"Okay. Now then, about the shoot tomorrow—"

"If Seth is refusing to be there, then cancel it. I'll speak to Dex and Luca, but I guarantee you they're going to agree with me. If Seth is done, we're all done."

"You're willing to end Forgotten Legacy because of Seth?"

"I don't know what to tell you, Karl. We're not bringing in another guitarist to take his place."

"Let's not make any rash decisions."

"Without Seth, there is no Forgotten Legacy. The same if any of us leave. One goes, we're all done."

CHAPTER 25

SHARKS - IMAGINE DRAGONS

Gabe

Dex and Luca met me at the studio. The door was unlocked when I arrived, and I found them both inside.

"Have you spoken to Seth?" Dex asked when I walked through the door.

"He's not taking my calls, and he's changed the code on his gates so I can't get in. You?"

"I spoke to him this morning. He told me to fuck off and hung up on me."

We both looked at Luca. "I haven't tried." When we both nailed him with matching glares, he shrugged. "Look, when I left town and you guys chased me, I'm not gonna lie, it was fucking annoying. I needed to get things straight in my head and I couldn't do that with you all breathing down my neck. Maybe he needs the same. Leave him alone. If he's still acting like this in a couple of weeks, then we'll start pushing. Carter is there, so we know someone is keeping him alive."

"What about Riley?"

Luca shook his head. "Ever said he's kicked her out. She turned up at the bookstore yesterday in tears. There were bruises on her throat."

"*Bruises?*" I jumped on the word.

"Not sure if it was playful bruising or not. Knowing Seth, I'd say not. It's not the first time he's had her in a chokehold."

I thought back, trying to remember when that had happened. "The tour bus ... he was drinking back then, and it's the only time he's done anything like that, as far as I'm aware." That didn't excuse what he'd done, and he'd been horrified about it the morning after. "He's never been violent to any woman. That's not who he is."

"She said he was drunk, and angry. Claims he didn't hurt her and that they had a conversation, but she wouldn't share what it was and Ever said she was definitely upset."

"So we're just supposed to ignore that?" Dex asked.

"For now."

"He told Karl we needed to audition for a new guitarist," I told them.

"Fuck that." Both men spoke at once.

"That's what I told Karl." I flicked open my lighter, stared into the flame, then snapped it closed. "If we agree to give him space and not contact him ... how long do we wait?" I looked at Luca.

"Two weeks. Give him that long. He needs to work through the shit that's been plastered all over the news. And it gives us time to deal with it as well. Did you read it? That's a lot to fucking take in, Gabe. I didn't know half of it."

"Me either," Dex added quietly. "I found Siobhan fucking sobbing over the newspaper."

"Ever was the same. It's going to take time for the girls to be able to look at him without all of them feeling uncomfortable, and that's not fair on Seth. No matter how everyone feels, all he's going to see is pity. So let him have this time. Carter will report back if anything is wrong."

I hated how logical Luca was being, but I couldn't argue with anything he said. I nodded. "Okay, fine. I just want it on record that I don't fucking like it."

"Of course you don't. You're fucking married to the guy. All of the relationship, none of the sex." Luca stood and patted my shoulder. "We'll be okay, Gabe."

"How is Everleigh?" I changed the subject. "Haven't seen her for a few weeks."

"Hormonal. So *fucking* hormonal. I swear, she cries when a flower loses a petal." Luca laughed. "And horny. I never thought a woman could wear me out, but she's relentless." From the grin splitting his face in half, he wasn't *that* worn out. "I always thought pregnant women would rather eat than have sex, but Ever's all about the D."

"I mean, if you want to get technical about it, she's still *eating*." Dex snickered. "Make the most of it. Once those babies arrive, you won't be getting any for a while."

***

The house was empty when I got home. I climbed out of the car, left Remy to go and check in with the extra security he had patrolling the grounds, and walked inside. I dropped Harper a text to let her know I was back and headed down to my studio for a couple of hours. If I couldn't hang out with Seth, then losing myself in music and writing was the next best thing ... at least until Harper came home.

"Gabe?" Harper's voice roused me from the semi-doze I was in, and I shoved up off the couch in the studio, rubbing my eyes.

"Hey, Frosty," I greeted her around a yawn, crossed the room to wrap an arm around her waist and pulled her against me. "What time is it?"

"Four. I texted you, but you didn't answer. I assumed you fell asleep." She reached up to kiss me. "Guess you didn't make it to the bedroom."

"Guess not." The last thing I remembered was sitting down to write some lyrics. Seems my body decided otherwise. That wasn't unusual, especially with the stress of the past few days. I squeezed her waist, then dropped my arm so I could take her hand. "How was your day?"

"We've *finally* got permission to extend Bea's place. I went with her to pick the kids' bedroom furniture and the jungle gym for outside." She laughed softly. "I'm not sure who was more excited. Bea or the kids."

"That's good." I yawned again. "The shoot tomorrow is canceled. Seth refused to go."

"You spoke to him?"

I shook my head. "No, he left a message with Karl." I ignored the stab of pain saying that caused. Her fingers squeezed mine gently, letting me know she knew how I felt.

We walked along the hallway and into the living room. I flopped onto the couch and pulled Harper down beside me. "Karl said there are some crazies coming out of the woodwork on the tail-end of the news about Seth."

"What kind of crazies?" She settled beside me, lifting her legs and curling into my side.

I wrapped my arm around her shoulders and propped my feet up on the coffee table. Tipping my head back, I yawned again. "Some kid taking a chance and claiming his mom knew my da, and wants to meet me."

"*Really*? What did you say?"

"Told Karl to let the PR or legal team deal with it. Not making the same mistake I made last time."

"The only mistake you made last time was not telling me." Her head rested against my shoulder. "*Could* his mom have known your dad?"

"I guess so. Who knows?"

"Aren't you curious?"

"It'll just be another scam. What's the point?"

"I don't know. It'd make me wonder. Your dad used to have women over to your apartment all the time. What if—"

I rolled my eyes. "Come on, Frosty. You think my da has a

litter of unwanted kids scattered around the city and not one of them has ever made the connection between me and him?"

"It could happen."

I snorted.

"I'm serious!" She shifted from where she sat, twisted, and climbed over my lap until she straddled my legs.

"Hmmm, I like this development. Keep going." My hands curved over her hips and pulled her more snugly against me. It was her turn to roll her eyes.

"What harm would it be to meet with him?"

"Have you forgotten the part where I'm a multi-millionaire asshole rock star?" I cocked an eyebrow.

"Like you would let *anyone* forget that. I think you should meet with him."

"What would it achieve?" I let my fingers trail over her ass, up to the waistband of her pants, and tugged out the hem of the blouse she was wearing so I could slide my fingers beneath the silk.

"What would it *harm*? Maybe he's lying. Maybe he's confused. Maybe he just wants someone to *see* he exists."

"And maybe he's a crazy stalker who has concocted a fantasy world." My fingers found the clasp on her bra and I unhooked it. "Open your blouse."

She popped the first button, then a second. I licked my lips at the creamy skin being revealed.

"But what if he's *not* lying?" she continued as the third button opened, and the blouse separated to reveal the valley between her breasts.

"Of course he's lying, either intentionally or because his mom fed him bullshit for breakfast." I slid a finger into the gap parting the front of her blouse and slowly dragged it to one side, uncovering a nipple. Lifting my hand, I pressed a finger against her lips. "Lick."

Her lips parted and she sucked it into her mouth. I laughed quietly. "I said lick, not suck." Her teeth nipped at my fingertip, and she leaned back.

"End result is the same. Your finger is wet."

"Is your pussy?" I used my finger to circle her nipple. It tightened under my touch.

"I'm trying to have a serious conversation with you."

I lifted my gaze to hers and smiled. "I'm multitasking. You didn't finish unbuttoning your blouse."

"You didn't answer my question." Her fingers returned to the buttons and made quick work of popping them through the material.

"Take it off."

She let the silk slide down her arms and it fell against my legs. The bra, no longer restricted by the blouse, followed it, and I admired the view in front of me.

Could you be addicted to a person? Their body, their eyes, their lips, their voice, their personality? I was. Everything that made Harper *Harper* attracted me.

I licked my lips. "Play with your nipples."

"What if he's not lying?"

"Then I have a half-brother running around L.A." I caught her wrists and lifted her hands to her breasts. "Play."

She rolled her nipples between thumb and forefinger. "Arrange to meet him."

"Tell me your pussy is wet."

"Your dick is pressing against it, making all kinds of promises. Of course it's wet. So we'll tell Karl you're willing to meet with the boy, okay?"

I laughed at how matter-of-fact she sounded. "I love you, Frosty."

***

As it turned out, I didn't need Karl to arrange a meeting. Remy strolled into the room a couple of hours later. Thankfully, we'd done fooling around, showered together and were clothed, and sprawled on the couch watching a movie.

"Gabe. There's a kid hanging around outside the gates. Keeps pushing the buzzer and asking to speak to you. He's been asked to move along three times now, but keeps coming back. We could call the police and get him moved officially, or—"

"Claims he's got something to say about my da?"

"That's right."

I slanted a look at Harper. "Guess you got your wish sooner than both of us expected." I untangled myself from her and stood. "Stay here."

"But—"

"No. We don't know who he is. I'll take Remy. I don't want him anywhere near you." I walked to the door, paused and turned. "You know … if we'd kept the penthouse, this shit wouldn't happen."

She poked her tongue out at me. I blew her a kiss, and followed Remy out of the house. It took a few minutes to reach the end of the drive, but I could see the figure sitting on the sidewalk on the opposite side of the road before I reached the gates.

First impression showed me dark jeans torn at the knees, dirty sneakers, and a black t-shirt torn across the ribs. Dark hair flopped down over his forehead and sunglasses covered his eyes.

"Stay on this side of the gate," Remy cautioned.

I rolled my eyes but didn't argue. "Hey, kid. You wanted to speak to me?"

His head jerked up at the sound of my voice, and he scrambled to his feet. "Gabe!" He shot across the road and skidded to a stop on the other side of the gate. "My name is Tate. I think we have the same dad." The words tripped over each other in his hurry to get them out.

"That right?" I studied him.

Dark hair, couldn't see his eyes, lanky—all arms and legs, hadn't really grown into his height yet—skinny. I didn't see myself in him. He looked like every other Forgotten Legacy fan.

"I've been trying to find Thomas Mercer for about a year now. I found a photograph of my mom with him and asked her about it. She told me he was my dad."

"He's dead."

"I know. Took me a while to trace him, but—"

"Look, I'm sorry, kid, but whatever your mom told you is wrong, or maybe it was a different Thomas Mercer. But my da never had any other kids. And, trust me, that's a good thing."

"She never told him."

"Of course she didn't." I didn't even try to hide the disbelief in my voice.

"When she found out she was pregnant, she said she went to tell him, but he was drunk. She didn't think he'd make a good father, so she left without saying anything."

The hairs rose on the back of my neck. There was something about his words that stirred a memory. A vague recollection of seeing a woman standing by our apartment door. "No. I'm not feeding into this bullshit. Go home." I turned on my heel and walked away.

Neglected Consequences

CHAPTER 26

MORBID MIND - JACK KAYS

Seth

I hadn't been to Lexi's grave since the funeral. I didn't even know why I was bothering now. Carter was a quiet presence behind me as I walked through the cemetery. I wasn't concerned about being recognized—who would expect to find me here—but I'd selected a pair of sunglasses and a dark suit to blend in with the other people. I'd been sure at least one funeral would be in progress, and I'd been right. Not far from where Lexi had been laid to rest, there were people clustered around an open grave while the priest gave his sermon.

When I reached Lexi's resting place, Carter dropped back to give me privacy while staying close enough that should anyone recognize or approach me, he would be able to intercept them. I stood in front of the marble gravestone and read the inscription.

Beloved daughter and sister
You were never for this world.
Our hope is that you find happiness in the next.
Never forgotten.

Lexi Olivia Hawkins

Unlike me, she hadn't wanted to wipe her original name out of existence and kept it when our identities were changed.

Beneath the inscription was her date of birth and death. She'd been twenty-seven. *Fucking* twenty-seven.

There were flowers in front of the gravestone, and the grass was neat and devoid of weeds and leaves. Evidence that my mom and dad—my adoptive parents, the only ones who mattered—were regular visitors.

I walked around, letting my fingers trail over the top of the marble. It was cool beneath my touch.

"I hope you *are* happy, Lex," I whispered. "I'm glad you're not here right now. What would you do if you were in my place? I'd like to think you wouldn't want to see either of them, but I know you would. I'm sorry I didn't tell you I'd found her. I thought we had time, that I could make sure she wasn't going to hurt you." I laughed quietly.

"I was blind to the fact *I* was the one hurting you … just by being there, reminding you every single fucking day of what we had to do to survive. I wish you'd said something. Did you behave like you needed me there because you thought it was what *I* needed? Or did you really need me that much?" I returned to the front of the grave. "I have so many questions that you can never answer. Was it a moment of weakness or utter strength that made you finally take that step? Did I drive you to it? You know I'd never have left you, right? My love for Riley would never have stopped me from loving you, too."

I sank down to my knees and rested my head against the cold marble, my hands on the wet grass. "What am I supposed to do, Lex? Everyone says I need to move on, act like he isn't here watching my every fucking move, making my skin crawl. But I *can't*. I can't rest knowing he's so close. He's already got her back under his spell. How the fuck did he do that? She was getting better, and now he's back she's acting like he's the love of her fucking life and not the man who abused her and her kids."

My cell vibrated in my pocket. I pulled it out and checked, unsurprised to find it was Gabe trying to call again. I sent it to voicemail. I could almost *feel* my sister's disapproval over ignoring my best friend.

"I know. I need to talk to him. But he'll want to dissect everything, and I just can't think about that right now. I can't think about *anything*. How am I supposed to move forward, Lex? Our names were changed for a reason. What was she *thinking*? I wish I understood *why* she'd tell everyone what happened and then behave like he didn't fuck us all over. I want to ask him why. *Why* did he do that to us? To *her*?"

I sucked in a breath. "But he walked out of her condo, and I froze. All these years, I've said if I ever had the chance to face him, I'd demand answers ... but I fucking *froze*. I was Nate in that moment, and I was so fucking scared again. It was embarrassing."

"Seth ..." Carter's voice was quiet, but there was a warning tone to it. I twisted my head to search him out. "We've been spotted." He jerked his chin toward two people heading toward us. "They look like reporters. It's time we left. They've probably been lurking, hoping you'd show up here."

I pressed my palm to the gravestone. "I love you, Olivia. I hope you're happy now, wherever you are." Pushing to my feet, I turned and crossed to where Carter waited.

"Seth! Seth, can we have a word?"

I swung to face the two men, one snapping photographs as they scurried over the grass, uncaring of the graves they traipsed over.

"You can have two." I pushed my sunglasses on top of my head and nailed them with a glare. "Fuck and Off." I raised my middle finger, just to emphasize my mood, knowing that would be the photograph they'd run with, and stalked past Carter, leaving him to deal with them. He caught up to me just as I climbed into the back of the car.

"The headline should be fun tomorrow."

I tipped my head back against the seat. "Don't give a fuck."

***

I locked myself inside my studio when we got back to the house, after telling Carter I was done for the day and to go find something else to do. I knew he would lurk, though, and materialize as soon as I thought about going outside, so I spent some time retuning my guitars and fooling around with demo tracks I had lying around. Anything to keep my mind off the fucked-up mess my life was in.

The screen on my cell brightened with an incoming text

message.

SHUTTERBUG - I'll give you space, but I need you to tell me you're alive once a day. Can you do that?

I stroked my thumb over her name, warmth flooding me. No matter what I did, how nasty I got, she saw through it. I had a lot of making up to do, and I would, but not yet.

ME - I can do that. I'm still alive.

I hit send, stared down at the message, then added another.

ME - I love you, Shutterbug. That hasn't changed.

SHUTTERBUG - I know. I love you too. I just wish you would let me be there for you.

ME - You are. Just knowing you are out there helps, I swear.

I switched off my cell after sending the message, because talking to her via text would eventually turn into a call, and then I wouldn't be able to resist inviting her over. Pocketing it, I left my studio.

I must have wandered the entire house three times over before the answer came to me. And it was so simple ... so *obvious* ... I didn't understand how I hadn't figured it out sooner. Actually, that was a lie. I knew why I hadn't thought about it. The idea sent terror coursing through my veins. But if I didn't do it. If I didn't face the monster from my past, I would never be able to move forward.

I snatched up my car keys and walked out of the house after

checking to make sure Carter's car wasn't there.

An incoming call broke the silence inside my car, my mom's cell number displaying on the screen. After a second's hesitation, I accepted the call.

"Mom, I'm driving. Can I call you later?"

"I'm worried about you. Why don't you come home for dinner?"

"I'm fine, I promise."

"I don't see how you are even remotely okay. Not knowing that bastard is in town."

My eyebrows rose at the venom in her voice. She'd always been very careful in how she spoke about our biological parents, if she ever mentioned them at all.

"I love you, Mom. Tell Dad I'll see him soon, okay?" I ended the call before she could say anything more.

Neglected Consequences

CHAPTER 27

RUNAWAY - MOD SUN

Gabe

I was roused from sleep by my cell's ringtone shattering the silence. I groped around behind me until my fingers found it and I lifted it to my ear.

"What?"

"Seth's disappeared," Remy said.

Sleep dissipated, and my eyes snapped open. I sat up. "What the fuck do you mean he's *disappeared*?"

"Carter called me around one am. He left Seth in his studio and stuck around for a few hours. When Seth didn't come out, he did a food run. When he came back, Seth's car was gone. Carter has checked all his usual haunts, but he's not at any of them."

"I'll make sure he's not here."

"He's not. I've already checked. I also went to Riley's, his parents, *and* Marcie's. He's not been seen by any of them."

"Is Raphael still at Marcie's?"

"No. There was no sign of him. Security on the gate said he hasn't been seen since we sent him away the other day. They also confirmed Seth hasn't visited either. Have you got any idea where else he might have gone?"

"Stupid question, but have you tried calling him?" I swung my legs off the bed and grabbed the nearest pair of sweats and dragged them on.

"Of course we have."

"Where are you? There's a place he might have gone that no one else will know about, but it's back where we grew up."

"I'm about five minutes away. I'd say give me the location, but you're going to insist on coming with me."

"You got that right. I'll be waiting. Hurry the fuck up." I ended the call, pulled on a t-shirt and jogged down the hallway. "Harper?" I called her name, and she appeared in the doorway to the kitchen. "Babe, I have to go out."

"To look for Seth, I know. Remy called to see if he was here. You don't think he's done something stupid, do you?"

"Define stupid." I kissed her cheek before heading down the hallway to the front door. My sneakers were beside the door. I pushed my feet into them. "Stay home today, okay?"

"Why?"

"I dunno. I just ... I have a bad feeling. Is there anything you need to do today?"

She shook her head. "No. I was going to come to the photoshoot with you, but since that's been canceled, my day is free."

"Okay. Keep your cell on. I'll call you if I find him."

"Gabe." Her hand caught my arm. "Be careful."

I pressed another kiss to her lips. "Always, Frosty."

***

I had the car door open before it stopped.

"Gabe, slow down."

I ignored Remy's words and jumped out. I'd opted to sit in the front passenger seat instead of the back, and headed into the small wooded area without waiting for him. I didn't pause to look around, make comparisons between the last time I'd been here as a teen and now, or reminisce. Not that there was anything good to reminisce about. The last time we'd been here had been when we were fourteen and I'd talked Seth out of killing himself.

I walked through the trees, the path to the clearing imprinted in my brain. I didn't even need to think about when to turn. There was no path to follow, and I pushed through the undergrowth until I finally broke through into the small secluded area... and stopped.

"He hasn't been here," Remy said from behind me.

I'd been *sure* this was where he'd head to. I turned in a slow circle, running my bottom lip between my teeth as I thought.

What if he wasn't suicidal? I thought back over the last few interactions we'd had. He'd been angry, full of misplaced guilt, but not suicidal.

I scowled. Where else would he go? And then it came to me.

"Fuck." I patted my pockets, looking for my cell, fished it out and opened a browser. Tapping in Marcus DeMario's name, I found his business number and dialed.

"DeMario Investigations, how may I help you?" The sing-song voice of his receptionist answered.

"I need to speak to Marcus."

"Who's calling, please?"

"Gabe Mercer. Tell him it's about Seth Hawkins. And it's an emergency."

"Please hold." Her voice gave no indication of whether she recognized our names.

I held ... but I wasn't pleased about it. I paced around the clearing, badly recorded instrumental music playing down my ear.

"Mr. Mercer?" A male voice came onto the line. I assumed it was the man I'd asked for.

"DeMario? I need to know if Seth's been in touch with you."

"I'm sorry, Mr. Mercer, I can't discuss clients with you."

"If you know Seth, then you know who I am to him. He's missing. I need to know where he is. Did he sic you onto his father?"

"Mr. Mercer—"

"Do *not* fucking tell me about client privilege. Just answer the fucking question."

There was a long silence, and I pulled my cell from my ear to check he hadn't cut me off.

"Look, Mr. Mercer, I pride myself on the fact I do not break a confidence."

"This is a unique situation."

"I agree. While I will not disclose what Seth hired me for, I *will* send you an address that may answer your questions."

"Don't talk in fucking riddles."

"I'm afraid it's that or nothing."

I clenched my jaw to stop myself from threatening him, and sucked in a deep breath through my nose. "Okay, fine."

"I'll need your number."

I told him. He repeated it back to me.

"A pleasure talking to you, Mr. Mercer." He ended the call and a few seconds later a text came through ... but it wasn't the one I was expecting.

CHAPTER 28

THE DEVIL DOESN'T BARGAIN - ALEC BENJAMIN

Seth

I sat in my car outside the motel room. I couldn't see any movement, but from what I could tell, the curtains were closed. My fingers drummed on the steering wheel. I should leave before he came out. Before he saw me. But I couldn't make myself turn the key to start the engine. So I sat there and stared.

Ten minutes passed, thirty, an hour. People came and went. The sun set. I slid down in my seat, sunglasses still covering my face and tried to look as inconspicuous as possible. No one cared enough to even glance in my direction. I doubted a man sitting in a car was the weirdest thing that had happened at this particular motel.

At four am, the door opened and *he* walked out—tall, dark-haired, slim build. It was like looking into a fucking mirror. My heart jumped in my chest and a lump blocked my throat. A cold chill crept up my spine and I shivered. He stood in the doorway, looking left and right and then came straight toward me.

He stopped a couple of feet away, illuminated by the street light, but his face was still in shadows. Not that I needed to see it. I *knew* what he looked like. It was the face I saw in the mirror every morning, just a little older.

"Do you intend to sit out here all night? Or did you piss your pants and are too scared to move?" That mocking voice threw me back into the past, and I fought against it.

Stop sniveling, Nathaniel. You're embarrassing me.

Stop struggling and relax.

That's a good boy. Now give us a smile. You're so pretty when you smile.

I shoved the memories back into their box and my fingers tightened their grip on the steering wheel, knuckles white.

"I assume you're here to talk to me or kill me. Pick one. I have better things to do than wait out here while you build up the nerve to face me." His head canted, and his teeth flashed as he smiled. "From what I've read about you, I didn't think you'd be this much of a pussy. I always knew your sister was the stronger one. Shame you drove her to kill herself. She clearly couldn't watch your pathetic attempt to be *normal* any longer." He chuckled.

"Not that you could ever be normal, right, Nate? Not after the things you did. You're wasted in the music industry. Porn would have been a better fit. Especially with the skills you learned."

I threw open the car door and climbed out. His smile broadened.

"That's a good boy. Come inside."

Like a fucking idiot I was halfway to the door before I realized what I was doing. I stopped, fingers curling into fists.

"You don't control me anymore." My voice was low.

One side of his mouth tipped up. "Don't I? Are you sure? Starlight ... Masterpiece ... and what was the third?" He tapped a finger against his lip. "Oh, I remember. *Penalty.* Do you remember what the commands meant? Can you still follow instructions?"

"Shut the fuck up."

"Do you need me to remind you what each word means, Nate? Starlight ... strip. Masterpiece ... on your knees ... *Penalty* ... come."

"I *said* shut the fuck up!" I shouted, my hands over my ears.

He laughed. "Are you *sure* I don't control you? Are you brave enough to come inside and find out for sure?"

I stiffened my spine, threw my shoulders back and followed him inside.

"Close the door, Nathaniel." He turned his back on me, a clear message that I was nothing to fear.

My jaw clenched, but I did as he said. Let him believe I wasn't dangerous. He'd learn the truth soon enough.

"Good boy." I tensed at the words, at the approval in his voice and the quick stab of relief that I'd done something right. I shoved the feeling aside. It was ingrained, instinctive, and fucking wrong. "Now then, what do you want to say to me? We should get that out of the way. Clear the air. That's what you want, yes?" He sat on the edge of the bed, elbows resting on his knees and his eyes raked over me.

"Tell me why." I stayed near the door.

"You'll have to be more specific than that. And stop hovering. I thought you were a man now. Wasn't that what you claimed?

You're all grown up and not scared of the monsters under the bed anymore." He laughed. "Or should that be the monsters *in* your bed?"

I refused to react, holding myself still while he chuckled at his own joke.

"Alright. Why did you force us to do the things you did? We were children, *your* children. Why would you do that? What kind of fucking monster are you?"

His laughter cut off abruptly. "I'll accept the monster tag. I don't deny my ... tastes are not acceptable to most. But *force* you? Nathaniel, what have you convinced yourself? There was *never* any force. You were more than willing to join in. Open a woman's legs and you were more than eager to please."

"Not through choice." I was surprised at how calm I sounded.

"You were always given a choice. What happened when you said no, Nate? Were you punished? Think carefully, now."

I didn't need to think. I knew the answer. "You put me back in the basement, and took someone else."

"Exactly. You went back to your room. If you didn't want to play with the adults, you were sent back to be with the children. What's wrong with that?"

"Fucking everything!"

"It was how I was raised. Why wouldn't I want the same for you? I turned out—"

"If you say you're fine, I'm going to fucking kill you."

He quirked an eyebrow. "Nathaniel." His voice was calm,

almost gentle. "I understand how this is difficult for you, but it need not be. You were taught all the skills you needed to perform well in life, and you brought so many people pleasure. How is that different from what you do now?"

"It's completely different."

"How? Didn't you and … *Gabe, is it?* … Didn't you and Gabe explore when you were kids? I bet you taught him all his tricks. I've seen the pieces written about him. How many lessons did it take to train him? What about all those fans who stare at your body and think about the things they want to do to you. What they'd like *you* to do to them. I'm sure a lot of them are young. Do you think about them touching themselves under their sheets at night?"

His smile turned my stomach. "Your girlfriend is much younger than you, isn't she? There's something special about that, isn't there?"

"Don't fucking talk about her."

"Why not? You are standing there accusing me of being a monster, yet the woman who shares your bed wasn't much more than a child when you first stuck your dick into her."

"That's not true."

"Lie to yourself, if that makes it easier for you. But believe me, son, once you accept who you are, you'll hate yourself less."

"And who am I?"

"You really need to ask? You're just like me."

CHAPTER 29

BLOOD - CALL ME KARIZMA

Gabe

I stared down at my cell, the single word of the text the only thing I could see.

SETH - Nightingale

"We need to find Seth *now*." I didn't even recognize my own voice. That one word had made my stomach bottom out and tightened my throat.

"We're *trying* to. But without a clue on where we should be heading, it's going to be difficult."

My cell chimed while he spoke and the promised address from DeMario popped up. I forwarded it to Remy. "We have an address. Get moving."

Did I know Seth would be there? No, but my gut screamed at me that it was where we needed to go. I didn't wait for Remy to argue with me over it, and set off back toward the car at a jog.

The lights on the car flashed as I reached it and I pulled open the door and threw myself into the passenger seat. Remy joined me seconds later, jammed his key into the ignition and started the engine.

"Why are we rushing?"

"Seth has a word... It means he's in trouble."

"O...kay?"

"He just sent it to me. Hurry up."

He cast me a sidelong look, but didn't increase his speed. "If I *hurry up*, we'll get pulled over and then it'll take longer to get there. We could get there faster if you set up the GPS and stopped telling me how to drive."

I stabbed at the monitor on the dashboard, typed in the address of the motel and hit the directions button. The female voice came through the speakers with a direction to turn right.

"Thank you. Now put your seatbelt on and stop scowling."

I glared at him and yanked the belt over my chest, and slammed it into the lock.

"You said Seth sent you a text. Have you tried to call him?"

"Have I tried—" My mouth snapped shut with a click of teeth. I'd been thrown so hard by the text I hadn't even considered it. I grabbed my cell and hit the speed dial. It went through to his voicemail.

"Not here. Leave a message."

"Fuck's sake. Where the fuck are you? Answer your fucking phone! Why the fuck send me a text and then not have your cell switched on? Jesus fucking Christ." I caught the look Remy shot at me and stopped talking. "You better fucking be at the address I have," I growled, then ended the call and tossed my cell down onto my lap so I could reach for my lighter.

My foot tapped on the floor, my leg bounced, the lighter flicked open and closed on repeat, and I stared straight ahead.

"Your destination is straight ahead." The robotic female voice intoned.

I sat up straighter, my free hand gripping the seatbelt. "There's Seth's car."

Remy pulled into the space beside it. "Let me go in first."

I ignored him and threw myself out of the car. Somehow Remy still managed to get to the door of the room before me. He held out a hand, forcing me to stand behind him, and he knocked on the door.

"Seth?"

No answer.

"Just open the fucking door."

He lifted a finger to his lips and slowly, so fucking slowly, turned the doorknob. "Wait here." Remy's voice was a low warning and he slipped through the gap.

I stood, holding my breath. Five seconds, ten, twenty… and then I followed him inside. My eyes darted around the room. My eyes registered nothing other than the body slumped on the bed with Remy bending over it.

"Seth?" I shot forward and Remy held out a hand.

"Not Seth. Check the bathroom."

I hurried across the room and tried the door. It wouldn't open so I rapped on it. "Seth? Are you in there?"

There was a grunt, a thud, and then a click as the door was

unlocked. I shoved it open, stepped inside, and slipped.

"What the—" I caught the wash basin, steadied myself, and looked around. "Fuck. Seth!"

He was on the floor beside the door, head drooping against his chest, a red stain spreading out across the front of his shirt.

I dropped to my knees in front of him. "Fuck. Seth?" I caught his shoulder, and shook. "Open your fucking eyes."

His eyelashes fluttered, and his tongue came out to wet his lips. "I think ... I'm bleeding."

My laugh was part-relieved and part-hysterical. "No shit. What happened?"

"Is ... he dead?"

I didn't need to ask who he meant. "Well, he sure as shit wasn't fucking moving when I got here." He nodded, eyes slipping closed again. I tapped his cheek. "Don't close your eyes. We need to get you out of here."

"I'm good. The floor is ... more comfortable ... than it looks." His lips curled up.

"You're such a fucking idiot. Let me see." I carefully eased his hand away from his side. "Tell me what happened."

"Oh, you know ..." He paused to take a breath and frowned down at his shirt. "Father and son reunion ... Gabe?"

"Yeah." I pulled off my t-shirt and bunched it against his side. I wasn't sure where all the blood had come from, but there was a definite gash across his ribs, and I wasn't taking any chances.

"I think I killed him." He frowned. "Did I?" He lifted his head, and there was a soft thud as he let it drop back against the wall. "Karl is going to fucking kill me."

"*I'm* going to fucking kill you, if you don't tell me what happened."

CHAPTER 30

DON'T LET THE LIGHT GO OUT – PANIC! AT THE DISCO

Seth

Focusing on Gabe was difficult. My eyes wanted to close, pain burned my hands and ribs. Maybe I was dying. I wasn't entirely sure. When Gabe pressed his shirt against my ribs, I hissed.

"No. Don't you dare fucking close your eyes on me." His snarl brought my gaze up to search out his face.

I wondered if I was as pale as him.

"Talk to me, Seth. What the fuck happened?"

I gave a small headshake. It was all I could manage without the room swimming. Was it blood loss? How red was the floor? I shifted my attention from Gabe to the floor.

"Hmmm."

"Hmmm? What the fuck does *hmmm* mean?"

"Less blood... than I thought."

"We need to get you to the hospital."

"No. Just... take me home."

"What? *No*. What the fuck?" He pulled out his cell.

"Gabe." I kept my voice soft, repeating his name when he ignored me. "Gabe, please. No hospital."

"You're losing blood. You probably need stitches. You *still* haven't explained what happened."

"Gabe." Remy's voice cut him off. "We either need to call the police or get out of here."

Gabe's eyes darted from me to his bodyguard and back again. His hand rubbed the back of his neck, and then sighed. "Can you hold this against your ribs?" He guided my hand over the shirt soaking up the blood. "Just for a couple of minutes, okay?"

I nodded. "Okay."

He sprang to his feet, caught Remy's arm and pulled him out of the room. Their voices were too low for me to understand the words, but it sounded like they were arguing. Gabe came back just as my hand fell away from my ribs. He darted forward and caught the bloody t-shirt before it hit the floor.

"Okay, we're getting you out of here. Do you think you can stand?"

"Maybe?"

Remy crouched, pulled my arm across his shoulders, and slowly rose to his feet, pulling me with him. I sucked in a breath against the pain, and by the time we were both upright, I was panting and swearing.

Gabe kept one hand braced against my ribs, and we made our slow way through the motel room. I avoided looking at the bed, my attention focused on the door.

"Just a few more steps. We're parked right outside," Gabe said when I stopped.

I took another deep breath and we set off again. It seemed like hours, but eventually, we were beside the car. Remy unlocked the back door, and they both eased me onto the seat. Gabe slipped onto it beside me.

"What about …?" I glanced toward the motel room.

"Remy's got it handled," Gabe said, the words curt. He pulled out his cell.

"No hospital, Gabe."

"I'm calling Harper."

I let my head drop against the back of the seat.

"Hey, Frosty. Do we have anything you could use to stitch up a wound? … Yes, Seth … Frosty … Frosty … *Harper*, stop asking questions," he barked. "Just get some stuff together and be ready to stitch him up." He fell silent, and I cracked open one eye.

"I'm sorry."

His head turned in my direction. "What for?"

"Everything."

***

I must have passed out because when I next opened my eyes it was to Gabe shaking me, voice full of panic when he said my name.

"I'm awake."

"Don't fucking *do* that," he snapped.

I forced a laugh. "Sorry. I'll try and warn you before I die."

"Not fucking funny." He didn't share my humor. "We're here.

Don't move. We're going to get you out of the car and inside."

Not moving seemed like the perfect idea, so I didn't argue. I think I passed out again. Voices swam in and out.

"... blood ... hospital ... need supplies ..."

"Oh my god!"

"Harper ... Baby, *focus!*"

Voices, words, all blending together in a confusing jumble. I didn't know if I was awake or dreaming, conscious or passed out, but I needed to say something. It was important.

I threw out a hand and gripped a wrist. I wasn't sure whose. *"No hospital."*

"Seth." A female voice. I frowned. Was it Harper? "You've lost a lot of blood. It might not be a choice."

"Stitch me up. You're a nurse."

"*Was*. And I'm not sure I have what I need for this."

I tugged on her wrist, pulling her closer until I could focus on her face. "Harper, just stitch me up. Worry about the rest later."

Her teeth worried at her lip, then she nodded.

"And please try and make my tattoos line up." I closed my eyes and let unconsciousness pull me under.

Neglected Consequences

CHAPTER 31

I'M STILL HERE - BOY EPIC

Gabe

I kept my voice steady as I explained to Harper what she needed to do. Her eyes darted to Seth, where we'd put him on the kitchen table, then to me. Her hand was steady when she peeled back his clothes and looked at his chest.

"It's not as deep as it looks. Drinking heavily would have made him bleed more. Maybe he won't need an infusion, but I can't be sure. If he does … and we leave it …" She faced me. "I'm scared it'll kill him."

"He's insisting on no hospital. Do what you can." I kissed her forehead. "I trust you, Harper."

She gave me an unhappy smile. "I don't like this."

"Me either."

"If we take him to the hospital, then we have to explain what happened." Remy walked into the room. "Someone will leak it to the press, and then we'll have another round of fuckery to deal with. Seth's right. We need to keep this contained. That way I can get everything cleaned up. I've spoken to Asher, who will look at the security footage and see what needs to be removed. And I have ... people going to the motel room to ..." His smile was a baring of teeth. "Well, they'll sanitize it. Carter has already gone to pick up Seth's car."

I didn't ask for details. The less I knew, the better. "Thanks, Remy."

"Do you know what happened?" Harper asked as she probed around the wound across Seth's ribs. Mercifully, he wasn't conscious because we had nothing to numb the pain he was sure to be feeling.

"Not yet."

"Have you seen his hands? It looks like he grabbed something ... a knife? ... Combined with the slash across his ribs, I'd say he was trying to defend himself against an attack."

"His *hands*? Let me see." I strode across the room and picked up one of Seth's wrists, turned his hand so it was palm up, and winced at the lacerations across his palm. "Fuck. Will that heal okay? He'll still be able to play guitar, won't he?"

"I think so. I'm not a doctor, but I don't think it'll be too bad. I'm sure there will be some scarring, but nothing that will restrict his fingers." She pressed a finger to his throat. "His pulse is strong. My concern is that I don't know if he's passing out from blood loss or the pain or something that we don't know about."

"Just do what you can. Stop the bleeding, stitch him up while he's not conscious. What do you need me to do?"

"Be ready in case he wakes up. You might need to hold him

still. Keep a check on his pulse. We have no machines here that can tell me what is happening with his heart."

I reached out, caught her hand and squeezed. "You can do this, Harper."

Her lips pressed together, then she nodded. "Okay." She took a deep breath. "Okay." Her voice was firmer that time. She looked around. "Can you bring one of the lamps from the living room? I need it to be brighter so I can see what I'm doing.

"You got it." I spun away and went to do as she asked, returning a couple of minutes later, lamp in tow. I positioned it beside the table, found a power outlet and plugged it in. "What else?"

"Warm water, towels." She gave a small shrug. "Prayers?"

***

"I'm done." At Harper's voice, I straightened from my slouch and looked at her. There was a crease between her eyebrows, her eyes were dull, and her lips compressed into a downward curve. "I don't *think* the slashes on his ribs were deep enough to do internal damage, and the blood had already stopped flowing once he stopped moving around."

She touched Seth's face and turned it toward her. His face was pale, almost white, and his dark lashes stood out in stark contrast where they rested against his skin. "I'm worried that he hasn't come around, though." Her fingers pressed against the pulse in his throat. I stayed silent while she counted. "His pulse is good, strong, but ..." She bit her lip. "I don't know, Gabe. We need a doctor to look at him."

"And you have one." A new voice intruded, and my head snapped sideways to see Remy and an unfamiliar man.

"Remy?" I queried.

"This is Chase. I did some calling around, and found out he was in town." My bodyguard's eyes drilled into mine. "He's a friend of Shaun and Deacon's."

The man, Chase, stepped up to the table and placed a heavy black bag down onto the floor. "I was in town for a conference. Deacon asked me to stop by. He said you'd prefer this kept under the radar." A smile flickered over his lips. "That's something I can do." He studied the stitches Harper had done. "This your work?" He glanced at her.

Harper nodded.

"Nicely done." He repeated Harper's action of checking Seth's pulse, then pulled each lid up to look at his eyes. "Can we get him somewhere more comfortable? A bed, maybe?"

"Are we okay to move him?" I stood, rubbing at the ache in my back.

"We just need to be careful about it. But he's not going to thank you for the extra aches that come from sleeping on a hard surface, so let's relocate him."

Between the three of us, with Harper supervising, we managed to get him to one of the guest bedrooms. Thankfully, Harper always kept one of them made up, just in case. I wasn't sure what that 'just in case' was about, because I sure as fuck didn't want anyone visiting or staying over. But my girl liked to be ready for everything including, apparently, stitching up rock stars without too much hysteria. I guessed after years of playing nurse to me when we were growing up, she had just learned to take it in her stride.

Maybe it was like riding a bike and never really left you.

I was pulled out of my musing by Harper's touch on my arm. "Are you listening?"

"Sorry, I zoned out." I redirected my attention to the sandy-haired doctor standing beside the bed.

"Harper did a good job. Blood loss looked more than it actually was, probably due to excessive alcohol consumption in the past twenty-four hours. He's going to be sore. I can give you something for that. We just need to wrap the wounds on his hands."

"Will they heal okay?" I looked at my friend, at his hands, and my stomach twisted.

"They should. They're relatively superficial. Again, they look worse than they are. Did he tell you what happened?"

I shook my head.

"From the appearance of them, I'd say someone came at him with a knife. He lifted his hands to defend his face, and the attacker slashed downward across his palms, then horizontally over his ribs." Chase mimicked the action. "What happened to the other guy?"

"He's dead," Remy replied.

Chase chuckled. "Good man. You have that all in order?"

Remy nodded.

"Do I need to talk to Mac?"

"No, we're covered. Asher is dealing with the tech side to remove any evidence. I called in one of our clean-up teams from Disperser Security." Remy mentioned the business he co-owned with Deacon and Asher—the security firm Forgotten Legacy hired as bodyguards. I forgot, often, that Remy was one of the owners. He was so self-effacing. The polar opposite of Deacon, whose personality was as big as his mouth.

"What do we do now?"

Two sets of eyes turned to me, but it was Remy who answered. "We can keep Seth unconnected to the death as long as *he* keeps quiet about it. If he wakes up and decides he needs to confess, then we might have a problem. If he's happy to say nothing, we can make it go away."

"Is this one of the things I don't want to question?"

Both men nodded. "We'll sniff around the scene and see what we can find out. Then make a decision on how we need to deal with it."

"Like you did for Dex." It wasn't a question, but Remy gave another nod.

"This will be easier in some ways. The man wasn't supposed to be here. He registered at the motel under an assumed name. There's no evidence of Raphael Vasari ever traveling to Los Angeles. I made contact with Marcus DeMario and we traded information. Looks like his release came with the stipulation that he didn't leave South Carolina. DeMario believes he paid someone to pretend to be him so no questions were raised."

"Gabe?" Seth's voice, low and croaky, sent anything else I had to say flying into the ether, and I turned to my friend.

CHAPTER 32

WHAT DID I DO? - HAVD

Seth

Voices pierced the darkness first, and I listened for a while, content to float in the emptiness where pain was a distant memory. But then my father's name was mentioned, and reality forced its way into my peaceful existence.

"Gabe?" The word came out as a croak.

Hands touched my face, and the familiar fragrance of cotton candy informed me that Harper was nearby seconds before she spoke. "Seth, can you open your eyes?"

I *could*, but I didn't want to. If I opened my eyes, then I'd have to face the full truth of the past twenty-four hours. If I didn't, I could pretend this was all a dream.

"Seth?" Gabe's voice, familiar and comforting. The random thought that he'd love the fact I was relieved to hear him flitted through my mind, and I laughed to myself. "What the fuck, man? Me almost killing myself wasn't enough? You had to try and top it?" His tone was light, but I knew him too well and could hear the distress beneath the humor.

"Wasn't planned." I cleared my throat.

"Someone get him a drink."

I tried to smile at Gabe's demand, but everything hurt too much.

A hand curved beneath my head and lifted, then a glass was pressed to my lips. I took a sip, swallowed, savoring the cool water as it slid down my throat. A pillow was propped under my head, and I finally opened my eyes.

Gabe's concerned face was the first thing I saw, followed by Harper's, Remy's, and a blond guy I didn't recognize. Gabe must have seen the confusion in my expression, because he waved a hand.

"That's Chase. Private doctor. We needed to make sure you didn't require more than we had the ability to do here."

"What's the verdict, doc?" It was an effort to speak.

"You'll live, but I recommend not getting into any more knife fights."

I tried to laugh, and pain ricocheted through my body. My eyes drifted closed. "I'm so tired."

"That's the blood loss, pain, and whatever else you've been abusing your body with for the past few days." There was a bite to Gabe's voice.

"Sleep. You'll feel better." A hand touched my forehead, then down to the pulse in my throat. "I've given Harper some painkillers for you to take, which should help. Take it easy for a couple of days. Keep an eye on the stitches, and make sure you don't pull them. Keep them wrapped for forty-eight hours. Don't do *anything* strenuous. Be careful not to bump or knock them once you're back on your feet. They should be ready to get removed in ten days. Harper can do that, but I'll leave my number with Gabe in case there are any problems. I'm going to be in town until the end of the month. If you need anything, call me."

"Thanks, doc," I whispered and let sleep pull me back under.

***

When I next woke, the room was empty aside from Gabe, who was sprawled in a chair beside the bed. He sat up when I opened my eyes.

"Hey."

"My hands hurt." In fact, it felt like they were on fire.

"You cut them up pretty bad. Chase said it's all superficial and should heal okay, though. They're bandaged up." He paused. "What the fuck were you thinking going to see him?"

"I wanted him to leave."

"Did you mean to kill him?"

"He's dead, then?" I'd wondered, but I hadn't been sure or in any condition to check for myself at the time.

"Very much so."

"Do the police know?"

"Fuck no. Remy will deal with it."

"How?"

"I didn't ask. Are you ready to tell me what happened?"

I wasn't sure I'd *ever* be ready to talk about it, but I owed him an explanation.

"I needed to face him, face my past. Since everything got out,

I've been going around and around in my head. Even though it's been over twenty years since I got out of there, it's always been hanging over me." I used my elbows to lift myself up and frowned down at my bare chest. The bandages wrapped around my ribs were my only covering. I glanced at Gabe.

He stood and crossed the room. Pulling open the door, he disappeared through it and returned a minute later, t-shirt in hand. It was a struggle, but between us we got it over my head and in place without too much swearing on my part. I fell back against the pillows, panting.

"Do you want a couple of those painkillers Chase left?" He jerked his chin toward the nightstand.

I nodded, then glared down at my bandaged hands.

Gabe gave a quiet laugh. "Looks like you're gonna have to suck it up and accept help. Open wide, honey." He scooped up two pills and the glass of water.

I glared at him but ignored the endearment and did as he said. He dropped the pills onto my tongue, and held the glass close to my mouth.

"Give them a few minutes to kick in."

I tipped my head back, and closed my eyes. Sure enough, after a few minutes, the pain began to ease to a dull throb.

"I guess you got DeMario to track him down and that's how you knew where he was?"

"Yeah. I thought if I faced him, forced him to acknowledge what he'd done, maybe he'd... I don't know ... show remorse? Regret?"

"I guess he didn't?"

"Fuck, no. He spoke to me like he was still in charge, still in control. He told me I was complicit in everything I took part in. That by not refusing, it made me willing."

"That's fucked up."

"At first, it rocked me, threw me back to that time, but the more he talked, the angrier I got. He admitted he lied about Marcie staying in contact with him, and that he'd tracked her after figuring out who I was. He said he recognized me and could not have denied our relationship. Finding Marcie wasn't difficult as she never changed her name, and the paper trail was easy to follow. She tried to run from him, Gabe, but he caught her and drugged her. That article going out is my fault. If I'd kept in touch, tried harder to spend time with her, he wouldn't have been able to get to her."

"You know that isn't true. He'd have found a way."

"Maybe. Anyway, by the time we both showed up at her condo, he had her so high she was living back in the past. He thought it was fucking funny. He said he planned on getting her pregnant again, because she made pretty children and he needed some new toys. Ones that weren't broken like I was."

"And you lost your shit."

CHAPTER 33

MAYBE - MACHINE GUN KELLY

Gabe

Seth's smile was barely a twitch of his lips. "Something like that."

"Who had the knife first?"

"He did. I punched him. He fell back onto the bed. I think the knife was on there. I don't know. I wasn't paying attention to the room. When I went to hit him again, he had it in his hand and went for my face. I blocked him, and he aimed for my chest." Seth licked his lips, glancing away.

"I tried to get the knife from him, but he's stronger than he looks or maybe all the years inside taught him how to fight, I don't know." He paused to suck in a breath. "I *don't* know what happened, Gabe. I was losing blood. I kept going dizzy. Maybe I passed out? The next thing I remember is Raphael on the bed, and Marcie was standing over him. She pulled me into the bathroom and told me to lock the door. I was in a daze, barely thinking, so I did what she said … and then you were there."

I sat forward. "Wait. *Marcie* was there?"

"I think so. *I don't know.* Maybe I was seeing things. That's been happening a lot lately."

I wanted to ask what else he'd been seeing, but filed it away for later. Finding out what happened was more important. "She wasn't there when we arrived. Just you and him. I'll ask Remy to check in on her, though. Could she have been there all along?"

"If she was there, she must have been hiding in the bathroom while I was talking to him. And where would she have gone afterward?"

"If *you* didn't kill him, and she did, then maybe she ran."

"*If* she was even there." His gaze met mine. "What if I killed him, Gabe, and I'm just trying to convince myself that Marcie did?"

"Fucker deserved it, no matter who did it." The expression on his face made it clear he didn't agree. "Look, don't worry about it right now. Get some rest. When Remy comes back, we'll know more."

"But—"

"Don't screw with your own head like that. He's dead, and you're hurt. I think it's a pretty safe bet you didn't imagine Marcie being there; otherwise, you'd probably be the one who was dead."

"I guess."

I moved to sit on the edge of the bed. "Seth, listen to me." I dropped the light tone from my voice. "Even if you did kill him, it's *not* your fault. He put you in that position. He attacked you. It's self-defense."

"I'm not sure the police will see it that way."

"Fuck the police. They don't need to know." I grabbed the television remote from the nightstand, twisted to sit beside him and propped my back against the headboard. Tapping the power button, I tossed the remote control onto Seth's lap. "Find a movie, and stop talking shit."

***

The television screen was dark. I lay on my back and stared up at the ceiling, waiting for my mind to wake up. A low grunt beside me caused my brows to pull together and I rolled my head sideways, then laughed quietly. Well, that sure as shit *wasn't* Harper. I must have fallen asleep during the movie.

I nudged Seth's leg with my foot.

"Don't touch me, Mercer."

The dark hid my smile. *Someone* was feeling better. "I love you, Seth."

"I'll still break your fingers if you touch me."

I chuckled. "How are you feeling?"

"Sore." There was a pause. "I think Marcie *was* there, Gabe. The more I think about it, the more I'm certain I wasn't the one to kill him. After he slashed my hands, I could barely move them. There's no way I could have gripped the knife."

"I agree. I'll text Remy and see if he has any news." I rolled off the bed and stood. "Do you need any painkillers?"

"Not right now. It's not unbearable."

I switched on the bedside lamp. "But there's no need to suffer if you don't have to." I uncapped the pill bottle and shook two out. "Take them. Don't you think you've gone through enough?"

Our gazes met, clashed, and I held out my palm and waited. When he sighed and reached out to snatch the pills off me, I lifted them out of his reach, turned to grab the bottle of water from the nightstand and cocked an eyebrow. "Open wide, sweetheart."

"When did you become so responsible?" he grumbled and let me drop the pills into his mouth, then took a mouthful of water.

I shrugged. "Having a near-death experience changes things."

"I guess."

I stared at him for a second, debating whether to voice my next question.

"Spit it out, Mercer. I can hear you thinking from here."

"You and Riley… I haven't told her you're here. What do you want me to do?"

His head dropped back against the pillows. "Fuck."

"You treated her badly, Seth."

"I know."

"You bruised her throat, you know? You better hope her mom doesn't see it."

"What? When?"

"She said it wasn't anything important and you didn't mean it. But you choked her a little too hard. I'm not kink-shaming or anything, man, but you have to watch what you're doing."

"Fuck off, Gabe. I wasn't choking her for kicks."

"But you *did* choke her?"

"No … yes …" His sigh was heavy. "I don't remember."

"You need to talk to her. Do you want me to bring her here?"

"I should go home."

"Once we know you're on the road to recovery. I'd rather you stayed here for a couple of days."

He wanted to argue. I could see it in his eyes as he glared at me, but he nodded. "Call Riley."

I nodded, checked the time, and pursed my lips. "I'll check in with Remy, and get Carter to go and pick Riley up."

CHAPTER 34

SWEET HEROINE – YUNGBLUD

Riley

My cell's ringtone jolted me out of sleep, and I groped around for it so I could squint at the screen. Gabe's name showed on the display. I hit answer.

"Is Seth okay?"

"I have him with me. I'm sending Carter to pick you up. Try not to disturb your mom or Karl, if he's there. We don't want them asking questions."

"Questions … what?"

"Carter will explain everything to you. He'll be outside the house in a few minutes. Go and meet him."

"Gabe, is Seth *okay*?" My heart hammered against my ribs.

"He's alive and irritable, so he's on the way to being okay, yeah. I'll speak to you soon." He ended the call before I could question him further.

I dressed on autopilot, my mind concocting all kinds of scenarios in my head for why Seth was with Gabe, and why

I'd been summoned in the middle of the night. When I crept through the house and sneaked out of the front door, a flash of lights told me where Carter was parked, and I hurried across the street to the car.

He leaned across the seat and threw open the passenger door. "Get in."

When I was settled, with my seatbelt in place, he started the car.

"Seth was hurt earlier today. He reached out to Gabe," he began without waiting for me to ask. "When Gabe and Remy got to him, everything except making sure he was safe and cleaned up was forgotten. Gabe wants me to tell you that not contacting you wasn't a conscious decision. They just had other things going on."

"How was he hurt?"

"He went to see Raphael. They ended up arguing, then Raphael attacked Seth, and they fought. Harper cleaned him up and a doctor has seen him. He'll be okay, but he's sore and tired, so go easy on him when we get there, okay?"

"Why would he go and see that man? He's *evil!*"

Carter glanced at me. "Sometimes the heart wants answers and doesn't listen to the head. I think Seth got answers that hurt more than not having them. So, I'm asking you as his friend, not his bodyguard, to give him some leeway. I know he's acted like an asshole. I know he hurt you. But his entire world was rocked off its axis."

"I know." My voice was soft. I *did* know. Seth had done what he thought was the best thing. He pushed both me and Gabe away because he didn't want us caught in the crossfire. Had he always planned on facing the monster who'd raised him?

My guess was he had.

The second he saw the man outside Marcie's condo, his attitude had changed from being ready to face the world after the article landed, to wanting no one around him. "Where are they?"

"Gabe's house. He insisted on no hospital, so the only other option was to see if Harper could stitch him up."

"*Stitch him up?*" My voice rose.

"Raphael had a knife."

"Oh my god!" I covered my mouth with my hand, nausea a heavy lump in my throat.

"He's okay, Riley. Harper was able to stitch him up. The knife caught him across the ribs, and his hands were cut up. Chase, the doctor, says he's going to be alright. He just needs to take it easy for a couple of weeks."

The gates leading to Gabe's house slid open silently, and we drove through. Gabe was standing outside when we pulled up. He strode across and opened the door to help me out.

"Did Carter tell you?"

I nodded.

"Don't throw yourself at him. We don't want the stitches coming apart. He's tired and surly. Just tell him to shut the fuck up if he gets snappy."

My laugh was a little choked. Gabe slung an arm across my shoulders. "He's okay, Ri. He just lost his way for a while there.

But we have him back now."

We walked inside the house, and Gabe led me along the hallway. He paused outside a door. "Ready?"

I took a deep breath. "Ready."

He opened the door, and gave me a gentle push forward. I stepped through into the room, and the whole world receded until the only thing I could see was the man semi-reclining on the bed. The door behind me clicked shut and I took another step deeper into the room. Seth watched me, but didn't speak. His gaze moved over my face, dipped down, and he frowned, lips pressing into a thin line.

"Are you—"

"I'm sorry."

We spoke at the same time. I moved closer. "Are you okay?"

"I've been better."

"Gabe said you hurt your hands." I looked down to where they rested against the mattress.

"It was a choice between my hands or my face." He lifted one hand and turned it to show the bandage covering his palm. "The doctor said they're not deep and will heal. I should still be able to play guitar." But there was a hint of fear in his voice.

I reached out but stopped before I touched his fingers. "Nothing will stop you from playing guitar."

There was a short awkward silence. I wasn't sure what to say. Seth was hard to read in a normal situation. His face was utterly blank, eyes dark. I sat on the chair next to the bed.

"Thank you for coming."

"I was worried about you."

He nodded. "I know. I'm sorry." His voice cracked. "Fuck, Riley. I have so many apologies to make. Can you forgive me or have I broken us forever?"

"We're no more broken than before all this happened. I understand why you pushed me away. I don't like it, but I understand."

"I hurt you."

I leaned forward and rested my hand on his wrist, just above the bandages. "I told you before, Lucifer, you didn't hurt me. You hurt yourself."

His dark eyes glanced at me, at my throat, then away. "I don't remember doing that."

"It was the day you almost drowned in the pool. Do you remember that? I think you were drunk."

He shook his head. "The last week is mostly a blur. I'm so fucking sorry, Riley."

"Can I ask you something?"

"Anything."

"Why did you go to see him?"

There was no hesitation in his reply. "I wanted answers. I needed to know if *I* was remembering things wrong. Was he as much of a monster as I had built him up to be?"

"What did you find out?"

His smile was unhappy. "He was worse than I ever imagined."

CHAPTER 35

WHERE WERE YOU? - GIRLFRIENDS

Seth

Hearing that admission come out of my mouth unlocked something inside of me. I talked for what seemed like hours, telling Riley everything about my childhood. The things I'd done, the choices I'd made so Lexi was protected, the way it made me feel. She already knew a little, but she didn't know it all. I told her about the conversation with Raphael, and how he'd said no one forced me to do the things I did.

She said nothing and let me speak. At some point, she climbed onto the bed beside me, took my hand carefully between hers and stroked over my wrist with her thumb.

I talked until I was hoarse, until my voice trembled with exhaustion and my eyes burned with unshed tears for the boy I'd been. I fought against crying. I didn't *want* to cry, and it felt like a victory when I pushed through. But then Riley's hand curved over my jaw, and she turned my head toward her.

Her green eyes were wet, tear stains tracked down her cheeks, and she leaned close so she could press her forehead against mine.

"Don't cry," I whispered. "I didn't tell you to make you cry."

"I'm crying because you won't allow yourself to." Her palms were warm against my cheeks. "I wish you would, just once. Stop holding it all inside, Seth."

I swallowed against the lump in my throat and shook my head.

"It doesn't make you weak, Lucifer." Her lips touched mine. "The things you lived through, that you *survived* ... I'm in awe of how strong you are."

"But I'm not strong. That's just it. If I was strong, I wouldn't have done the things I did."

"You were a *child*, Seth. You did what you had to do so you and your sister could survive. You might not have said no, but it was still manipulation. You understand that, don't you? You were a child, raised to believe what you suffered was normal. But it wasn't. And against all the odds stacked against you, you fought against it and you're here."

I dropped my head against her shoulder. "You sound like you really believe that."

"I *do*. I wish you could see what I see when I look at you."

"What do you see?"

"I see a man who was taught that love meant pain, but instead of repeating the cycle, he removed himself from the risk of falling in love so he didn't hurt anyone."

"But I *did* fall in love." I needed her to know that.

"I know." She sounded so smug I couldn't help but laugh.

"But you fought against it for a long time. But I *saw* you, Seth. I saw beyond The Devil you show everyone. I saw your heart." Her head turned and her lips touched the top of my head. "I saw how much you love Gabe and the band, and I wanted you to see how much *you* were loved in return."

"You're a special kind of woman, Shutterbug." I lifted my head to smile at her.

"I must be, because I made The Devil fall in love with me." Her fingers caressed mine, but before I could say anything the door opened and Gabe walked in.

His gray eyes swept over the pair of us. "All good?"

"I think so," Riley answered for us both.

Gabe nodded. "Okay. Remy's just checked in. They've confirmed Marcie *was* at the motel. They're trying to track her down now."

I sat up, and winced when the movement pulled at my stitches. "How can they tell?"

"I don't know, didn't ask. I guess it's part of what they do. They don't just offer bodyguard services. Remy thinks after she killed Raphael, her flight instinct took over from fight, and she ran. They're going back to her condo to see if she found her way back there. He says most people always return to what they're most familiar with and that's her most recent home."

He moved to sit on the opposite side of the bed from Riley. "How are you feeling?"

"Same as I was last time you asked."

"Seth—"

"I know." I cut in before he could say anything more. I could guess by the tone of his voice he wanted to say how worried he'd been. "I'm sorry for cutting you out. I wasn't thinking straight."

"I've done the same thing, more than once. I get it."

We locked eyes. He smiled.

I shook my head. "Don't do it."

His smile turned into a grin, and he leaned forward so he could lick his way up my throat and slap a kiss on my cheek. "I love you, man."

"No press here, asshole."

"You know it has nothing to do with the press." He chuckled. "Don't you remember why I really started doing that?"

Neglected Consequences

CHAPTER 36

MEMORIES - YUNGBLUD

Seth

AGE 12

I threw my bag against the wall and slammed the bedroom door. Another day over. I pulled the nightstand away from the wall, grabbed the pencil from the floor and marked a little line on the paint.

One-hundred-fifty-three days. That's how long we'd been with the Hawkins family. And, so far, everything seemed perfect. It made me nervous. Lexi had embraced the whole family thing, but I was waiting for the bomb to drop. *No one* was that nice without wanting something in return. Jake and Annabelle Hawkins had to be building up to something. I just couldn't figure out what it was.

"Seth?"

I shoved the nightstand back against the wall, hiding my counter, and straightened seconds before there was a tap at the door. I crossed the room and threw it open, revealing Jake Hawkins, my foster dad.

He smiled. "I thought I heard you come home. I'm about to head out and grab some groceries. Is there anything you'd like?"

I shook my head.

"Nothing you really want to eat?"

I fought not to roll my eyes. He did this at least once a week. Trying to discover the things I liked the most, probably so he could take them away later. Lexi bought into it. Not me, though. I had to stay on alert.

"He likes mac and cheese." Lexi's face popped up behind Jake, and she rested her head against his arm.

His smile broadened, and he reached out to stroke her hair. "Hello, honey. How was your day? Coming shopping with me?"

Her arms wound around his waist. "Yes, please. And it was good." I glared at her. She ignored me. "His favorite is when bacon is added to it."

"Mac and cheese with bacon." Jake nodded. "Got it. Come on then. Sure you don't want to come?" The question was sent to me.

I shrugged and turned away. Part of me wanted to go along, just to make sure nothing happened to Lexi. The rest of me couldn't wait for them to leave so I could have some time to myself. The house would be empty, *quiet*, until Annabelle arrived home.

Those snatches of time with nobody there were the only times I could let my guard down and relax. I could shower, change, and not worry about anyone walking in on me.

"I thought I'd go and see Gabe after dinner."

Jake smiled. "Why don't you invite him over *for* dinner?"

I frowned. "Why?"

"God, *Seth*, don't you know *anything?*" My sister rolled her eyes at me. "It's what having friends means. You hang out with each other."

"Now, now, young lady, don't be mean to your brother. Is there anyone you'd like to invite over?"

She grinned. "I could see if Haley wants to come over." She mentioned a girl who lived a couple of doors down from us. I'd seen them playing together in the yard, giggling and whispering.

Still frowning, I switched my attention back to Jake. "I'll ask him."

"Alright, son." He reached out to pat my shoulder. I took a step back and his hand hovered between us for a second. He dropped it and sighed. "Take your key. In case we're still out when you get back." He looped his arm through Lexi's and they left me alone.

I waited by the window, until I saw them both leave the house and climb into Jake's car. Only then did I grab my stuff and hurry into the bathroom to take a shower. I set an alarm on the cell phone Jake had given me. Ten minutes to shower. Long enough to get clean. Short enough to be out and dressed before anyone got back.

***

Gabe was sitting on the steps leading up to his apartment building when I got there. There was a fresh split in his lip and a bruise forming on his cheek. Harper, his eternal shadow, sat beside him. He hopped to his feet when he saw me, and Harper's lips turned downward. I didn't think she liked me very much. I took Gabe's attention away from her, but she never said anything, just leaned up on her toes to kiss his cheek and disappeared back inside.

"Fighting again?" I jerked my chin toward his face.

He shrugged.

"Jake wants to know if you want to come over for dinner." I expected him to refuse—who would want to owe a favor in return for food to someone else?—but he surprised me.

"S-sure. We c-can do the m-math homework." He grabbed his bag from the step and slung it over one shoulder.

The house was still empty when we got there, and we spread out our math homework across the kitchen table. We were bickering over the answer to a question when Annabelle got home.

"Hello, boys. Where's Jake and Lexi?"

"Shopping." I didn't look up.

The older woman moved around the kitchen, taking out a mug from one of the cabinets. "I think it's been *hours* since I last had a drink. Would you boys like something? I think there's Coca-Cola or juice."

"I'd l-love a coke, Mrs. H-Hawkins." Gabe tossed her a grin.

"Oh! Honey, what happened to your face?" She stopped making her drink and hurried across to him, captured his face between her palms and tilted his head back. "You need that cleaned up. Who hit you?"

"J-just fooling around with f-friends. It g-got out of h-hand." The lie rolled off Gabe's tongue easily, and Annabelle swallowed it whole.

She tutted. "Boys!"

Gabe raised an eyebrow at me when she spun away to grab tissues and antiseptic. I rolled my eyes. She was back a few minutes later and grasped Gabe's chin so she could lift his face and blot at his lip. He winced, the antiseptic stinging, and she chided him in a soft voice, lecturing him on fighting with his friends. He didn't argue or protest, and when she was done she ruffled his hair and he laughed quietly.

"Why did you let her do that?" I demanded in a low voice when she left the room.

"It m-made her f-feel good to h-help."

"What about when she wants to be paid for it? Are you willing to pay the price of her kindness?"

CHAPTER 37

PARANOID - PALAYE ROYALE

Gabe
AGE 12

Seth's question hung between us. There was a bite to his tone, but the fear hidden beneath it was obvious to me. As someone who also masked how I really felt behind sarcasm and attitude, I was attuned to the nuances of words in a way most kids our age weren't.

I turned on my chair to face him. "Do y-you think th-that she w-wants something in return f-for her h-help?"

"Of course she does! The more you let them give you, the bigger the price. *You*, of all people, should know that."

I considered how to reply carefully. My stutter made it hard to get things over quickly, so I had to choose my words well to stop Seth from shutting down on me. "K-kindness doesn't al-always m-mean pain. H-Harper taught m-me that."

He snorted. "I think you're wrong."

"I th-think *you're* wrong."

We glared at each other. Seth shook his head. "Let's just get this stupid math done." He dragged the book toward him, and bent his head over the equation.

I stared at him for a moment longer. I knew he'd come from some bad experiences, but as yet, we hadn't reached a point in our friendship where he was willing to talk about them. He knew about my da, about my mom, and about Harper, but only because he'd called for me during one of my da's episodes. I hadn't really had much choice but to tell him what had happened when I opened the door, bleeding and bloody, to go over to Harper's and he'd been standing there.

His foster dad and Lexi returned a short while later, bringing laughter and noise to the house, and Annabelle shooed us out of the kitchen to clean up and get ready for dinner. I followed Seth up to his bedroom and flopped onto his bed.

"Your p-parents are nice."

"They're *not* my parents." His denial was immediate and expected.

"As g-good as."

"We've been here five months. We haven't lasted a year at any foster home. I doubt we'll be here much longer."

"W-why?"

He leaned against the dresser and shoved his hands into the pockets of his sweats. "Because I'll fuck it up. They'll ask me for something I don't want to do, or try and get Lexi to do something, and when I fight back, they'll move us on."

"I d-don't think they're l-like that."

"*Everyone* wants something, Gabe."

"Some p-people just want f-friendship."

"With all the shit your dad puts you through, why are you so optimistic?"

I laughed. "Because if e-everyone is out to f-fuck us over, then w-we might as w-well just e-end it now and s-save ourselves th-the pain."

"Boys! Time to eat," Annabelle called up to us.

I pushed to my feet and crossed to where he stood.

He straightened, eyes on me as I moved closer, his expression one I knew well. He was waiting for the blow to land. Untrusting fucker. I spun and leaned beside him, shoving him over a little with my shoulder.

"What are you doing?" Suspicion laced his voice.

I rolled my eyes, and threw an arm across his shoulders. He tensed. "Ch-chill. I d-don't like b-boys that way."

"Then what are you doing?"

"Wh-when I met H-Harper, d-do you kn-know what the f-first th-thing she d-did was?"

"Why would I?"

"She h-hugged me. It h-hurt like a b-bitch. My r-ribs were still h-healing after a r-round with my da."

I tightened my grip and hauled him into a hug, one arm around his neck, the other around his ribs. He struggled to get free. I ignored him and held on.

"Th-thing is, Seth, sometimes a h-hug is just a h-hug." I bent closer, licked up the side of his face, then planted a wet kiss on his cheek, and stepped back. "And sometimes a k-kiss is a silent m-message of understanding."

His hand wiped his face and he scowled at me.

"I'm gonna d-do that every d-day until you f-figure it out." I walked to the door. "I'm st-starving. Let's go eat."

Neglected Consequences

CHAPTER 38

I DON'T CARE – FRIDAY PILOTS CLUB

Gabe

I stood beside Remy, watching the security footage from a couple of hours earlier.

"What the fuck is he thinking?" I said, as the kid who claimed we had the same da scaled the gates and hopped down on the other side. A quick glance left and right, and then he darted across the grass toward the house. "Is he stupid?"

"He *really* wants to talk to you again."

"What did you do with him?"

"Locked him up in the pool house. I think we may need to put a security hut near the gates to future proof against any further trespassing."

"Didn't have this problem when I lived in the penthouse."

"I remember hearing a story of a stalker breaking in and holding you at knifepoint, so are you sure about that?"

I grunted. "Fine. You made your point."

"Doesn't solve the immediate problem of what you want to do with him?" He flicked the screen with one finger. "We obviously have him on a trespassing charge, if you want to take that route."

I was shaking my head before he was done talking. "I don't think we need to give the kid a criminal record just yet. Throw him out, threaten him with the police if he continues." I checked the time on my cell. "I have to go to NFG. Get him out of here before Harper discovers him; otherwise, I'll come back to find he's moved in or something." The worst part of that was I wasn't even joking. Harper would take the kid's lies at face value and have him settled in before I could say a word against it.

"I'll drive you to NFG. I brought in extra security to patrol the grounds."

I tossed him my car keys. "Sometimes I question who's the employer in our relationship."

"We'll pretend it's you." He led the way out of the house. "Let me speak to security, and then we'll go." He unlocked his SUV instead of my car. "Get in."

I sighed, but didn't argue, and opened the door. Leaning on the top of it, I waited until he was halfway across the grass. "I'm not a child, you know," I called.

He didn't respond, and I glared at his back until it disappeared around the side of the house.

***

"Get in here!" Karl's acerbic command rang out the second I exited the elevator. "Explain to me why Riley was sneaking out of the house in the early hours of this morning." He pointed to the seat in front of his desk.

"You were there, huh?"

"Yes, I *was* there. I took Shirley out for dinner and then we went back to her—"

"Stop!" I held out a hand. "I don't want to know."

"What? We're not allowed to enjoy ourselves?"

"Sure you can. I just don't want to hear about it. It's like imagining parents doing the nasty." I shuddered. "In my head, you're above things like that."

He snorted. "So *I* have to live through your sexual exploits for years, but I can't say a word."

"Exactly. It's like hearing parents talk about their sex life. I don't want to know about it."

"Which takes us back to the original topic, so stop trying to change the subject."

"I wasn't! Riley came over to my place to see Seth."

"Seth's at *your* house?"

"Yeah. We …" I hesitated. What the fuck was I supposed to say? "We decided to talk things out." There, that sounded like something we'd do.

"And where does Riley fit into that?"

"Well, you know … he missed her. He felt bad for arguing with her. He wanted to apologize." I took the seat he waved at.

Karl rounded his desk and sat opposite me. I shifted uncomfortably under his glare. "And you're sticking with that story?"

"Yeah. Why wouldn't I?"

"Because you're trying to spin me bullshit. What's going on, Gabe?"

I forced a smile. "Nothing."

His eyes never left mine. I sat still, kept my hands loose on my lap and didn't reach for my lighter the way my instincts were screaming at me to do. After what felt like a thousand years, he sighed and looked away.

"Fine. But if whatever you're doing blows up in your faces, I'm going to come down hard on you."

"We're not doing anything, I swear."

"Don't dig the hole any deeper." He swiveled on his chair to face the computer screen on his desk. "I canceled all upcoming appearances for Forgotten Legacy for the month. With Seth all over the news, and then his refusal to be involved in anything band-related, I thought it was wise. We'll revisit them at a later date, when you're either ready to tell me what is going on *or* we're out of danger of something new being leaked. I'll let you decide which one."

"Karl—" I had to give him something, anything, but he spoke again before I could say anything more.

"I don't want to hear it. You've made your decision for now. Let's leave it at that. My door is open if you change your mind. In the meantime, what is happening with the kid and his claim? Remy said you met with him."

"Not really met with him, just spoke through the gates of the house. It's bullshit. He's still claiming his mom knew my da."

"Does he have proof?"

"He didn't show me any. He tried to break in this morning. Security caught him. They threw him out with a warning that next time we'll go to the police."

"Why are you the one who attracts the stalkers?" He waved a hand. "Don't answer that."

I laughed. "I don't *have* an answer to that."

"No, I don't suppose you do."

My cell burst into life. I didn't reach for it, and Karl sighed.

"Go on. Take your call. We're done here, anyway. I'll check in with you in a couple of days. Unless you have a change of heart about keeping me in the dark before then."

I was out of the door, my cell to my ear, before he finished talking. "Yeah?"

"Are you done? I'm outside with the car. I have news, but I don't want to tell you over the phone," Remy said.

"On my way."

CHAPTER 39

HAVE FAITH IN ME - A DAY TO REMEMBER

Harper

The commotion outside the house drew my attention, and I opened the doors leading out to the pool to investigate. Two of the security detail Remy had brought in after the news broke about Seth had their hands wrapped around the arms of a third person. I stepped outside, and one lifted their free hand.

"We have this under control, ma'am." My shoulders tightened at the formality, but I understood. It was protocol for the company Remy owned for his security teams to be formal. But it still felt really odd to me. I ignored his statement and moved closer.

"Who are you?" Had a journalist tried to break in? He looked too young to be a reporter.

The man's head rose, and I was struck by features that were as familiar to me as my own. I gasped. "*You're* the boy who wanted to speak to Gabe!"

"My name is Tate." His sullen growl sounded just like Gabe had at the same age.

"Let him go," I instructed the two men holding him.

"I'm sorry, ma'am, we're under instruction to remove him from the premises."

"From who? Remy?" Their expressions didn't change. I shook my head. "No, it was Gabe, wasn't it?" I stepped closer, and one of the security guards moved in front of the boy ... *Tate* ... blocking him from my view.

"I want to speak to him. I doubt he's going to try and hurt me. Not if he wants Gabe to listen to him. Let me see him." I held his gaze, and tried to look confident. After a second, he sighed and stepped to the side.

Tate scowled at me. I studied him. I could see Gabe in the shape of his face—his jawline and lips, the same sharp cheekbones. But his eyes were a slightly different shape, and his hair was dark brown instead of black.

"Finished looking?" The raised eyebrow was a pure Gabe look, and I couldn't stop a laugh from bursting out.

"Come and sit down." I turned and walked to where three sun loungers were placed and sank onto one.

The two security guards hovered, then moved forward with him. He sat opposite me, looking at me just as curiously as I was him. His eyes were a golden brown, very different from Gabe's stormy gray ones.

"Why do you think you're related to Gabe?"

"My mom told me about my real dad. It took months, but I finally tracked him down, only to find out he was dead."

"Real dad?"

"She's married. My dad ... I mean *step*-dad, raised me as his own. But I found my birth certificate, and it didn't have his name on it. So I confronted them both."

The anger over the discovery was clear in his voice.

"You didn't know he wasn't your real dad? That must have been a shock."

"No shit," he snapped.

"You know ..." I kept my voice gentle. "I'm your best shot at getting Gabe to listen to what you have to say. You really don't want to alienate me." I couldn't believe how much he reminded me of Gabe when we were younger—full of arrogance, anger, and attitude.

He glared at me. I smiled at him.

"You said your name is Tate. Who's your mom?"

"Florence Danvers. But back then, she would have been known as Florence Reynolds."

"How old are you?"

"Why?"

"I'm just trying to figure out the timeline of events, that's all. I've known Gabe since he was ten. We grew up together. I was wondering how old he would have been when you were born."

His jaw clenched as he thought about my words, then he

nodded. "I'm seventeen. Eighteen next month."

I did the calculation in my head. "So Gabe would have been fourteen when you were born. Maybe thirteen when his dad knew your mom."

"*Our* dad."

"You understand why Gabe needs more than just your word, don't you? It's easy for someone to walk up and claim they're related, but he needs proof."

"I *have* proof."

"What do you have?"

"Photographs of Thomas Mercer and my mom together. My mom's word that he's my dad should be enough!"

"Why? She's *your* mom, not Gabe's. He doesn't even know her."

"He just doesn't want to know because he has money and we don't."

I shook my head. "That's not it, at all. But you have to understand that because he *is* a celebrity, he gets a lot of people claiming all sorts of things just *because* he has money."

The muscle in his jaw moved, and he swallowed, the anger in his eyes fading. "I guess."

"Do you have photographs with you? Would you show me? Maybe I'll recognize your mom. I lived in the apartment opposite Gabe when we were growing up. I might have seen her."

He reached into his back pocket, and both security guards straightened and moved closer. I frowned at them, and they stopped.

Tate held out a folded photograph to me. I took it and opened it up. It was old, faded, and creased but clearly showed an image of Thomas Mercer with his arm around a dark-haired woman. They were in a bar, that was obvious, with glasses of beer and bottles on the table. The woman was laughing up at Thomas. My heart lurched at the smile on his face. Gabe's smile set in the features of a man who I *knew* had made his life a living hell.

"Well, that's definitely Gabe's dad," I said. "That's your mom? I don't remember ever seeing her at the apartment."

"I don't think she ever went there. She had her own place, I think."

"I don't remember Thomas Mercer ever having a serious relationship with anything other than alcohol." I looked down at the photograph again. "Can I keep hold of this to show Gabe?"

He shrugged. "I have more, so if he destroys it it won't matter. There are others."

"He won't destroy it, I promise. Do you have a cell number?"

"Why?"

"If you give it to me, I can call you and let you know whether I managed to convince Gabe to sit down with you. Where are you staying?"

His eyes slid away from mine.

"Tate?" I took another look at him. His clothes were scruffy, the knees showing through the rips of his dirty jeans. I sighed. "You're sleeping rough, aren't you. Does your mom even know you're here?"

"You're not my family."

"If Gabe *is* your brother, then we *are* family. Do you even live in L.A.?"

"Does it matter?"

"Of course it matters. It's not safe on the streets. Let me book you into a hotel."

"Why would you do that if you don't believe me?"

"I never said I don't believe you. And even if I didn't, I don't like the thought of you sleeping on the streets. Call your mom and let her know you're safe. What did you do? Find out your stepdad isn't your dad, then lose your temper over it and run away?"

The red tinge to his cheeks told me I'd guessed right.

"Oh, Tate. That's such a Gabe thing to do." I stood. "Come inside. You can have something to eat and drink, and I'll get you booked into a hotel room. You should call your mom and explain where you are."

"Ms. Jackson?" One of the security guards spoke up. "I'm not sure we can approve that."

"I don't think it's part of your job description to tell me what I can and can't do in my own home." I held out a hand to Tate. "Come on. I think you need to take a shower as well. We'll steal something of Gabe's for you to wear."

Neglected Consequences

CHAPTER 40

BOIS LIE - AVRIL LAVIGNE

Gabe

"So, the good news is that we found Marcie," Remy said as soon as I got into the car.

"Where?"

"Back at her condo." He twisted on his seat to look at me.

"You said the good news. That means there's bad news?"

"She's dead. From what we can tell, she fought with Raphael. He stabbed her multiple times. She somehow got the knife away from him, killed him, then fled."

"Fuck." I rubbed a hand down my face. "How would she have managed that?"

"Fear and adrenaline add strength. I'm sure you've seen the stories of people lifting cars and things to get a kid out. Maybe her maternal instinct kicked in. We'll never know. But her injuries suggest there was a struggle. The angle of the wounds are consistent with a man of Raphael's height."

"What happens now?"

"We have two options. Stick with the original plan and

make Raphael's body disappear. The motel room has already been cleaned. Nothing will be found there, no matter how hard anyone tries. Then wait for Marcie to be discovered and wait and see what the police do."

"What's option two?"

"We place Raphael's body in the condo and stage it so it looks like the fight went down there."

"You can do that?"

A quick smile crossed his lips. "We can. We'll have to move fast, though. It might be the better option. He's already been seen at the condo, so there's history already. And it gives less of a reason for anyone to look deeper."

I nodded slowly. "Makes sense. Let's do that, and I'll tell Seth."

"You don't think you should tell him first?"

I hesitated, then blew out a breath. "Do we have time for that? We can head back now and I can talk to him, if so. Otherwise, get on with it, and I'll beg for forgiveness afterward."

"There's time. A couple of hours won't make any difference." He turned back to the front of the car and started the engine. "Make sure it's what he wants first. We don't want to make things worse for him."

"Okay." I dropped my head against the seat and closed my eyes. Although I'd grabbed a couple of hours of sleep during the movie with Seth, I could feel exhaustion trying to pull me under. I didn't have time to sleep yet, though. There were still too many things to sort out. I stifled a yawn and rubbed my eyes. "I'll call

Harper and let her know I'm on my way back."

Remy nodded and pushed a button to lift the privacy glass. I called Harper.

"Hey, Frosty."

"Hey yourself. I need to talk to you. When will you be back?"

"On my way now. Can it wait? I have to speak to Seth, and there's kind of a time limit on it."

"Yeah, it'll keep for a little while."

"Okay. I'll see you in about ten minutes. Love you, Harper." Another yawn cracked my jaw and she laughed.

"I love you, too. See you soon."

***

I went straight up to the room Seth was using when we got back. The door was open, so I didn't knock and walked straight in. Riley was beside him on the bed, and she smiled when she saw me.

"Hey, Ri. Could I get five minutes alone with Seth? Why don't you go and find Harper and grab something to drink?"

"Sure." She kissed Seth's cheek and scrambled off the mattress. "Don't fight while I'm gone."

I grinned at her. "No promises. It's our love language."

She laughed and walked out. I kicked the door shut. Seth watched me, brows dipping as I turned the lock.

"Why the locked door?"

"I don't want us to be interrupted." I crossed the room and dropped onto the chair beside the bed. "Look, there's no way of softening this, so I'm just gonna spit it out, okay?"

"Okay."

"Marcie was definitely in the motel. They found her body back at her condo."

"Her body?"

I nodded. "Remy says it looks like she fought with Raphael, and he managed to stab her before she killed him, then she ran."

"After making sure I was safely away from him," Seth added softly.

"Yeah. So … Remy thought moving Raphael's body to the condo and restaging the fight so it looks like it happened there would ensure there's no link back to you." His eyes jerked up to meet mine. I curled my fingers around the lighter in my pocket. "I told him to go ahead and do that, but—"

"It's a good idea."

"Are you sure?"

"Yeah. I don't need any more attention, Gabe. I don't think I can deal with it anymore."

"I understand that. I'll tell him you're okay with it then. He wanted to wait for your agreement before issuing instructions."

"He can guarantee there'll be no trace back to me?"

"He says so, yeah."

Seth nodded. "Okay." He took a deep breath and winced. "Okay." His voice was firmer.

"I'll let him know." I stood.

"Gabe?"

"Yeah?" I turned and he lifted a hand. I bent, and he hooked an arm around my neck, pulled me closer, then kissed my cheek.

"I remember," he whispered.

I straightened and grinned. The expression on his face warned me not to say anything, so I patted his shoulder and walked toward the door.

"Send Riley in, would you?"

"You got it."

I called Remy on my way through the house, telling him to go ahead with the plan for Raphael and Marcie. By the time I hung up, I was in the kitchen. I could hear voices and followed the sound outside, where Harper and Riley sat beside the pool.

"Seth is summoning you," I told Riley, skirting around the loungers to drop a kiss onto Harper's shoulder. "Take a coffee for him. We'll order food in later." I sat behind Harper, legs either side of hers and looped my arms around her waist. "What did you want to talk about?"

She leaned back against me, hands covering mine where they rested against her stomach. "Promise you won't be mad."

"And that's where I leave you guys to it." Riley hopped to her feet and bolted indoors.

I frowned after her. "What's happened?"

"I want to talk to you about Tate."

I sighed. "Harper."

"No, listen. I met him today."

I dropped my head against her shoulder, groaning. "I fucking told them to make sure you didn't see him. I *knew* you'd talk to him. What did you do?"

"We talked. He showed me a photograph. I have it. It's of his mom and your dad."

"It's of a *woman* and my da, you mean."

"Why are you so *against* the idea of him being related to you?" She twisted in my arms to face me, kneeling up on the lounger. I tightened my hold on her waist, so she didn't topple off.

"I'm not. I'm just being realistic. You've seen the claims that get made. What makes this one any different?"

"Did you *see* him? He's almost your double when you were seventeen. He even has your bad attitude."

I snorted. "I didn't have a bad attitude."

"Oh *please*, don't talk nonsense. You were the ultimate high school bad boy. That's why you had no shortage of girlfriends."

"I didn't have *any* girlfriends."

She punched my shoulder. "Stop avoiding the subject, Gabriel."

"Oh, it's *Gabriel* now, is it?" I adjusted my hold on her waist, toppled her back onto the lounger, and straddled her hips. My fingers stroked over her stomach, hooked into the hem of her shirt and dragged it up her body. When I uncovered the curve of her breast, I smiled. "Hello. No bra. This is getting interesting. What else aren't you wearing?"

"You're not going to distract me. I want you to sit down with Tate and *talk* to him properly."

I leaned forward to kiss the soft skin I'd revealed, then nudged the material the rest of the way off her breast so I could lick over her nipple. It beaded under my tongue. "I'm not trying to distract you." My lips brushed over her skin as I spoke. "Lift your arms and hold onto the top of the lounger."

She did, the move lifting her shirt, baring both her breasts. I licked my lips. It didn't matter how many times I saw her naked. I didn't think I'd ever get used to how beautiful she was. Leaning back on my heels, I stared down at her. My dick strained against the front of my jeans. I wanted to strip her, rip off my clothes and bury myself inside her. I wanted to spend hours worshiping her. I wanted her hands all over me, her scent marking me.

I twirled a lock of lavender hair around my finger, and gave it a gentle tug. "Why don't you ever sunbathe naked?"

Her lips tilted up. "Because I'd never get a tan. There would always be this Gabe-shaped shadow blocking the light."

"True." I lowered my head again and caught a nipple between my teeth, nipping just hard enough to make her gasp.

"Stop distracting me." But she didn't push me away.

"Sorry, can't do that. Take your clothes off and lay back down."

She pulled the t-shirt over her head, and I climbed off so she could shimmy out of her jeans and panties.

"Now what?" She arched a brow.

"Open your legs. Put them on either side of the lounger." I moved to the foot of the sun lounger, my eyes on her pussy as she spread her legs. "I could stand here and stare at you for hours. You look like a fucking angel."

"An angel wouldn't be having the thoughts I am."

I put one knee onto the lounger. "Oh? What are you thinking about, Frosty?"

"You, and the things I want you to do."

"Tell me what they are."

Her cheeks turned pink. She was still so awkward about sharing her fantasies, but we were getting there ... slowly.

"I can see how wet you are. Your legs are wide open, everything on display. Are you wet because you want me to fuck you, or because you're naked outside where security could walk past at any moment?" They wouldn't. They'd left with Remy, and the only security guard remaining was stationed at the gate at the end of the drive. Unless Riley or Seth came outside, *no one* would see Harper. I would never put her in a position where someone would see her without her permission, and she knew it. But the words, the *fantasy,* were enough.

Her nipples tightened and her hips shifted.

"Know what I'd love to see right now?"

Her tongue swept over her lips as she waited for me to continue.

"Your fingers on your clit. I want to see just how wet you can get before I touch you."

Neglected Consequences

CHAPTER 41

PLAY WITH FIRE - SAM TINNESZ

Harper

ow did he do that?

One minute I was intent on having a serious conversation with him. The next I'm naked, touching myself while he stood at the end of the lounger and watched me fall apart to the sound of his voice.

He smiled when he caught me looking at him, and reached back to drag his t-shirt over his head. When his hands dropped to the button on his jeans, I licked my lips. Gabe naked was one of my favorite things to look at. His smile widened.

"Want me, Harper?"

I nodded, not sure I could trust my voice. Thankfully, he wasn't in the mood to demand words and kicked out of his jeans to crawl on top of me. My legs hooked around his hips, and I reached between us to curl my fingers around his erection and drag him against me.

His mouth trailed kisses over my shoulder, up my throat, then my lips. "Ready?" he whispered, and pushed inside me.

We groaned in tandem. How long had it been? Twenty-four hours? Two days? Longer? It *seemed* longer, with everything that had gone on, and I was more than ready to have this moment, this *reconnection* with him.

I touched his face, and stroked my hands over his shoulders, along his arms and his ribs. "I love you," I whispered against his throat.

His head turned, tongue licking over my ear. "Always and forever, Frosty."

And then all words were forgotten as he drove us both to an orgasm that left me gasping for breath.

"So, will you meet with him?" I asked when I was finally able to speak again.

Gabe's laugh was warm, and he shoved up on one hand to look down at me. "You're trouble, Harper. My dick is still inside you and you're already back to business. But no, I spoke to him outside the house. I have nothing more to say."

"Please."

He shook his head, rolling off me and reaching for his clothes. "I'm sorry, Frosty. I'm not changing my mind on this." He handed me my clothes. "Get dressed. I'm going to see what Seth wants to eat and then place an order."

And just like that the heat, the passion of earlier was gone, and Gabe Mercer, *rock star*, was firmly in the ascendant.

I shoved upright and caught his arm. "Gabe, stop."

"Harper." He swung back to face me, and ran his knuckles

down my cheek. "Baby, I get what you're doing. I *do*. But you can't rescue every single stray with a sob story."

"He's not a stray."

"*Yes*, he is. I'm sorry, but you have no idea who he is other than whatever tale he's told you. I fucking knew you'd buy into it if you saw him."

"He looks just like you!"

"Does he? Or is it because *that's* what you expect to see?"

I grabbed my jeans and pulled out the photograph Tate had given me. "At least *look* at the photograph."

"Harper, come on."

"No, Gabe. *Look* at it."

He dragged a hand through his hair and sighed. "Fine. Give it to me." He snatched it out of my hand. "What am I looking at, exactly?"

"Your dad and a woman."

"I can see that. It could be anyone. I don't recognize her."

"It's Tate's mom."

"Or so he claims."

I jumped to my feet. "What is *wrong* with you? Why can't you just admit that the kid looks like you, sounds like you, and *might* be related to you?"

"Because if I do that and it's more fucking bullshit, what then?" He snapped. "I think I have a blood relation." He dropped the photograph onto the lounger. "Oh no, sorry, you don't! My bad."

We glared at each other. "Meet him."

"No."

"For me."

"*No.*"

I cast around for something I could use, something that would make him see this could be a good thing. "What if he agreed to a DNA test?"

Gabe threw his head back, staring up into the sky. I could almost hear him pleading *'why me'* with the universe. I ran my palm up his arm.

"You know I wouldn't push if I didn't think he was telling the truth."

"Okay. Fine." He lowered his head, and his eyes burned into mine. "If you can get him to agree to a DNA test, then we'll talk about it."

My moment of triumph was cut off abruptly by his next sentence, delivered in a hard tone.

"But if he's fucking around and lying, I'm not going to let him get away with it. Not now he's forced you to be a part of his scheme."

***

"What do I need to do?" Tate sounded more curious than angry over the DNA test suggestion.

"It's straightforward. It's just a swab of your mouth, and then they run the test."

"I can do that. When?"

"I need to find out where to get it done. How's the hotel?"

He laughed down the line. "The bed is way more comfortable than a sheet of cardboard on the ground. Food's better, too."

"I should hope so." I walked down the hallway to Gabe's studio. "Okay. Let me figure out where we can get it done, and I'll let you know."

"Hey, Harper?"

My finger hovered over the 'end call' button. "Yeah?"

"Thank you."

"You're welcome. I'll talk to you later." I ended the call and tapped on the studio door. "Gabe?" I could just walk in, but if he was deep in writing or recording, I didn't want to disturb him. Not that he'd complain, but I preferred not to disturb him.

The door swung open, and Gabe smiled at me. "You don't need to knock, Frosty."

"I don't like disturbing you."

His arm slid around my waist and pulled me against him so he could kiss me. "You *always* disturb me … in all the right ways."

I laughed. "Would you like a burger with that cheese?"

"Wow. I'm giving you a compliment and you just cut me down." His smile lit up his eyes, and the sheer devilry in his expression woke up the butterflies in my stomach.

"You are trouble, Gabriel Mercer." I looped my arms around his neck.

He bent his head and kissed me. "You wouldn't have me any other way."

CHAPTER 42

PRETEND - NOTHING/NOWHERE

Seth

I stayed at Gabe's place for another two days, before Harper said she was comfortable with the idea of me going home. I think Gabe might have had something to do with her decision. He knew I needed my space, and her mothering was pushing me to the point of snapping. She meant well, and I didn't want to upset her, but there was only so much concern and sympathy I could stomach.

Carter steadied my balance as I stepped out of the car and looked up at my house. A hand touched my back, and then the citrus scent of Riley's perfume surrounded me as she came to a stop beside me.

"Ready to go inside?"

Riley had stayed with me at Gabe's, her quiet presence soothing me in ways I doubted she realized. We'd talked through the night, or more accurately, *I* talked while she listened. To begin with, when I started telling her about my childhood, I was on edge, waiting for signs of disgust or accusations. But the deeper into it we got, the more I realized that the only emotions she felt were concern, sadness, and love. A love I had never expected to be the recipient of.

I stripped myself bare and showed her everything, and she didn't run. Even now, days later, I found that hard to believe.

As we walked toward the house, I reached out and ran my fingertips down her arm. She turned to look at me, and smiled.

"You're an incredible woman. Do you know that?"

She stopped walking, her head tilting, then her palm covered my jaw. "You're not so bad yourself."

"I want to show you something when we go inside."

She didn't ask what it was, just followed me inside and up the stairs. The box I'd pulled out from beneath the bed was still on the floor. I crossed the room and crouched to pick it up, and flipped open the lid. "Sometimes I think about finding the other kids in this photograph." I handed it to her. "But then I wonder whether they'd prefer not to have the reminder of that part of their lives."

"Because you don't like the reminder." She took it from me and looked at it. "When was this taken?"

"After we were rescued." A smile twisted my lips. "*Rescued*. Didn't feel like much of a rescue at the time. But the detective who handled me and Lexi was a good man. He did everything he could, but once we were moved out of South Carolina, it was out of his jurisdiction."

"Isn't it unusual to get moved that far away?"

"It was an unusual case. I think they thought changing our identities wasn't enough. We needed to have a completely fresh start... which would have been great *if* the foster homes we were placed in were any good."

Riley perched on the edge of the bed. "Do you remember the detective's name?"

I nodded. "Mark Peterson. I'll never forget it. I sometimes wonder if he's still around and whether he thought about us once the case was closed."

"It would be easy to find out. Do you think you'd want to do that?" She placed the photograph beside her. "I bet if we asked Marcus DeMario, he'd be able to track him down."

"You don't think it would be weird?"

"Not at all. I'm sure he'd love to discover that at least one of the kids he helped rescue had made something of himself. I bet he'd be very proud of you."

"That's not—"

"I know it's not." She held out a hand. "Come and sit with me."

I sank onto the mattress beside her, the box on my lap.

"I've been thinking, and this sounds terrible, but in some ways, I think everything finally becoming public and, to a lesser extent, Raphael showing up might have been a good thing."

I frowned. "A *good* thing?"

She nodded. "You've been carrying this weight around for so long, Seth, always on edge and waiting for something to slip. Now you don't have to. You can relax. It's out there and, d'you know what? It's only made your fans love you more. It's made you *real* to them. You don't have to wonder whether Raphael will appear or if Marcie will slip. You're free, Seth. You're finally free of it all."

It took a moment for what she was saying to really connect with me, but when it did and I realized what she meant, something unlocked inside me.

"I don't ... I need time to process that," I said slowly.

"You've got all the time in the world, Lucifer." She leaned closer to press a kiss to my cheek. "And, if you want, we can ask Marcus to find this detective of yours. He could fill in some of the details that you maybe saw differently as a kid. It might give you some closure."

"Closure," I repeated.

"I think it would be good for you. You don't have to decide now. But think about it, okay?" She tapped the box. "Do you want to show me what else is in there?"

I handed it to her. I knew what she'd find inside. Birth Certificates for Nathaniel and Olivia Enshaw, two faded photographs of Marcie. One was of Marcie cradling Lexi as a baby. A child holding a child. The second was of a two-year-old dark-haired, dark-eyed boy leaning against a girl of around twelve, who held a baby in her arms. Me, Marcie, and Lexi. Marcus DeMario had used those images to help him find her for me. A flash drive was at the bottom of the box, video footage Raphael had taken of his *entertainment* evenings. I don't know why I didn't destroy that. I should ... in case it fell into the wrong hands. I'd stolen it one night before we were taken away by the police, and watched it more than once over the years to remind myself it hadn't just been a bad nightmare. The final thing in the box was Lexi's letter. The one she'd sent to me after she died.

"I don't feel sad." I hadn't meant to say that out loud.

Riley lifted her head and looked at me. "About what?"

"Marcie. I should ... right? I should be sad that she died." I frowned, examining the way I *did* feel. "I'm relieved."

She set the box down on the floor near her feet and twisted to face me. "I don't think there's any right or wrong way you should feel. I'd have been surprised if you did feel sad about it, though. She's not your mom. That's Annabelle."

Hearing my mom's name made me smile. "I need to call her. Let her know I'm okay."

"Are you going to tell her and Jake what happened?"

I shook my head. "I'm not sure. In some ways, I think the less they know the better. But on the other hand, I don't want to lie to them." I rubbed a hand over my jaw, stifling a yawn.

"You should rest." She stood. "Harper said it's going to take a few days to get back to normal. Why don't you try to sleep for a while?" She crouched in front of me and pulled off my sneakers, laughing when I grumbled in protest. "You're a terrible patient. Come on, feet on the bed."

"You know," I eyed her as she lifted my legs onto the bed. "I understand Gabe's nurse fantasies a little better now."

She turned pink.

"Can I ask you something?"

"I'm not borrowing a nurse's outfit from Harper."

I laughed. "That wasn't quite what I was going to ask, but now you've put the thought into my head, I like that idea. I'll text Gabe later."

"Don't you dare! Anyway, you can't do anything strenuous until you've healed more."

"I'm sure there are workarounds. Gabe will know. He was on limited activity for a while when he fractured his femur." I eased back against the pillows. "Will you move in with me? Not just a couple of nights here and there. Properly... All in?"

Her jaw dropped. "All in?" she repeated.

I nodded. "No more fucking around and bullshit excuses. Move in with me."

Neglected Consequences

CHAPTER 43

CHASING CARS - SNOW PATROL

Seth

I wanted to go with Riley back to her mom's place to help pack up her stuff, but both she and Carter insisted I stay home. Their reasoning wasn't wrong—I was still sore, I shouldn't overdo moving around, I tired easily, and most importantly, I'd have to explain why my hands were bandaged.

The fewer people who knew I was injured, the less likely it was to become public knowledge. It minimized the risk of me being linked to the deaths of Marcie and Raphael. *Not* that I had actually killed either of them, but as Carter pointed out, the police couldn't charge either of them and I'd be an easy target. Faced with those facts, I didn't really have any choice but to agree to stay where I was.

I dozed on and off, and was woken up by the smell of Italian food a few hours later. I opened my eyes to Riley waving a takeout container under my nose. She grinned at the unholy noise my stomach made.

"Wake up, sleeping beauty."

"I'm awake."

"And hungry," she noted when my stomach rumbled again. "Do you want to come downstairs to eat, or stay here?"

"Downstairs. I'm tired of being an invalid. A short walk won't hurt me." I sat up carefully, and swung my legs off the bed. Riley ducked beneath my arm, and helped me stand. "I fucking hate this."

"It won't be for long." She wrapped an arm around my waist, and we made our way downstairs slowly.

The rest of the meal was laid out on the low coffee table in the living room. I dropped onto the couch with a sigh of relief. Just the short walk had used up what energy I had.

"Did you get everything packed?" I asked while she stacked food onto plates.

She nodded. "It's all in the main entrance hall. I'll sort it out tomorrow."

"How angry was your mom?"

Riley handed me a plate. "She wasn't, which was a surprise. She just muttered something about how it's taken long enough."

"Guess she didn't see that, then." I pointed at her throat. "I'm sorry, Riley. I didn't mean to hurt you."

"I wore high-necked shirts at home. And I know you didn't. You were drunk and confused." She bit her lip.

"What?"

"Nothing."

"Shutterbug, you're moving in with me. If there's something

wrong, tell me. I can't fix what I don't know about."

"It's nothing like that. Just something you said that day."

"What did I say?" Most of the day we were talking about was blank, forgotten with the events that happened after. If I'd done or *said* something to scare her, I needed to know.

"You said there was a reason everyone called you The Devil, that there were things you like to do that meant girls didn't want to be with you."

"I said that?" I frowned.

"I just … if there's something you want to do … you know, that we don't do already … I don't want you to hide your needs from me."

"My … needs?" And then her meaning hit me. "Fuck, no. You fulfill my needs more than you know."

"You'd tell me if you wanted me to do something, right?"

"Of course I would."

"Even if it was …" She swallowed and glanced away. "Even if it was unusual."

I set my plate down and caught her hands with mine, ignoring the small sting of pain the action caused. "Riley, I don't have *any* unusual kinks. Believe me, if I had, they would have burned out of me a long time ago from overuse." A small part of my mind noted how light I sounded. A week ago, I'd never have joked about the things I'd been forced to do. "I'm happy with what we do, *more* than satisfied. I don't need anything more."

"Then what did you mean?"

"I wasn't thinking straight, you know that. I don't remember that day, but I remember how I felt leading up to it. I was driving everyone away from me. If I thought claiming I had dark and twisted desires would send you running from me, I'd have used it."

Her eyes scanned my face. Whatever she saw must have satisfied her because she nodded. "Okay. "

"Okay? You believe me?"

"I do. I should have thought about it, really. If you'd been weird about sex, someone would have sold *that* story years ago."

I snorted and, just like that, the atmosphere in the room lightened and we ate in a contented silence.

***

"Your hands are healing nicely. We can leave the bandages off now. How do your fingers feel?" The doctor I'd met at Gabe's turned my hand palm up. "Bend them. Let's see the movement."

I made a fist, straightened my fingers, then curled them again.

"Any pain?"

"No."

"That's good. I didn't think it would take long. Don't play guitar for another week or so. But I think you'll make a full recovery. Let's take a look at your ribs."

I pushed aside the desire not to take my shirt off, and unbuttoned it. Chase ummed and ahhed as he prodded and examined the stitches, then leaned back.

"Very good. Nothing to be worried about. You're on course to getting those stitches out on schedule."

"Great."

"Seth. A police car has just pulled up." Carter came into the kitchen.

"You think they've—"

"I'd say it's very likely," he cut in. "All you have to do is act surprised. No one is going to expect you to break down in tears. Not after what was splashed across the news."

"Do you want me to stick around?" Chase asked.

Carter shook his head. "I think we'll be okay. I'll walk out with you and let the cops in."

Chase nodded and they both left me alone. I pulled on my shirt and waited, drawing the mantle of *The Devil* around me. Gabe called it our rock star personas. I called it protection. I was known for not giving much away, so they wouldn't expect an emotional response. Carter was right about that.

Grabbing my cell off the table, I dropped a text to Riley.

ME - Stay in your studio until I come for you.

SHUTTERBUG - Why?

ME - Cops are here.

SHUTTERBUG - OMG, are you sure you don't want me to be with you?

ME - No, stay put.

Riley had a terrible poker face. If I wanted to pull this off, I couldn't risk her attracting the attention of the cops.

"Seth? This is Officer Stevens and Officer Ryan." Carter

escorted the two cops, one male and one female, into the kitchen.

I tossed my cell back onto the table and stood.

"Good afternoon, officers. Is there something I can help you with?"

"Mr. Hawkins?" The female cop spoke.

I nodded.

"Can we sit down?"

"Sure." I waved a hand around the table.

"When did you last speak to your mother, Mr. Hawkins?"

"I spoke to my mom three days ago. I dropped by their house."

"I'm sorry," she said. "I should have been more clear. I mean Marcie Enshaw."

"I see. I went to see Marcie about a week ago. We don't talk much."

"Do you have any witnesses to that meeting?"

"Quite a few, actually. My girlfriend was with me, my bodyguard,"—I nodded toward Carter—"Gabe Mercer and his bodyguard were also there."

"Did you see anyone else there?"

"Yes. Raphael Vasari was there."

"Your father."

"My *biological* father, yes." My voice remained steady.

"Did you leave at the same time as Mr. Mercer?"

"We *did* leave at the same time, yes." I glanced at the wall clock and injected a note of impatience into my tone. "Look, officer, I have things to do. Can you tell me why you're here?"

"There's no easy way to say this, Mr. Hawkins." The female cop spoke again. "Your biological parents were found dead in her condo early this morning."

"What?" I gripped the table's edge, my nerves real as I waited for them to arrest me.

"Security at the community confirmed that you had left instructions for Raphael Vasari to be kept out. Understandable, given the reasons he spent the last twenty years incarcerated. We believe he managed to sneak onto the property. Forensics think that Ms. Enshaw tried to defend herself against Vasari and lost her life while taking his."

I shoved to my feet. "How?"

"Seth." Carter moved around the table and caught my arm. "Officers, you can see this is a shock to my employer. Is there anything else you need?"

The two police officers stood. "We're really sorry to have to ask, but we need you to identify the bodies. You're the next living kin to both of them."

"No."

"Sir—"

Carter moved to stand between us. "Have you any idea what you're asking of Mr. Hawkins?"

"We're aware of the history, yes."

"Then you'll understand why asking him to do this is inappropriate. You can get anyone from the complex Ms. Enshaw lived in to identify her. As for Vasari, he's in the system.

I'm sure you can identify him yourself." As he spoke, he guided both officers toward the door. "We appreciate you letting Mr. Hawkins know of the situation, and ask for your understanding in light of the lack of relationship between him and his biological parents. If that's not sufficient, then we'll need to bring Mr. Hawkins' lawyer in to discuss the next step."

Their voices faded as Carter herded them toward the front of the house, closing the kitchen door behind him. I sank back down onto the seat and let out a breath. My hand shook when I reached for my cell.

ME - It's clear now.

Riley came through the door seconds later. Her eyes darted around the room. "What happened?"

"The police came to tell me Marcie was dead."

She gasped and caught my hand. "What?"

"They wanted me to go and identify her body. I said no."

Neglected Consequences

CHAPTER 44

SCREAMAGER - THERAPY?

Gabe

I wedged my cell against my ear, listening to Seth as he told me about the update from the police, and pulled on a pair of jeans.

"So, they've said they're not pursuing an investigation further because it looks like it was just the two of them." He couldn't mask the relief in his voice.

"Good." I left the bedroom and wandered, barefoot, along the hallway. "How are you feeling?"

"Stitches are itching, which is annoying. My hands are almost clear now. I'm thinking about heading into my studio later and picking up a guitar."

"Don't rush it."

Seth chuckled. "Yes, dad."

"You know what I mean. You bitched at me when I pushed too hard after my accident. Learn from my stupidity." I bent to kiss Harper's cheek, who was seated at the kitchen table when I entered the room. "Did I tell you Harper forced me to take a DNA test a couple of days ago?" I grinned at her eye roll.

"No. What's that about? Does she think you're an alien or something?"

"She probably *does* think that, but no. Some kid keeps claiming he's related to me." My stomach twisted as I said the words out loud.

"*Really?* There are two of you running around? Not sure the world can handle that, Gabe."

Not sure I can handle it, either. I didn't say that out loud. I was being careful not to dwell on the idea of having a blood relation out there, because if the results came back and they proved he was full of shit ... Well, let's just say I preferred thinking the worst.

"Does Harper think he's telling the truth?"

"Yeah. She met him. He showed her a photograph of some woman with my da. That was enough for her." I dodged the punch she aimed at my shoulder and winked at her. "You know what a soft touch she can be. Now she's got him staying at a hotel *and* gave him my clothes to wear."

"You know she wouldn't go to those lengths if she didn't really think there was a chance he was telling the truth."

I walked across the kitchen and out through the doors, which led to the pool, so I could sit on one of the loungers. "I know. I just like teasing her about it." I lay back and threw an arm over my face, shielding my eyes from the sun.

"My turn to ask you how *you're* feeling."

I sighed. "Worried. If he's full of shit, it's going to hurt

Harper, and she'll feel guilty for making me consider it."

"But what if he isn't?"

"I'm trying not to think about that."

"Why not? I'm guessing he's saying you have the same dad, right?"

"That's right."

"So let's talk about that. What if he does? What if you have a brother out there?"

My heart lurched. I squashed down the surge of emotion before I could acknowledge what it was. "I don't. It's going to be bullshit."

"And if it's not?"

"I don't know, Seth. Has his life been like mine? Where are his parents? Harper said he has a stepdad, and they don't live in L.A. Why aren't they looking for him? Do they give a shit?"

"Are you worried he's had a fucked-up childhood just like yours or scared you'll be jealous that he didn't?"

"He didn't live with my da, so I doubt his life has been that bad." *But what if it had? What if he was reaching out because his family life was as fucked up as mine and I was denying his existence?*

"When are the results due?"

"I'm not sure. Today or tomorrow, I think. Harper found somewhere that will do it quickly and privately."

"Which leads back to my original question. How do you feel about it?"

"Fucking terrified." I lowered my voice, glancing back toward the house to make sure Harper wasn't on her way out.

"That's stupid, right? But it's worse than all those baby claims. They annoyed me. This fucking scares me, Seth."

***

By the end of the day, I was on edge, snapping at anyone who spoke to me. Every time I heard Harper's cell ring, I stopped what I was doing, held my breath, and waited for her to find me. Waited for the news telling me the kid was full of shit.

I swam laps, spent an hour in my studio, showered ... *twice* ... and prowled around the grounds of the house. *Anything* in an attempt to keep my mind off the DNA test I'd submitted.

What if he *was* my da's kid? What if he was my half-brother? What then? What was I supposed to do? He didn't need someone as fucked up as me in their life. What would his parents say? Would they look at my past behavior—it was hard to miss, emblazoned across the internet—and tell him to stay away from me? Or would they hold out their hands and demand money?

Would I pay it? Was I willing to hand over money in return for having someone who has connected to me through blood? Did I want that?

I scrubbed a hand down my face.

But what if he *was* lying? Or maybe it was his mother who was telling him lies. What then? Would I need to deal with that? *How* would I deal with that?

My nerves were shot, and my brain scrambled from going through all the different scenarios in my head, so when Harper did finally search me out, I didn't notice her until she touched my arm.

"I called you," she said when I finished swearing.

"I didn't hear you."

"Clearly." Her fingers slid down my arm and linked with mine. "The results came in."

I swallowed, but didn't ask. I *couldn't*. My mouth was dry, and my heart was beating so rapidly that I was lightheaded. What did I want the result to be?

"Hey." She palmed my cheek. "Gabe, look at me. You're okay."

"Just tell me." I forced the words out from between dry lips. Why the fuck was I so scared by this?

"He's your brother … well, half-brother."

"Fuck."

CHAPTER 45

LEVEL OF CONCERN - TWENTY-ONE PILOTS

Harper

We sat in a booth at the back of Charlie's Bistro, where I'd told Tate to meet us for lunch.

"This is a mistake." Gabe started to stand, and I caught his arm. "We should do this somewhere else. Somewhere less likely to attract attention."

"We talked about this. No one is going to pay any attention to us here. Charlie's sectioned it off, so we have privacy. And the only other alternatives were NFG, the hotel, or home. This is neutral. And you can both walk away, if you need to." I squeezed his arm. "Sit down, Gabe."

"I told him he was *lying*, Harper. I disowned him before even giving him a chance."

I released his arm and grabbed his hand. "That's not what you did. It'll be okay."

"This way, my darling." Charlie's voice reached us seconds

before the woman came into view, Tate a step behind her. Gabe stiffened beside me. I kept hold of his hand beneath the table.

"Tate." I smiled up at the younger boy ... well, young *man*, really, and was struck again by how similar he looked to Gabe. Same messy hair, same shuttered expression. "Come and sit with us."

He took the seat opposite us in silence and stared at Gabe. Gabe drew his celebrity shield around himself, obvious to me but probably unnoticed by anyone else. His body relaxed, a relaxed smile tugged one corner of his mouth up, and the death grip he had on my hand loosened.

"I guess I owe you an apology." Gabe was the first to break the silence.

"I told you I wasn't lying."

"I had to be sure. A lot of claims get made."

"Yeah, I've read about some of them." The derisive smile curling up Tate's lip was identical to the one Gabe used when he was on the defensive.

"Would you like something to drink?" I jumped in before the inevitable argument began.

Two sets of eyes focused on me, one pair a familiar gray, the other golden brown.

"Coffee? Something cold?"

"I'll take a beer if you're buying."

"You're underage," Gabe said.

Tate laughed. "Because *you* were an angel when you were seventeen, of course."

"I didn't say that." Gabe's voice was mild. "Charlie won't serve you."

"But she'll serve *her*." He jerked his chin toward me.

"She will, but I'm not buying you alcohol. So, coffee or cola?" I folded my arms, and stared him down.

"Whatever!" He threw himself back against the seat.

"Careful." Gabe's voice lost its friendly tone. "You show her respect or I walk away. I don't give a fuck what the DNA test said. You say one word that upsets Harper, and we're done."

They glared at each other. I sighed.

"Stop it, both of you." I stood. "Do you think you can control yourselves while I go and place an order?"

Gabe grunted. Tate's lip curled.

"Boys!" I snapped the word and Gabe laughed softly.

"Yes, Frosty. We'll behave."

"I thought her name was Harper."

"It is, but she's my snowflake. Unique, a one-off, and melts on my tongue."

"Gabe!" My cheeks heated at his words.

He smiled. "Go get the drinks, Harper. We'll be good."

I gave them both what I hoped was a stern look, then left them alone to order drinks at the counter. I could have waited for a server to come to us, but I felt that the quicker I got things moving, the better.

Charlie must have been watching because she met me before I reached the counter. "Is everything okay?"

"We just want to order some drinks."

"Coffee for you and Gabe? What shall I bring the boy?"

"Cola, please."

"You got it, darling. Go back to the table before Gabe says something to cause problems."

Neglected Consequences

CHAPTER 46

BETTER NOW - ETHAM
Seth

"Your parents are here." Carter popped his head around the door of my studio to say. "The police went to see them after coming here. Your mom said she tried to call you and when you didn't pick up, she got worried."

I frowned, and reached for my cell. It was off. "I think it's dead. I forgot to charge it." Setting the guitar back on its stand, I stood and stretched, careful not to pull the stitches still annoying the ever-loving fuck out of me. I'd be glad when they could come out. The itching drove me crazy, much to Riley's amusement.

"I've left them in the main living room and said I'd come and get you."

"Where's Riley?"

"Locked away in her studio, muttering about finding the perfect edit for a social media post."

I chuckled. "Can you text her or something and ask her to come inside? I would, except …" I waved a hand at my dead cell.

Carter nodded. "Your mom is going to want to hug you. How

are you going to get around that?"

"I'm not going to lie to them. They deserve to know the truth." I'd gone back and forth on it all for two days, before coming to a decision on what to tell them. They'd supported me for twenty years, and I doubted they would betray me now. It wasn't even a concern, not the way it would have been for my teenage self. My parents, and they *were* my parents in all the ways that mattered, loved me. It had taken me a long time to figure that out. Long years of bad behavior and displays of patience they deserved a medal for.

I locked up my studio and walked with Carter back to the main part of the house. We parted ways near the kitchen. He headed outside to collect Riley and I turned right to go into the living room.

My mom leapt to her feet the second I appeared, and hurried toward me. I held out a hand, stopping her before she wrapped her arms around me. She frowned.

"Don't freak out," I cautioned, then lifted the hem of my shirt to show her my ribs.

"Oh my god! What happened?" She caught my shirt and yanked it up further, fingers hovering over the stitches.

"I need you to sit down." I took her hand in mine and walked her back to the couch.

"Is this something to do with—" She bit her lip.

"It's okay, Mom. You can say their names. Carter said the police came to see you."

"They wanted to know if I was aware that *he* had come here. Did *you* know he was here, Seth?"

"I did. He was there when I went to see Marcie."

Her eyes closed. I touched her cheek. "Mom, it's okay, I swear."

My dad took his wife's hand and pulled her down to sit beside him. "Why don't you tell us what happened, son."

***

Riley arrived just as I reached the part where I contacted Gabe. She settled beside me silently, and linked her fingers with mine.

"Everything is a bit vague from that point. From what we've pieced together, Raphael had taken Marcie to the motel room for …" I shrugged. "I don't know why. When I turned up, she hid in the bathroom but, for whatever reason, when we fought she came out to stop him from hurting me. They fought, and I guess she managed to wrestle the knife from him and stabbed him."

"So how did they end up back at the condo?" my dad asked.

"Having friends in strange places is helpful sometimes. They restructured the events of the motel in the condo. Marcie was already there. It was just a case of transporting Raphael and making sure everything was laid out exactly the same to stop anyone from being suspicious. With both of them dead, the police might have tried to lay it all at my feet."

"What did the police say to you?" Riley asked.

"Only that they'd both been found dead, and they weren't treating it as suspicious. They were checking to see if we'd been aware that Vasari was here and whether we knew if he'd tried to initiate contact with you. We told them we had no idea," my dad said.

"Well, I'm glad he's dead!" My mom's eyes widened and her hand flew to her lips. It was almost comical the look of horror on her face at her own words, but I schooled my expression and didn't laugh. "I'm so sorry. I shouldn't have said that."

"Why? I'm glad he's dead, too. And, if I'm being honest, I think Marcie is better off, as well." My words were cool, calm, and emotionless.

Riley's fingers tightened on mine. I smiled at her. "Riley helped me to clear everything up in my head. They're gone, and it's like something heavy has been lifted off me. For the first time, I woke up this morning and my first thought wasn't, 'will this be the day I'm dragged back into the past?'"

A tear spilled from my mom's eye, and I reached forward to brush it away with my thumb. "I love you, Mom. Both of you. You started me on the path toward finding happiness. You showed me that not all families are full of pain and hate."

My mom surged forward and threw her arms around my shoulders. She buried her face against my throat and I could feel the wetness from her tears against my skin. I smoothed a hand down her back, and turned my head to press my lips to her hair.

"If it wasn't for you, I wouldn't be who I am today. I wouldn't *be* here at all."

Neglected Consequences

CHAPTER 47

AIN'T NO REST FOR THE WICKED - CAGE THE ELEPHANT

Gabe

The silence after Harper left was awkward, and I reached for the menu just for something to do. "Did you want something to eat?"

"No. I want you to tell me about our dad."

No small talk, then. Okay. This kid was abrasive. I wondered how much of it was a front, put on to hide the fear of rejection. Or was that just who he was? It was possible. My da was an asshole, after all, and so was I.

"What did your mom tell you?"

"Not a lot. His name, where he lived, and that she remembered him having a son called Gabriel." His lip curled. "That's *you,* in case you didn't realize."

"I figured that out." I didn't rise to the aggressive note in his voice. "How did they meet?"

He shrugged. "Didn't ask. Don't care. Just want to know what he was like, since they fucking lied about her husband being my dad for my entire life."

"What's your stepfather like?"

"He's okay. Until I found my birth certificate, I thought he *was* my dad. He never treated me like I wasn't."

"When did your mom meet him? I guess you were very young since you don't remember a time without him."

"She said she was pregnant with me when she met him." He sat up straighter on the seat. "Look, I didn't come here to talk about him. I want to know about *our* dad. I want to know what I missed out on."

I laughed, the sound sharp. "You didn't miss out on anything."

"You got signed by NFG Records when you were eighteen, didn't you? I bet Dad was excited about that."

"Not particularly, no." My hand reached for the lighter in my pocket. Where was Harper? She would be better at this than me. How long did it take to order drinks?

"No way! His son gets signed to a record label, and he wasn't excited by it? I don't believe that."

"Sorry, kid. He couldn't give a fuck. Not until he realized how much money I was making, anyway."

"No way. You're just saying that."

"Why would I? I've got nothing to gain by it. The man is dead." Harper rounded the corner then, and I breathed a sigh of relief. "If you don't believe me, ask Harper. She lived opposite me when I was a kid."

"Ask me what?" She sat beside me. "Charlie's bringing drinks over."

"About my da. He doesn't believe me."

"What have you told him?"

"Not a lot. Just that he was an asshole."

Her hand rested on my thigh and she squeezed gently. "He was definitely an asshole," she agreed.

"What did he die of?"

"I'd like to think the Devil came to get him."

"Gabe!" Harper snapped my name.

"There's no point in sugarcoating it, Frosty. Look, *Tate*, our dad was a fucking asshole, okay? From the age of four to eighteen, he beat the shit out of me on the regular. It was only when I moved out that he stopped, and even then, we clashed heads a few times."

Tate's jaw dropped at my clipped words. He swallowed a couple of times, then licked his lips. Any response he had to make was stalled by Charlie arriving with our drinks. She smiled around the table, set down the tray, and pulled off my ball cap to ruffle my hair.

"Stop hiding that beautiful face of yours, Gabriel."

"If anyone sees my *beautiful* face in here, you'll have a mob forming and Remy will complain."

She huffed. "Fine. If you need refills, let me know." She slapped the cap back into place, and then she was gone.

"Where was your mom?" Tate demanded the second she was out of sight.

"She died when I was four." I was amazed at how calm I

sounded, because my fingers were curled tight around my lighter.

"Were you a bad kid?"

"At times, sure."

"What? Gabe, no!" Harper cut in. "No, he wasn't a bad kid. Why are you asking that?"

"Well, why else would his dad beat him?"

"Thomas Mercer was *not* a good man, Tate. Maybe that's why your mom never told him about you, or you about him. Have you asked her?"

Tate dropped his gaze. I leaned forward. "Have you spoken to your mom at all since coming here?"

"I sent her a text after Harper took me to the hotel."

"A *text*? That's it? Saying what?"

"That I was alive, and I might have found a brother." He muttered the words.

"Fuck's sake." I rubbed a hand down my face. "Call your fucking mother, Tate."

His head came up, the muscle clenched in his jaw, and I waited for him to storm out.

"My mom died when I was twenty-two," Harper said softly. "I'd give anything to talk to her one last time. Gabe was at school when his mom died. She dropped him off, and he never saw her again."

My heart faltered at her words, and I looked away. That day was burned into my memory, the confusion, the heartbreak, the *loss*.

"Call your mom, Tate. Let her hear your voice so she knows you're okay." Her voice was insistent.

Tate cleared his throat. "Okay, *okay*."

I hid a smile. Harper had always had a way of getting me to do what she wanted at that age, too.

"Do you want to use my phone?"

His eyes widened, and I had to smother a laugh by picking up my coffee.

"You mean you want me to call her *now?*"

I set the mug down. "I'd like to speak to her, so yeah, call her now."

He pulled his cell out of a pocket and placed it on the tabletop, scrolled through his contacts and then hit call on a number, followed by the speaker image. When it connected and we heard it ring, he tapped the volume to lower it a little so it didn't echo around the bistro.

"*Tate?* Oh my god, Tate, is that you?" A woman's voice came through the speaker.

Tate's eyes darted up to mine, then down to the cell. "Hi, Mom. Yeah, it's me."

CHAPTER 48

TEENAGERS - MY CHEMICAL ROMANCE

Tate

I hadn't heard my mom's voice for two weeks, and it shook me more than I thought it would. There was a suspicious burn at the back of my eyes, and I blinked rapidly.

"Tate? Tate, where are you? Are you okay? God, I've been so worried." She sounded it, her voice trembling and soft.

"I sent you a text." I, on the other hand, sounded angry.

I'd been angry for six months. Ever since I found my birth certificate and it *didn't* have my dad's name on it. It didn't have *anybody's* name on it. I'd been listed as Tate Reynolds, *not* Tate Danvers, which was my dad's last name. The night I pulled my birth certificate out of the folder my mom kept all official documents in, my world had imploded. My entire life was based on a lie.

I'd thrust the birth certificate at her and demanded to know why my dad's name wasn't listed, why *I* wasn't named after him, and she'd folded like a bad hand of poker. She'd turned white, dropped onto the nearest seat, and clutched the paper to her chest. My dad, *Oscar*, had come inside from his workshop to investigate what the shouting was about, and found me yelling while my mom cried.

He'd moved between us, told me to take a walk and cool off, then wrapped his arms around my mom and took her out of the room. I didn't take a walk. I trashed the kitchen, smashing china, slamming doors, and kicking the table and chairs until he came back in.

"A text after *two weeks*. I thought you were *dead!*" My mom's voice snapped my attention back to the moment.

"Yeah, well, clearly I'm not."

"Where are you?"

"Los Angeles. I told you I was going to find my dad… my *real* dad, not the bullshit lie you gave me."

"Oscar has always been your dad."

"But he's not, is he?" Something moved at the edge of my vision and I looked up to see Gabe Mercer—Gabe *Fucking* Mercer, lead singer of Forgotten Legacy and my long-lost half-brother—stretch out a hand and pick up my cell.

"What's your mom's name?" he asked me.

"Florence."

He took the call off speaker and lifted the cell to his ear. "Hi. My name is Gabe Mercer. I believe you knew my father. Tate is safe. He's been making a nuisance of himself outside my home for the past week." He caught my eye, and one side of his mouth curled up. "Yes, I am *that* Gabe Mercer." His smile stretched wide. "Is that right? A fan, huh? From the mouth on him, I'd never have guessed."

"What is she saying?" I demanded. Gabe ignored me.

"My fiance put him into a hotel. How about we bring him home tomorrow?"

I reached for my phone and Gabe leaned back out of reach, one eyebrow arching. "I think you're right. It shocked me as well, so I know a little of what he's feeling … no, it's not a problem. I'm looking forward to meeting you as well. We'll speak tomorrow." He held the phone out. "Your mom wants a word."

I went to take it, and he held it up. "Be *nice*. You don't know what could be your last words to her."

I snatched my cell from him. "Hi."

"Tate, is it true? Thomas' son is the singer from that band you like?"

"Yeah."

"He sounds nice."

"He's an asshole."

Gabe snorted, and Harper sighed.

"Don't talk that way. He could have had you arrested or refused to talk to you."

"He *did* refuse to talk to me. It was his girlfriend who got him to listen. Then we did a DNA test to prove I was right."

Her sigh was soft. "Oh, Tate. I wish—"

"Don't. There's no point in wishing you'd done things differently. You didn't. You lied and I found out."

"Enough." Gabe snapped. "Tell your mom you love her and

let's get the fuck out of here. People are starting to notice us."

"Just because we're related doesn't mean you get to boss me around."

"Actually, big brother rules state I can do whatever the fuck I like. And since I'm new to this whole thing, I have a lot of years worth of being annoying to pack in. So do as you're fucking told."

"Gabe." His girlfriend put her hand on his arm, and his features immediately softened.

I rolled my eyes. Pussy-whipped asshole.

"Tate, I love you. *We* both love you. You know that, don't you?" My mom's voice was quiet.

"I guess so."

Gabe cleared his throat. I sighed.

"I love you too, Mom. I guess I'll see you tomorrow." I ended the call and pocketed my cell. "Now what?"

"Now we go back to my place and clear some shit up." He tossed money onto the table and stood. "Let's get out of here. There are fans heading our way."

I followed the direction of his gaze to see three girls, weaving through the tables, their eyes on Gabe. A dark-suited man unfolded himself from a seat at the counter and intercepted them.

What the fuck? Was that a bodyguard? He glanced back, one eyebrow raised.

"We almost made it out," Gabe muttered. I looked at him. He shrugged. "Time to put on a show." He tossed me a smile. "Welcome to the high life, kid." He straightened and a change swept over him. I swear he *became* the lead singer of Forgotten Legacy in front of my eyes. The changes were subtle, but they were there. A cocky grin, a wicked gleam in his eyes, casual confidence in his stance, and arrogance in his expression as he strode forward to meet the girls clutching napkins and pens.

Gabe Fucking Mercer. Front man of Forgotten Legacy. My brother.

What the actual fuck?

CHAPTER 49

ORIGINAL ME – YUNGBLUD & DAN REYNOLDS

Gabe

It took over thirty minutes to get out of the bistro. I posed for photographs, signed napkins, receipts, and arms, answered questions and made myself available to the fans who crowded around. Harper was dragged into the chaos because so many of our fans had embraced our chosen partners. Our female fans, especially, wanted to meet the women who had tamed the rock stars. She dealt with the attention with her usual charm and warmth. By the time we escaped, I was sure the girls were more in love with her than they were with me.

I was conscious of Tate's presence the entire time, wondering whether he'd use it as an opportunity to tell people who he was. But he stayed beside the table and said nothing, watching everything out of guarded eyes. A flash of relief crossed his face when Remy finally put a stop to the horde of people, and hustled us outside.

Tate followed us to the car. When he didn't stop beside it, I caught his arm. "Get in."

"Why?"

"Do you want to do this or not? You've just seen how it can get when people notice I'm here. You pushed to meet me, insisted we were related, and now you've got my attention, you're what? Skipping out? Either you want to know where you came from, or you're just punishing your mom and don't actually give a fuck. I'm not going to chase you on this, Tate. If you want me to keep on acknowledging you exist, then get in the fucking car."

Could I have been nicer? Sure. Would it have been effective? If he was anything like me, not in the slightest.

I climbed into the car after Harper, and left Tate to make up his mind. I wasn't joking when I said I wasn't going to chase him. I'd lived thirty-two years without a brother. I could live the rest of my life without one. Especially an annoying teenage one.

He didn't move from where he stood. I ground my teeth. I *would not* back down on this.

"Tate?" Harper leaned past me to call his name, one hand resting against my thigh. "Come back to the house with us."

I caught her sidelong glance and rolled my eyes.

"Fuck's sake," I muttered. "Tate, get in the fucking car."

"Stop pretending you don't want to get to know him," she murmured, low enough so that only I could hear her. "He doesn't need to meet Gabe Mercer, the singer, rock star, and asshole, right now. He needs Gabriel... his brother. This is just as strange for him as you."

"You know, Frosty, I'm not sure it is." But I knew what she

meant. I raised my voice. "Tate, let's try this again, okay? Come back to the house. We'll sit down and talk. I'll answer any question you have, and we'll drive you home tomorrow and talk to your parents together. I have a few questions of my own. How's that sound?"

I bit back a relieved sigh when the kid finally got into the car. Remy slammed the door, closing us inside.

"Your mom said you have posters of the band on your bedroom wall."

He shrugged.

"Come on, man. You gotta meet me halfway here. The whole angsty teen thing isn't going to work. It's not my fault your mom didn't tell you who your dad was."

"You didn't believe me."

"Look at it from my point of view. I get people claiming all sorts of weird shit all the time. Some kid saying they're my brother without any proof—"

"I *have* proof."

"No, you had photographs of your mom with my da. There are probably thousands of similar photographs of him with people. I doubt they all had kids with him. The DNA test we did is proof, so we've passed that hurdle now."

"Honestly, looking at the pair of you together, it's impossible not to see the resemblance," Harper said. "You even have the same mannerisms."

I snorted ... so did Tate, and Harper laughed. "See!"

"The *point* is we have a lot to figure out. I know you want me to tell you that my da was perfect. You want to hear that he would have been devastated to know you were out there and he wasn't aware of you. But the sad truth is ... I'm sorry, but he wouldn't have given a single fuck. Maybe once he might have, but after my mom died *nothing* mattered to him. Nothing except losing himself to drink. You were better off without him in your life."

His jaw clenched, and his lips set into a thin line. He wanted to argue. It was right there in the set of his features.

"The first time he hit me was around four months after my mom died," I said quietly. "I tried to make breakfast and ended up making a mess instead. From that point on, I don't think a week went by where I didn't have bruised ribs, or a black eye, or a split lip from him."

I sat back on the car seat, and pulled my lighter from out of my pocket. I held it out to him. "I stole this from him. He tore the apartment apart looking for it. When I disappeared for a weekend, he didn't even notice. Not until I got back and was in his line of sight, anyway."

"And then what happened?"

"He beat the shit out of me for daring to stay out of his way." My voice was casual, but my grip on the lighter was tight.

"Didn't anyone do anything?"

I laughed. "It rarely works that way. It doesn't matter. It was a long time ago."

"Gabe got into fights a lot. It hid where the bruises and broken bones came from." I should have known Harper would take the explanation deeper. "Thomas Mercer was an alcoholic. He was mean and cruel. He scared me."

I reached out and curled my fingers around hers. "I got a call ... around seven years ago, I think, from the hospital to tell me he'd been taken in. Someone found him collapsed outside his apartment. He never woke up. I paid for the hospital to keep him on life support for years. They kept trying to talk me into switching it off and letting him go, but ..." I shrugged.

"It was weird, I'll be honest. I hated the bastard. He made my life a living hell. But I couldn't do it." I glanced out of the window, saw the gates opening which would lead us to the house, then turned back to face Tate. "Anyway, he died in the hospital a few years ago. I can take you to where he's buried if you want. I don't know if that will help, but it's something we could do."

"Do you ever go there?"

"Fuck, no. Haven't been there since I put him in the ground."

CHAPTER 50

THE HYPE - TWENTY-ONE PILOTS

Tate

The first time I'd been in Gabe's house was with Harper. I didn't get much chance to look around. Harper dragged me down the hallway and tossed me into the bathroom to shower and then had me taken to a hotel.

This time I wasn't climbing over the fence and being locked in the pool house for hours. I was walking in through the front door, a couple of steps behind Forgotten Legacy's frontman.

My fucking brother.

That sentence kept rattling around my brain. I was related to a rock star and, truthfully, I didn't know how to deal with that. When he'd been denying my existence, refusing to speak to me, it was easy to wrap myself up in anger, call him names, and ignore the reality of who he was. But now... now he was looking at me, *talking* to me, and I was struggling to hide my awe.

He was an asshole. He didn't deny it. But there was something else there, something hidden just below the surface. It came forward anytime he spoke or paid attention to his girlfriend, a slight softening of the hard outer shell. His voice lost its sarcastic edge, and he became a different person.

When he'd dealt with the fans who invaded the bistro, he became the rock star I recognized from interviews and concerts. And, inside, where he couldn't see it, I admitted that he was fascinating and complex. Way more complicated than I expected him to be.

"Through here." Gabe threw open a door and led me into a room.

I looked around curiously. There was a pool table on one side, the latest games consoles set up in front of a large television mounted to the wall. Bookcases lined one wall, and gold and platinum discs in frames covered the other. A shelf held various awards, surrounded by photographs of Forgotten Legacy in various poses.

A circular couch separated the room into two halves. Gabe rounded it and sat down. Harper tugged her hand free from his and walked back toward the door.

"I'm going to leave the two of you alone for a while. I have a few calls to make for the foundation. Do you think you could manage *not* to kill each other while I'm gone?"

"No promises, Frosty." He winked at me.

"*Try*." Her eyes moved to me. "*Both* of you."

"You said she knew you when you were kids. I remember you did an interview years ago asking people to tell you if they knew where she lived."

He tipped his head back against the couch and looked at me. "Not my best moment. I hadn't seen her in years, and she showed up at my club one night. I thought I had it all worked out. She'd come to the club, I'd sweep her off her feet and she'd remember how much she loved me." A grin pulled his lips up. "Fucked that right up. She remembered me alright. She remembered how much of an asshole I was, slugged me and walked out. It all worked out in the end, though. Just took a few years to get to the same place."

I moved around the room, stopped in front of the awards and looked at the photographs surrounding them. "Is it weird? The fame, I mean."

"It was. When we first started being recognized, there's a rush. We did stupid shit. Fame goes to your head. Anyone who tells you otherwise is lying. You're surrounded by people who constantly tell you how amazing, sexy, and talented you are. And for a while you believe the hype. Some people don't ever get beyond that stage, others figure it out."

"Which one are you?"

He laughed. "Most days I have it figured out, but I'll admit it does the ego good to hear the screams sometimes. I try to contain it unless we're on stage, though. Harper won't put up with my shit." His smile said he was okay with that.

"Did your dad really hit you?" I crossed to where he sat and stared down at him.

"All the fucking time." He peeled back the bands wrapped

around one wrist and held it up to me. There were faint scars beneath the tattoos, only visible if I looked close. "There were times when it got too much, and I tried to check out." The lightness in his voice was at odds with the words he was saying. "I like to think being successful really pissed him off. What did your mom tell you about him?"

I dropped onto the opposite end of the couch. "Not a lot. His name. That she didn't tell him about me. And the photograph I showed you."

"You're seventeen, right?"

I nodded.

"When is your birthday?"

"September."

"So I'd have been …" He paused, pursing his lips. "Fourteen when she got pregnant. Could have even happened on my birthday." He laughed. "That'd be just like him."

"What do you mean?"

"We had a fight on my fourteenth birthday." He frowned. "Yeah, I remember. He'd actually been in a decent mood. Almost like the da I had before my mom died. He even gave me a gift." His laugh that time was bitter. "He'd found a photograph of my mom and wrapped it. But his good mood didn't last long. We ended up fighting and he left." His fingers traced the scars on his wrist. "I cut myself that night. Wasn't really trying to end things, just needed to feel a different kind of pain."

"That sounds pretty shitty." Hearing about the way his dad

treated him made me feel bad about how I'd fought with *my* parents when I found out Oscar wasn't my real dad.

"Didn't know anything else. What's your stepdad like?"

"He's good … amazing, actually. I think that's why finding out he isn't my dad was such a shock. There was never any hint or reason to think he wasn't."

"Sounds like a good man."

"He is."

"Do you owe him an apology?" There was no condemnation in Gabe's voice, just curiosity.

"I probably do. I said some shit that I didn't mean." I rubbed the back of my neck. "I fucked up, didn't I?"

"Probably, but I'm sure they'll forgive you. Your mom sounded more worried than angry." His smirk was wicked. "Although once they've got you back safe and sound, I'm sure she'll make it clear how she feels."

"Yeah." I sighed. "She's gonna kill me."

Gabe laughed. "It might feel that way, but I doubt it." He pulled out his cell. "Your mom said you're a fan of the band. Let me see if any of them are free. We might as well get all the hero worship out of the way in one go."

"I'm not starstruck!" I was absolutely starstruck. My brother was a fucking rock star.

He ignored my outburst and tapped around on his cell. It chimed less than ten seconds later. "They'll be here in about an hour." He stood. "Let me show you my studio. Do you play any instruments?"

"I've been playing guitar since I was five." I followed him out of the room.

"Lots in common with Seth, then."

"You can play too, can't you?"

He nodded. "Guitar, piano, bass. I even dabble with the drums, although Luca will tell you I'm shit at it."

We walked along the hallways, up four steps and into another room. I turned in a circle, jaw dropping at the instruments, microphones, and technology for recording packed into it.

Gabe waved a hand. "Pick a guitar. Let's see what you can do."

Neglected Consequences

CHAPTER 51

SEX & CANDY - MARCY PLAYGROUND

Gabe

"Holy fuck." Dex walked in a circle around Tate. "You have a mini-me. If one of you put in colored contact lenses, we wouldn't be able to tell you apart."

"Apart from his hair being brown and not having any tattoos, you mean," I pointed out. "He's also shorter than me."

"He's still growing. You're not. He'll be taller than you before he's twenty."

"I'm also better looking," Tate added.

Dex laughed. "He has your ego, as well."

"I'm not sure the world is ready for a Gabe Mercer two point zero," Luca said.

"The world wasn't ready for Gabe Mercer, original version." Seth's voice was dry.

I leaned against the wall and watched my bandmates and friends eye Tate curiously. I had to give the kid his due, he didn't show any signs of discomfort. He held their gaze, hands shoved into the pockets of his jeans, and let them stare.

"He plays guitar," I told Seth.

"Oh?" Seth's eyes returned to Tate, a spark of interest in his gaze.

"Might replace you with him. He's not as mean as you."

"The fans would eat him for breakfast."

"Maybe if *you* ate *me* for breakfast ..." I cocked an eyebrow.

"Still not sucking your dick, Gabe."

"Wait." Tate spun to face me. "The rumors about you two—"

"Are just rumors that Gabe likes to stoke the fires on," Seth finished for him. "I have never, and *will* never suck his dick."

I sighed. "Spoilsport." I pushed away from the wall and walked closer to my best friend. "How are your ribs?"

"Getting there. Moving doesn't hurt anymore. Hands are almost clear." He held out his palms to show me. "Just need the stitches out. Considering doing it myself."

"Don't do that. Harper will lose her shit. Why not ask her to take a look and see if you're healed enough for them to come out early?"

He nodded. "I might do that." He glanced toward Tate, then back at me. "I asked Riley to move in with me."

"About time."

"Yeah. The last couple of weeks has made me realize a few things."

"Oh?"

"Life's too short to live in fear of what might happen." He patted my shoulder. "Let's see what your kid brother can do with a guitar."

Kid brother.

My gaze went to Tate, who was laughing at something Dex was saying. I was curious to meet his mom and see what she had to say about her time with my da. Did she know he was a drunk? Was that why she hadn't told him about Tate? I wouldn't hold it against her if that was the reason.

"Stop daydreaming, asshole." Seth's voice snapped me out of my thoughts. "Grab a mic and let's put this kid through his paces."

***

"I'm thinking about setting up a trust fund for Tate. What do you think?" I'd been thinking about it all afternoon, but didn't want to say anything until I'd talked it over with Harper.

She paused in the middle of unwrapping the towel from her hair, and straightened to look at me. "Maybe wait to meet his parents first? Get a feel for who they are. People can be weird. They might be insulted by it."

I folded my hands behind my head and stared up at the ceiling. "Good point. You'll come with us tomorrow, right?"

The bed dipped as she climbed onto it, and I rolled my head sideways to look at her.

"Of course I will."

I reached out to wrap a lock of still-damp hair around my finger, and used it to draw her toward me. My other hand found the knot in the towel wrapped around her body and loosened it.

"Are you trying to seduce me, Ms. Jackson?"

She laughed. "Sure. With my skin red from the shower, wet hair, and no makeup."

"Skin *flushed* from the shower. And you don't need makeup."

"I'm thirty next month. I absolutely need makeup. I'm sure I have gray hairs as well. Most of them are caused by *you*."

"You could be bald and look like a prune, and I'd still think you were the most beautiful woman in the world. I'd still want to fuck you until you screamed my name."

"Are *you* trying to seduce me now?"

I arched my brow. "Is it working?"

"I've heard better dirty talk from prank callers."

"Challenge accepted." I curved a hand over her shoulder and pushed her down against the pillows so I could pull open the towel covering her body. "Where shall I start?" I braced myself on one hand and leaned over her.

Those gorgeous purple-blue eyes gazed up at me. I studied her, eyes drifting over the curve of her breasts, the dip of her stomach, and down to the fine blonde landing strip between her thighs, then back up to her face. I smiled.

"The first time I saw you, I thought you were an angel. That maybe it was my time to die and you'd come to guide my way. Then I reminded myself that something so beautiful wouldn't have come for me. I was dirty, tainted, and destined for hell. If something was going to be sent for me, it wouldn't be a being as pure as you."

"That's lousy dirty talk, Gabe."

"Hush." I brushed a finger over her lips. "You hugged me and it *hurt*. Not just because my ribs were sore. It hurt my soul ... my heart. And I knew in that second, that *single moment*, the course of my life had changed. *You* had changed it. How could I check out of life when the universe had placed you into my path?"

"Gabe." She tried again, and I pressed my palm over her mouth.

"Not done. We'll get to the dirty talk. I'm building up to it." Lowering my head, I kissed her cheek, the tip of her nose, then moved my hand and kissed each corner of her mouth. "You became my north star, my guiding light, my reason to carry on breathing." I brushed my knuckles down her cheek.

"I lost you twice. Both times due to my own stupidity. I can't promise I won't mess up again, because we both know I'm an idiot. But I'm trying, Harper. I'm listening, and I'm trying to be better. For you. For us." I reached for her hands and lifted them above her head.

"Thank you for trusting me." I pulled out a silk tie from beneath the pillows and wrapped it around her wrists. "Thank you for giving me your first time." I tied it around the headboard. "Thank you for loving me." I kissed my way down her arms, across her shoulders and down to her breasts. "Thank you for saving me." I ran my tongue over her nipples, and teased them into peaks with my teeth and fingers. "Tell me you love me."

She didn't hesitate. "I love you."

"Always and forever?" I kissed my way down her ribs, licked a circle around her navel, then dipped lower so I could nibble my way over her hips.

"Always and forever."

"Do you remember the night Draven watched you suck my dick?" Draven was the drummer in a rock band called Climax Seduction. They were signed with NFG Records. Me and Draven had become friends, talking often. Not as often as I spoke to Seth or the other members of Forgotten Legacy, but we hung out whenever we were in the same location. We *never* talked about or repeated the events of that night, though.

I pushed a hand between her legs and slid my fingertips along her pussy. "Do you think he'd have been as excited if he'd walked in on me eating you out?"

"No." She gasped when I pushed one finger inside her. Her wetness made it slide in easily. "He was only interested in you."

"But if I had been eating your pussy, would you have been okay with him watching?"

"I don't know."

I added a second finger, pumped it in and out, and pressed my thumb against her clit. "You looked fucking amazing that night, you know. Your tits were spilling out of your dress. Your lips wet with my cum. If I could have captured it on film, I would have. The only thing that would have made it better was if you'd been the one spread out for me to feast on. Would you have got off on him watching my tongue fucking you?" A third finger joined the two already inside and I curled them, making her back arch and her fingers clutch the pillow above her head.

"What if the door had been open wider? Anyone walking past could have seen what we were doing. Or when Seth called and I was buried deep inside you. You liked that. You liked me talking to him while I was fucking you. The thought of him overhearing your moans made you so fucking wet, I almost slipped out. And when he told you to come…"

"He didn't." She gasped when I pinched her clit.

"As good as. He just didn't know what the instruction meant. Maybe I should call him, put him on speaker."

"Don't you dare!"

I wouldn't. She knew it. I knew it. But that wasn't what this was about. This was just using words to build a fantasy. One we would never turn into a reality. Seth wouldn't cross that line, and I would never share her with anyone. And Harper, for all her enjoyment of my dirty words, wouldn't be comfortable doing something like that. But she liked the teasing, the feeling of not knowing how far I'd push, and I liked how she fell apart for me.

I pulled my fingers free and licked them. "You taste sublime. Open your legs. I need more."

Her legs parted, giving me a glimpse of heaven, and I bent my head and swept my tongue over her, thrust it inside her, and swirled it around her clit, until she was writhing beneath me and pulling on the silk rope around her wrists.

"If Remy walked in now, he'd see everything. Your pussy is wet. Your clit is begging for attention. Your nipples are hard. I think you should get them pierced. It would give me something to play with. I'd say get a clit piercing, but I'm not sure I could stay away from it that long. I need you spread open like this for me more than I need to breathe. I love how you look. All wet and willing." I rose from the bed, stripped out of my clothes, then settled back between her thighs, I lined up my dick and thrust inside her.

Her eyelashes lowered and she moaned, hips lifting to meet my thrusts. I leaned down over her, caught her chin in one hand and tipped her head up.

"Open your eyes." I waited until she did, her gaze dark and passion-filled. I lowered my head until my lips hovered just above hers. "Still think prank callers talk dirty better than I do?"

Neglected Consequences

CHAPTER 52

HEROIN - BADFLOWER

Seth

I paced the small waiting room, hands shoved into my pockets, counting the steps beneath my breath. Thirty-five steps from one wall to the other, fifty-seven from the door to the reception desk. Seventeen from the desk back to the seat I'd been told to take.

My appointment was at ten. It was nine-fifty-five, and I was giving serious thought to walking out. This was a stupid idea. I'd been here before and it hadn't worked. Why would it be different this time?

"Seth?" The quiet voice of Dr. Santos broke the silence and I spun to face him. "Would you like to come inside?"

No, I fucking wouldn't. But my feet had other ideas, and I was inside the room before I could stop myself. The door closing behind me was like the clang of a prison cell, locking me inside.

"Why don't we go over to the couch?" He crossed the room to where a sleek leather couch and a matching chair were placed.

"It's good to see you again. How are you?"

"If I was okay, I wouldn't be here."

Instead of being offended, he laughed. "Very true. Was it your decision this time or at the suggestion of your record label?"

"I talked it over with my girlfriend, and she said it might be a good idea."

"Do you? Or are you here because she wanted you to be?"

"No, I think it is a good idea. I just..." I licked my lips. "It feels weird, that's all."

"Take a seat." He sank onto the chair.

I hesitated, then sat on the edge of the couch.

"Why do you think it's weird coming to talk to me?"

"No offense, doc, but talking about shit isn't something I do."

"Needing to talk things through with someone isn't something you should be ashamed of, Seth."

"I know that. And I know you've really helped Dex and Gabe." I shrugged. "But they're more people-friendly as a whole. I don't really... I'm just not good with people."

"Because of your past?"

"You know about that, huh?" I should have guessed, really. Who *didn't* know about it?

"I saw the articles in the news, but we had two brief sessions where we touched upon the things you went through."

"Oh... I didn't think you'd remember those."

He chuckled. "It's part of my job to remember; otherwise, we'd have to recap during every single session." He picked up a notepad from the side table beside his chair. "Do you mind if I take notes? It's solely so I don't keep interrupting you. I can jot down anything I'd like to talk more about."

I considered it, then nodded. "That sounds okay. So, what do I do? Just talk about whatever comes into my head, or do we look for a specific thing to start with?"

"There are no set rules. We can talk about anything you like. Is there anything in particular that made you decide that therapy was the right path for you today? We could start with that."

"I worry that Riley is going to realize that we're complete opposites and leave me." *Where the fuck had that come from?*

"Riley's your girlfriend. You mentioned her once before. How long have you been together?"

"Just over four years. I asked her to move in with me a couple of days ago. She stays over a lot, but I never suggested we take that final step. I have …" I thought about how to phrase my next words. "I fall into moods where having anyone around me makes me lash out. I know what to say to make it hurt the most. I didn't want to put her on the receiving end of that."

"Do you recognize when those moods are coming?"

I nodded. "Yeah, I start feeling out of sorts, restless, angry." Guilty, useless, *ashamed*. "When I get like that, I need to be alone. I don't like people touching me or being in my space."

"And you said you've asked her to move in now. What changed?"

"When The Inquisitor ran its story, Riley was there with me. She fought me when I tried to push her away. She wouldn't let me hide. When I did finally get her to leave, I realized I resented the fact she'd gone. I wanted her there. I wanted her to argue with me, to push against the boundaries I'd set up."

"You wanted to see that someone was willing to fight for you."

I glanced away and cleared my throat. "Don't get me wrong, doc, I am surrounded by people who will fight for me all the time. Gabe would never let me close myself off. But with Riley, it's different. I can lash out at Gabe and he'll bite back. We fight, maybe ignore each other for a day or two, and then we'll come back together. Hurting Riley hurt *me* in ways I don't understand."

"Do you think therapy will help you to stop that behavior, or help you understand it?"

"Hopefully, both."

"Why do you lash out? What is it that makes you drive people away? How do you feel? Can you tell me?"

I took a deep breath. "I feel weak." I lifted my gaze to meet his. "I don't want them to see how much of a fraud I am."

***

I felt wrung out, exhausted … drained. Carter pushed away from the wall when I left the therapist's office and fell into step beside me. A silent presence who kept anyone from approaching me as we returned to the car. I fell onto the back seat with a sigh of relief. Reading my mood, he kept the privacy glass up and left me to my own thoughts as he drove through the city back to my home.

I rested my head against the seat and closed my eyes. One hour-long session and I felt like I'd unpacked my entire life out of a mental box, tossed it to the floor and kicked it around. I wasn't stupid enough to believe that one session was enough to fix anything, if *fix* was even the right word. It probably wasn't.

Just before the session ended, Dr. Santos had handed me a booklet to read through and asked me to attempt to answer some of the questions inside it. We'd set a date for another appointment, and as I'd been about to open the door to leave, he touched my arm.

"Seth, remember this. You need to give yourself time. Allow yourself to grieve for the boy you were. Show yourself compassion. Be kind to yourself."

Those words swam around my head the entire journey back home, and I was still deep in thought when I entered the house. My cell rang as I walked along the hallway, and I fished it out of my pocket.

"Hey." Gabe greeted me. "Harper wants to know if you want her to come and check your stitches today."

My hand drifted over my ribs. "Only if she can get them out."

"She won't know until she looks. We're driving out to Lancaster later, to take Tate back to his parents, so I thought we could drop by now."

"Bringing the kid with you?"

"If you're okay with it."

"Sure. He reminds me of you when we were seventeen."

"Full of spunk and bullshit?"

I laughed. "Something like that." I stepped outside and followed the path to Riley's studio. The door was slightly ajar, so I pushed it open and walked in. "Come over and we'll let your baby brother loose on my guitar collection before he goes home."

"Alright, man. See you in an hour. Love you, Seth."

"Yeah, yeah."

"One day you'll tell me you love me."

"You already know I love you. Your ego doesn't need to hear it every five minutes." I ended the call with his laughter ringing in my ears. "Riley?" I called, and heard a muffled reply from the back of the studio. A door banged, and then she appeared, dressed in a pair of cut-off shorts and a Forgotten Legacy tank top.

Her hair was piled up on top of her head in some kind of messy ponytail and my fingers twitched with the desire to free her curls. She hurried across the carpet, threw her arms around my neck, and planted a firm kiss on my lips.

"How did it go?"

My hand smoothed down her spine and cupped her ass. "Good. I didn't break his arms or leave him bleeding."

She laughed. "A promising start."

The citrus scent of her perfume teased my nose, and I dipped my head to inhale more of it. My fingers flexed against her ass, squeezing. "Gabe and Harper are coming over. They're bringing Tate with them."

"Tate? That's Gabe's surprise brother, right?"

"That's right." My lips found the pulse in her throat and I pressed a kiss to it. My dick stirred against my jeans. When had I last touched her like this? I tightened my grip on her ass and pulled her against me.

Her eyes flew up to meet mine.

"We have an hour." I backed her toward the couch set against one wall.

"An hour for—" Her legs hit the back of the couch and she fell onto it. I followed her down, my hand finding the hem of her shirt and dragging it up to reveal her breasts. As usual, she wasn't wearing a bra. I bent my head and captured a nipple between my teeth, flicking my tongue across the tip, and worked at the button on her shorts so I could push my hand beneath the denim. She gasped when my fingers found her clit.

"Dr. Santos said my homework was to be kind to myself." That wasn't quite how he'd put it, but I'd modify it to fit my needs. I pushed two fingers inside her.

She caught my wrist. "Your ribs ..."

"My stitches don't even factor into my needs right now. Take your shirt off." She stared at me. I pushed a third finger inside her, and pumped them roughly in and out. "Today, Shutterbug."

She surged into motion, pulling the shirt over her head and tossing it to the floor. I pulled my fingers free, unzipped her shorts and yanked them down her legs, along with her panties.

Dropping to my knees beside the couch, I hooked my hands around her hips and dragged her forward. "Lift your legs onto my shoulders."

"Seth—"

"Unless you're about to tell me to fuck you, I don't care to hear it. I want my mouth on your pussy. Legs... shoulders."

Her eyes were wide as she did as I said. "Much better," I whispered, and bowed my head so I could run my tongue over her clit.

When was the last time I'd done this? Buried my face between her legs and fucked her with my tongue? I didn't remember. That was bad. The last two weeks had been a shitshow, and Riley had done everything to keep me from coming apart. What had I done for her other than take what she offered and pushed her away when it suited me?

Self-care started at home, right? And Riley was my home. In which case, my theory was sound. Making her come on my tongue, then fucking her until she couldn't walk, was the best possible self-care I could give myself.

Neglected Consequences

CHAPTER 53

LOVERBOY - YOU ME AT SIX

Gabe

It was the moaning that clued me in to what was going on.

"You two should probably wait here," I told Harper and Tate, and continued along the path to Riley's studio.

The moaning grew louder the closer I got, and I couldn't keep a grin off my face when I stepped through the door to find Riley bent over the couch and Seth balls deep inside her. I propped a shoulder against the doorframe, and cleared my throat.

The reaction was everything I could have hoped for. Riley shrieked, dislodging Seth's dick in her scramble to cover her tits and pussy. Seth merely sighed and glared at me.

"Fuck off, Mercer." He caught Riley by her waist and hauled her back into position in front of him.

"Seth! Not while Gabe's here." She shoved at his hip.

I snorted. Seth swatted her hand away, and pulled her back onto his dick.

"You're not Harper. He's not even looking at you."

He wasn't wrong. I wasn't interested in Riley, naked or

otherwise. My attention was mainly on Seth's face and the wall beyond the pair of them. Watching other people fuck wasn't my kink. "I'm just letting you know we're here. I'll go make coffee." I backed out of the studio and closed the door, laughing to myself.

Harper and Tate were seated at the kitchen table.

"They're just wrapping up." I was still grinning. Harper's eyes narrowed. "He's getting his dick wet, Harper."

She huffed. "Do you have to put it like that?"

"What would you prefer? They're fucking? He's nailing her? She's riding the happy train?"

"Stop talking like that in front of your brother."

I laughed. "Tate's seventeen years old. There's no way he's not a horny teenager. I'm sure he wishes he'd been the one to walk in on them."

"Uhh, no," Tate said. "Old people sex isn't hot."

"Fuck you." I crossed to the coffee maker and flicked it on. "Thirty-two isn't old. We're in our prime."

"Keep telling yourself that."

I didn't rise to the bait and focused on making coffee. Seth and Riley, her face glowing red, came through the door just as I was placing the mugs on the table.

"You said an hour." Seth nailed me with a glare.

"It's been an hour. Not my fault you decided right now was the time to get down and dirty. I *told* you we were coming. Guess you decided you needed to come too." I smirked. "Come, too. Get it?"

"What the fuck is wrong with you?" He snatched up a mug

and took a swallow of coffee. "Don't even try to answer that. We'll be here all day listing your issues."

"Love you, too." I blew him a kiss.

He rolled his eyes.

"Do you want to go into another room so I can check on your stitches?" Harper asked.

Seth's gaze moved from me to her, and he nodded. "Why don't you take Tate down to my studio. You know which guitars he shouldn't touch." He tossed me a key. "I'll catch up with you soon."

"You'll like Seth's guitar collection," I said to Tate, spinning the key ring around my finger. "He has some limited editions."

"Which will remain in their cases or I'll break your fingers," Seth warned me on his way out of the door.

I laughed. "You heard him. Come on, Tate. Let's go see what kind of trouble we can get into."

***

Harper refused to remove Seth's stitches, much to his disgust, and insisted she call Chase to do it properly. We left the house just as the doctor arrived, and I told Seth to call me and give me an update.

Tate was still floating on a high after a two-hour jamming session with the guitarist of Forgotten Legacy, and he spent most of the journey to Lancaster talking about Seth. Hero worship was clear in his voice, but I managed not to tease him about it. Mostly because Harper was throwing me looks that said, loud and clear, she'd cut my balls off if I said a word to ruin his excitement.

His chatter only slowed down as we reached the outskirts of the city, and he eventually fell silent and stared out of the window. When Remy brought the car to a stop outside a small one-story house set back a few yards from the sidewalk, he was scowling at the floor.

The privacy screen slid down. "This is it," Remy said.

Tate shifted on his seat. "My parents work hard. It might not look like your house, but—"

"I grew up in a shitty apartment in the Fashion District," I cut in. "It's not how it looks. It's whether it's a hellhole or a home. Which is it, Tate?"

He looked at me. "My parents are good people, Gabe."

"I know." I reached forward and patted his shoulder. "So, do you want to introduce me or... are we just dropping you here?" I added the second part hurriedly, in case the last thing he wanted was to put me in front of his parents.

Harper's head came up, and she frowned at me. She was that attuned to my moods, and she would know I was bracing myself, waiting for Tate to decide I wasn't worth knowing. I ignored her and waited to see how Tate replied.

"My mom and dad will want to meet you." Oblivious to my inner turmoil, he threw open the car door and climbed out.

Harper's hand caught my sleeve, stopping me before I followed him. "He's not your father, Gabriel." Her voice was soft. "They raised a good kid, even if he's manifesting Gabe Mercer asshole behavior. From everything Tate has said, they're decent people, *good* parents."

I patted her hand but didn't reply, and followed Tate out of the car. The front door opened as we walked up the path, and a woman with graying blonde hair came running out. She threw her arms around Tate, who stood stiffly for a second, then relaxed and wrapped his arms around her waist and held on tight. His mom, I guessed.

I stayed a few feet away, not wanting to interrupt their reunion. Harper joined me, her hand reaching for mine. We didn't speak, and watched as Tate's mom drew back and caught his face between her palms.

"Don't you *ever* do something so stupid again! I thought you were dead. I've been worried sick."

"I'm sorry. I just needed some time to think, to figure things out. I had to find him, you know?"

"Thomas Mercer isn't someone you want in your life. He changed after his wife died."

I held back a flinch at that. While I *knew* my da was a piece of shit, hearing it come out of someone else's mouth still hit me like an arrow. Harper's fingers tightened around mine.

"He's dead," Tate said. "But I found Gabe." He twisted out of his mom's grip and turned to me. "Mom, this is my brother."

I found myself engulfed in a flowery scent as she wrapped me in a hug. It wasn't lost on me that my immediate reaction was the same as Tate's. I stiffened, then relaxed. Unlike Tate, I didn't hug her back, but I dropped a kiss on the top of her head.

"Thank you for bringing him home."

Neglected Consequences

CHAPTER 54

THIS IS GOSPEL - PANIC! AT THE DISCO

Harper

Florence Danvers, Tate's mom, perched on the edge of the couch, one hand gripping Tate's. Her husband, Oscar, had disappeared into the kitchen to make drinks. Gabe, consummate performer that he was, sprawled on the only armchair, looking relaxed and at ease. But I recognized the showman smile he was wearing. It didn't make his eyes shine the way his real smile did. He was on edge, nervous, and I could guess why.

His experience around parents had never been positive—especially around fathers. My mom had liked him well enough, but she was barely around because she worked long hours and left me alone more often than not. His da ... Well, the less said about him, the better. The only truly *decent* parents he'd known were Seth's. So his natural first reaction was to watch and wait. Add discovering he had a brother into that mix, and he was on edge, waiting to see how the younger boy had been treated.

For all Gabe's talk about how he was sure Tate's parents were good and decent and nice, until he saw evidence of it, he wouldn't relax.

Florence touched Tate's face, and the teen rolled his eyes. "Come on, Mom. I'm not a ghost. Stop poking me."

"I'm just making sure you're here."

"If I wasn't, Dad would be calling for you to get psychiatric help."

"Be nice to your mom, Tate." Oscar walked back into the room, carrying a tray of drinks. "She's been worried about you. You should have called sooner."

Gabe tensed at the disapproval in the man's tone, but Tate just shrugged.

"Florry said you're a singer in a band?" He threw the question at Gabe as he placed the tray on the coffee table.

"Yes, sir."

"Is it a hobby? What do you do to earn a wage?"

"The band is my income."

"Dad, Gabe is the frontman for Forgotten Legacy. They're one of the biggest rock bands in the world right now."

The man's eyes grew wide. "I thought Florry was joking when she said that."

Gabe looked almost apologetic. "I'm afraid not."

Oscar swung to face Tate. "And you're sure you found the right man?"

"They both did a DNA test to confirm," I explained. "We had

to be certain, given Gabe's fame. You wouldn't believe some of the strange claims that are made."

"I'm so glad you became someone important, Gabriel," Florence said. "Your mom would be so proud of you. She loved to sing. I bet you got that from her."

Gabe's face drained of color. "You … knew my mom?"

"We grew up together. We lost touch shortly after you were born and I moved out of Los Angeles with my then-boyfriend. When I went back to visit many years later, I found out she'd died. That's when I reached out to Thomas. You look so much like her."

"I've heard that before." Nothing in his voice indicated how much hearing those words were hurting him. And they *were* hurting him. I could see it in his eyes. His father had told him often how much he looked like her, how he hated looking at him because of it.

"I was there the day she brought you home." Florence smiled. "She and Thomas were so proud. He insisted you were named after her, since—in his words—she put all the effort into bringing you into the world."

"He loved my mother very much."

I wanted to go to him, reach for his hand, *anything* to give him something to hold on to, while he heard this woman reminisce about his parents.

"She was the love of his life. When she died, something broke inside him."

I wanted to scream at her to stop talking, to stop hurting him. I wanted to grab Gabe and drag him out. But he sat there, a smile on his lips, and let her slice him to ribbons as she talked about Gabriella and her storybook love affair with Thomas Mercer.

"They were childhood sweethearts, always together. Joined at the hip, our moms would say. Thomas always said he took one look at her and lost his heart for life."

Gabe's gaze shifted to me and my heart skipped a beat. Tate's mom could have been talking about us.

"So how did …" Gabe waved a hand toward Tate. "How did you end up with him?"

Florence blushed. "Like I said, I had reason to go back to Los Angeles and I wanted to see Gabi. I went to the address I had when I lived there and found out that Gabi had died, and Thomas had taken his son and moved out. It took me a while, but eventually, I got contact details for him and went to the apartment."

"I don't recall seeing you." Gabe's voice was soft.

"You were at school. Thomas said it was your birthday and he was going to take you out to dinner to celebrate."

"Celebrate." He repeated, and his eyes found mine again.

He didn't set her straight and I bit down on my lip to stop myself from saying something. It wasn't my place, and Gabe didn't seem to want to correct her.

"I had a meeting to go to; otherwise, I'd have stayed to see you. Instead, I gave him a photograph I'd found of your mom holding you. I'd taken it not long after you both came home from the hospital, and asked him to pass it to you."

A muscle clenched in Gabe's jaw. "He gave it to me. Thank you."

"Later that evening, I was with friends. We'd been out for a meal and stopped at a local bar. Thomas came in. We spent hours talking, reminiscing, and ... I guess we were both lonely and sad, and ..." She sighed. "Sometimes you just need a connection. I'm sorry, Tate, I love you very much, but that night was a mistake and should never have happened. We had a little too much to drink."

"Yeah, I don't need to hear about your past, Mom," Tate grumbled, and shoved to his feet. "I was an accident. That's my takeaway from what you're saying."

"A *happy* accident," she countered. "I never regretted keeping you."

"Why didn't you tell him about Tate?" Nothing in Gabe's voice gave away what he was feeling. *I* couldn't even read the expression on his face.

"When I found out I was pregnant, I *did* go back to L.A. He was drunk, scary drunk, and I realized that he would never want to have a baby with me. I wasn't Gabriella." The look she gave Gabe was full of regret. "I'm sorry, Gabriel. I ran out of there without even thinking about what your life must have been like. It can't have been easy living with a man who still mourned the loss of his wife."

I waited for Gabe to tell her what living with him was like, but he didn't. "It had its moments," was all he said. He reached for the coffee mug in front of him and took a mouthful, then licked his lips. "You said you grew up with my mom. I was four when she died. I don't really remember much about her, other than her singing to me."

Florence jumped to her feet. "Oh, wait right here. I have photographs!" She darted out of the room before Gabe could say anything.

"Great," Tate groaned. "Now we're going to be treated to hours of endless stories of Mom when she was a kid."

"Leave her alone, Tate," Gabe's voice was quiet.

"You can't want to sit here and stare at photographs, surely?"

"If it makes your mom happy, then I'll do it. Why don't you go out to the car with Remy? There's something for you in the trunk. Maybe it'll keep you quiet for a while."

Neglected Consequences

CHAPTER 55

NO MORE - HUDDY
Gabe

My heart was shredded. I don't know how I managed to keep smiling, ask questions, and behave like every single turn of the page to display a fresh photograph of my mom wasn't tearing me apart inside. The two hours spent listening to Florence recount stories of her friendship with my mom was flaying the skin from my body. But it was the little stories and anecdotes about how in love my parents were that twisted the knife and made me bleed a little harder.

I wrapped myself in the mantle of Gabe *Fucking* Mercer, and gave the best fucking performance of my life, just so the woman perched on the arm of the chair beside me didn't realize how much she was killing me.

There was a pain behind my eyes, a throbbing that would have had me reaching for a bottle of whiskey a couple of years ago. But I didn't let any of it show. Instead, I smiled and laughed and showed interest in everything Florence said.

Tate had vacated the room a while ago, dragging Remy up

to his bedroom to help set up the latest games console I'd picked up for him. My response to Oscar's protest was that the band had an online games night at least once a week, and we wanted him to join us to play. I'd also bought him a new cell phone *and* given him one of my guitars.

I wanted to do more, but Harper had cautioned baby steps. Get to know Tate and his family first, and see how they felt about my presence in his life. For all I knew, Tate would be sick of me after a few days. Once the novelty of his brother being a rock star wore off.

"Gabe." Remy appeared in the doorway, and I looked up from the photograph album on my lap. "We need to think about heading back. You have a meeting at NFG in the morning."

"Right." I stroked a finger over the photograph of my mom. "Thank you for showing these to me."

"How about I get copies made for you? You can pick them up next time you see Tate."

I lifted my gaze to meet hers. "You'd do that?"

She reached out and patted my cheek. "Of course I will." She gave a small headshake. "I can't believe how much you look like her."

I forced myself to smile, closed the album and handed it to her. "Thank you. We need to get moving. Is it okay if I go and say goodbye to Tate?"

"Upstairs, third door on the right."

***

Tate walked out with us to the car, endured a hug from Harper before she climbed into the car, then stood there and looked at me. He kicked his foot against the dirt.

"Game night is Thursday. Text me when you have your account name sorted out. My number is programmed into your new cell."

"You didn't have to do that. I didn't want to meet you because of what you are."

"I know that. I did it because I wanted to. Anyway, you can team up with me and help kick Luca and Dex's ass when we play."

"The guitar, though ..."

"I don't play often. Seth gets angry with me if I steal his thunder. We'll be heading back into the studio to work on a new album in a couple of months. Maybe you can come and jam with us."

"Really?"

"Don't see why not. We'll see if your mom and dad are okay with it. If you're not busy next weekend, I'll come and pick you up. We'll hang out, and figure out how this brother shit is supposed to work."

"You're not just saying that?" The wonder in his voice settled some of the insecurities I was feeling.

"No. We'll figure it out. I'm bound to fuck up. I'm good at that. Ask Harper. So you might need to cut me some slack, okay? I'm new to this."

"Me too."

"Okay then."

Neither of us moved. He glanced at me, then away. I blew out a breath, reached out and hooked an arm around his neck so I could haul him into a hug. "We'll figure this shit out, Tate." I ruffled his hair and stepped away, turning toward the car. "I better get out of here before someone spots me ... Oh ..." I swung back.

"The press has a way of finding out about things like this. If you spot anyone lurking, or feel like something weird is going on, let me know. Even if it's just a feeling, okay? Our fans don't understand boundaries sometimes. If that happens, you might need a security detail. Keep an eye on your surroundings, and don't hesitate to call me."

I ducked my head and climbed into the car. Tate backed up the path to his house, and stood in the doorway waving as we pulled away.

Once we turned the corner and he was out of sight, I dropped my head against the seat and closed my eyes.

Harper's fingers touched my face. "Are you okay?"

I reached up, caught her hand without opening my eyes and pressed a kiss to her palm. "Just give me a minute, Frosty. I need to ..." Need to do what? Process? Rebuild my defenses? Cry? Scream? I wasn't sure. I just needed a minute to recenter myself.

The rumble of the car engine, the warmth of Harper's body close beside me, and the scent of cotton candy grounded me, slowed my racing heart, soothed my ragged nerves, and lulled me to sleep.

I woke up disoriented, my head thick and fuzzy, and it took me a second to figure out Harper was talking to me. I used the heel of my hands to rub my eyes, blinked and focused on her face.

"Did I fall asleep?" I yawned around the words. "I'm sorry."

"You did. I'd have left you to sleep, but we're home."

Another yawn cracked my jaw, and I fought to keep my eyes open. Her fingers linked with mine. "Let's go inside."

I nodded, and almost crawled out of the car behind her. Exhaustion made my limbs heavy, and I barely had the energy to put one foot in front of the other. Harper's hand in mine was the only thing keeping me moving forward. She led me into the living room, and I fell onto the couch. Her lips brushed over my forehead.

"Go back to sleep," she whispered, and my eyes were already drifting closed before she finished the instruction.

CHAPTER 56

I'M NOT OKAY (I PROMISE) - MY CHEMICAL ROMANCE

Seth

I twisted from side to side in front of the bathroom mirror, examining my ribs. The doctor had removed the stitches two days ago, and I was checking to make sure it hadn't fucked up my tattoo alignment. I was sure there was a slight difference, but nothing noticeable unless you were inches from my chest… and the only person getting that close would be Riley.

"Seth?" The woman I was thinking about poked her head around the door. "Marcus DeMario just called. He wants you to call him back."

I let my shirt drop and walked out of the bathroom.

"Are you still obsessing over your tattoos?" She lifted the hem and stroked a finger over the feathers tattooed across my ribs. "They look fine. You can barely see the scar. Harper did a good job."

I quirked a brow. "Don't tell her that. I need to have something I can hold over her if I need it."

Riley laughed. "That's mean."

"And expected. Gabe would be disappointed if I didn't." I looked around. "Where's my cell?"

"On the bed."

I walked over and stroked a finger over the lacy underwear next to my cell. "Strategic product placement?" I smirked at the way her jaw dropped and her cheeks heated.

"No! I was putting clothes away, and you'd left your phone in here when you took a shower."

"Don't need to explain, Shutterbug. If you want me naked, all you have to do is say so. There's no need to set the scene. I'm pretty easy."

She stared at me. "Who *are* you?"

It was a good question. I felt different. It had been gradual over the past couple of weeks. A lightening of the burden that had weighed on me since childhood. I hadn't completely let go of everything, and I doubted I'd ever truly be *fixed* or get over what I'd lived through. But instead of ignoring my experiences, I was acknowledging them, thinking about them, and most importantly, talking about them. With Riley. With the therapist.

And with that opening up, something had unlocked inside me. A part of me that I only really shared with Gabe. A lighthearted side that wanted to tease Riley until she blushed ... amongst other things.

I pressed a finger beneath her chin and pushed her mouth closed, then leaned forward and kissed her. "Have I thanked you at all?"

"For what?"

My fingers stroked over her cheek, down her nose, and traced the outline of her lips. "For being everything I need."

Her green eyes were wide. I pressed another kiss to her lips. "Get used to it, Shutterbug. I'm just getting started." I left her staring at me, and turned to grab my cell and return Marcus's call.

He answered straight away. "I found him. He's still on the force in South Carolina. I made contact and asked if he'd be interested in meeting you."

"What did he say?"

"No hesitation. He wants to meet. I didn't tell him who you are now. Do you want to fly out there, or bring him here?"

"I'll go to him. Send me the details. Thanks, Marcus." I cut the call and tossed my cell onto the bed. "Want to go on an adventure with me, Shutterbug?"

***

"Do you want me to come with you?" I knew that would be Gabe's first question when I called to tell him my plan.

"No. I can slip in under the radar. Both of us getting off a plane there will cause a commotion."

"Yeah, but—"

"I'll be okay. I'm taking Riley. Stop worrying."

"I just feel like I should be there. Just in case." Why hadn't I ever noticed that Gabe was the worrier? Always looking for ways to mitigate problems and ready to take the brunt of the consequences of any bad decisions.

"Gabe." I kept my voice soft. "I got this. You don't need to protect me."

"I know I don't, but—"

I chuckled. "But it's who you are, just like I'd do the same for you."

He sighed down the line. "Fine. But call me and let me know how it goes."

"I will. Our flight is boarding. I'll talk to you later." My lips twitched. "Love you, Gabe." I hung up on him swearing and demanding to know if I was dying. Riley was rolling her eyes when I looked up. "What?"

"You're really going all out to scare everyone, aren't you?"

"Have I really been that much of a hard-ass?"

"Hard-ass doesn't even come close to describing you. They call you The Devil for a reason, remember?"

I tapped her nose. "Ahhh, but *you* call me Lucifer. The Lightbringer. Someone told me once that names have meaning, and sometimes what you're called helps to define who you are."

"Is that why you chose the name Seth?"

I didn't answer her until we were settled into our seats on the plane and buckled in for take-off.

"I didn't pick the name Seth."

"Really? Who did?"

"The man we're going to meet. Detective Mark Peterson."

Neglected Consequences

CHAPTER 57

HOUSE OF MEMORIES - PANIC! AT THE DISCO

Seth

AGE 9

For two days, we'd been kept in this room. For two days, I'd stood guard beside the door so Olivia could sleep. For two days, adults came in and out, asking questions and bringing food, drinks, and fresh clothing. There was a small bathroom attached to the room. Olivia had spent hours in the tub, while I listened for the door being unlocked, and dressed in the clothes they left us.

Not me, though. I still wore the shirt and pants they found me in. I drank water from the faucet and didn't touch the food. I had no intention of owing them anything. I already expected to pay for the things Olivia had taken.

The click of the lock alerted me to visitors. I shifted my stance and braced myself, ready to take on whoever walked in.

"Still the last bastion of defense between the world and your sister, Nate?" A familiar voice, the detective who'd spent that first day with us. Mark something ... I didn't remember. Last names weren't important, only first names and what they wanted from me.

I didn't reply, lowering my eyes to the floor, and waited.

"Jenna said you haven't been eating."

"I have, Mr. Peterson." Olivia spoke from behind me.

"It's Detective Peterson, Olivia, but you can call me Mark." His voice was gentle, and I went on high alert. What did he want? "Jenna is outside with some new things for you. Why don't you go and see her while I speak to your brother?"

"No." I threw my head up. "Livvy stays with me." My fingers curled into fists.

"Ah, now you look at me." He smiled. "I thought that would get your attention. She'll be in sight all the time, Nate. We'll leave the door open. I just need to talk to you alone."

Alone. I knew what *that* meant. I took a step back. "Liv, go outside. Don't come back in until I tell you."

"But I want to stay with you."

"You heard the detective. The woman has something for you. Go and see what it is. It might be cake." The cakes they'd been bringing with dinner were her favorite thing.

"I'm sure Jenna can find some cake for you." The detective smiled, but his eyes were on me.

I held his gaze and refused to look away. Out of the corner of my eye, I could see Olivia walking toward the door. Her fingers brushed against mine as she passed. Sometimes I wondered how much she understood about what was happening in our lives. Sometimes I hoped she had no understanding at all.

She started to close the door, and the detective reached back to stop her. "Leave it open, honey. Can you see Jenna?" He pointed along the hallway. "She's just at the end. See her?" Olivia nodded. "See the bag on the table? That's all for you. Go and see what she has." He gave her a gentle push, then turned back to me. "Do you want to look and see where she is?"

I shook my head. He moved closer. I held my ground.

"You're losing weight, Nate. You can't really afford to do that. You need to put some weight on; otherwise, you'll get sick. Have you drank anything at all?"

"I drink the water."

"From the bathroom?" he glanced toward the bathroom door. "Nate, that's not drinking water. That's for washing. If you prefer water over the drinks you've been getting, I can arrange for you to get bottled water."

"I'm fine."

"You will be, but you're not there yet." He sat on the edge of one of the beds. "Did you know Nathaniel means 'gift of God?'"

I frowned, confused by the change of subject.

"Some people believe names have power. Do you think so?" He chuckled. "I can see from your expression that you don't."

"If God was real, he wouldn't have *gifted* me to Raphael. I would rather have a different name. I don't want to be anyone's gift."

"That's one of the things I wanted to talk to you about. To protect you, we want to take you out of South Carolina and move you far away from here so you can have a fresh start. How does that sound?"

"With Olivia?"

"That's the plan." But his eyes shifted from me, and I knew he was lying.

"You can't separate us. She needs me."

"I'll do my best to make that happen. But before we can do that, you need to stop worrying everyone and work on getting healthy. No one is going to hurt you here, Nate."

I laughed, and he sighed.

"I wish I could prove it to you, but the only way that's going to happen is if you trust me. All the words and promises in the world mean nothing unless you test them for yourself." He reached into a pocket, and I stiffened, but all he took out was a candy bar. He showed it to me, then tore off the wrapper and snapped a piece of chocolate off. "Small steps." He held it out to me.

My stomach grumbled.

"Take the chocolate. Let me show you there's nothing to be afraid of."

I shook my head. Chocolate had been a favorite tool Raphael used.

Do this, then you can have a treat, Nate.

I *hated* chocolate.

"You're hungry. I can hear your stomach protesting."

"Daddy gives Nate chocolate when he's a good boy." Olivia trotted back into the room, a woman behind her, and took the candy from the detective with a huge smile. "He doesn't like chocolate, so he always saves it for me."

Something passed across the detective's face, fury and something else I didn't recognize. Fear locked up my muscles and made my mind scream at me to run.

"Olivia..." My voice broke. I cleared my throat. "Get behind me."

"It's okay, Nate." The detective looked at me. His voice was soft. "I'm not angry with you. I should have realized you didn't like chocolate." He glanced at the woman. "Jenna, why don't you take Olivia out for some air. She's been cooped up in here for days. It's not good for a kid to stay indoors all the time."

Olivia bounced up and down on her toes beside me. "That's okay, isn't it, Nate? I can go? I like Jenna. She's nice to me." She tugged on my hand when I didn't reply. "Please, Nate?"

My nod was jerky and Olivia threw her arms around me. "Thank you! Thank you! I'll be good, I promise. Jenna will be happy with me." I tensed at her words. She was repeating what I said whenever I told them to take me instead of her.

"There's a play area not far from here," the detective told the woman... *Jenna*. "Take her for ice cream afterward."

"Come on, sweetheart." Jenna held out her hand for my sister, who took it happily in hers and walked out without looking back.

I waited for him to close the door. He didn't.

"There's a cafeteria downstairs. Why don't we take a walk and get some lunch?"

***

Every day after that, Detective Mark Peterson came to the room

I shared with Olivia, sent her off with Jenna and took me for lunch. For the first three days, he filled the silence on his own, talking about his own children, his job, and his wife. He ordered food for us both, a different meal every day, and wouldn't leave the table until I'd taken at least one bite.

By day seven, my stomach was rumbling before he even arrived. I recognized the pattern of conditioning. He was teaching my body to associate him with food, and it was working. It was getting harder to resist reaching for the food placed in front of me. The smells made my mouth water, teasing my senses, and I was starting to believe it would be worth what would invariably come after, just to have a full stomach.

"I thought we'd try their mac and cheese today." He greeted me with those words when the door swung open.

I was ready, waiting by the door, like I had been every other day. He held out a bag. "First, though, I want you to go and change. One of us is going to get arrested if you carry on wearing those pants. You've lost so much weight, they're barely staying up. And that shirt has seen better days. Go into the bathroom, lock the door, and get changed. Then we'll go and eat."

I stared at the bag. He seemed to hold his breath when I finally reached out to take it from him. When I started to strip out of my clothes, he held out a hand. "Not here, son. Go and do it in private. You don't need an audience to change."

"You don't want to watch me?" That made no sense to me. Someone always wanted to watch me.

"No, I don't. You have a right to privacy. Don't let anyone ever make you believe otherwise."

Privacy. I sampled the word. I knew what it meant. I wasn't stupid.

"You need to take a leap of faith at some point, son," he said quietly. "Go and change."

For the first time in my life, I turned my back on an adult and trusted that nothing would happen while I wasn't watching, and hurried into the bathroom. Closing the door, I turned the lock and leaned against it. I upturned the bag, tipping the clothes onto the floor. Underwear, a t-shirt, jeans, socks and sneakers. I stripped out of the rags I was wearing and reached down to pick up the underwear, then stopped, catching sight of my reflection.

Yellowing bruises covered my ribs and dirt smudged my skin. Did I have time to wash? I shouldn't put the new clothes on without being clean. I turned in a circle. There was a towel hanging on a bar on one wall. I chewed on my lip.

"Do I have time to wash?" I called out.

"Take as much time as you need," the detective replied.

I checked the door was locked, then stepped into the shower and switched it on. The sensation of hot water hitting my skin startled me. I'd been expecting it but actually *feeling* it was something else, something new. The showers back home were always ice-cold and came with other things I didn't want to think about.

I don't know how much time passed, but my skin was wrinkled when I finally dragged myself out of the small shower cubicle, dried, and pulled on the clothes.

I felt different. Almost as if the shower had washed away some of the things I'd lived through. I felt stronger. Ready to face the man waiting for me beyond the door. I felt *hungry*. I looked at my reflection, dragged a hand through my hair so it didn't flop down into my eyes, and took a deep breath.

"A leap of faith," I whispered to myself, then straightened and walked out of the bathroom.

***

I poked around the plate of gooey mess, unconvinced that it was edible. The detective laughed.

"Try it."

"It looks like vomit."

"It's pasta, cheese, and a magic sauce."

My lip curled. "There's no such thing as magic."

"Tell me that after you've tried it. Mac and cheese is a comfort food. I think you'll like it. One mouthful, Nate. That's our agreement. You'll try a mouthful of everything we order. That's what you said."

"What's comforting about it?" I was pushing it. I knew that. But my mood had changed since the shower and the fresh clothes. He'd told me to take a leap. If it backfired and I ended up hurt, at least I'd tried and proved no one could be trusted.

"It's warm and tasty and makes you feel good."

I sneered. "Madam Caroline described me like that."

"Then it's time to link that phrase with something better.

Try the mac and cheese, Nate."

He pushed the plate closer to me. I couldn't deny it smelled good.

"One mouthful," I said.

"One mouthful," he agreed, a slight smile tilting one side of his mouth.

I frowned. "What's funny?"

"Absolutely nothing. You're stalling." He tapped my fork. "Follow through on our agreement, Nate."

I shoved the fork into the food on the plate, then lifted it to my mouth. The flavor exploded on my tongue, my eyes widened, and I gasped, choked, spluttered, then caught myself. A second mouthful followed the first, then a third. When I cleared the plate, the detective silently slid his across to me and I devoured that one as well.

When I was finally done, I leaned back on the chair. My stomach ached. I didn't care. I'd never eaten anything so incredible.

"Mac and cheese was a hit, then. Maybe we should have started with that."

"It's how I imagine heaven would taste."

He chuckled. "I'm not sure we can top that, but would you like to try a dessert today? And something to drink other than water? Or is that pushing it too far?"

But I was nodding eagerly.

He gave me a wide smile, eyes dancing with humor. "Alright, then. Let's see what they have. You don't like chocolate, so chocolate cake is out. Do you want a hot or cold drink?"

"Hot."

"You're too young for coffee, really, but I think under the circumstances we can ignore that. How about apple pie and ice cream?"

"Okay."

I was contemplating licking my plate to make sure I got all the remaining drops of ice cream when he next spoke.

"Do you remember the conversation we had about names?"

I glanced up at him.

"I've noticed every time anyone says your name, you tense up. I have a pretty good idea of why that happens, so you don't need to explain. But I was thinking … Your name is linked with your experiences, with everything you have been through. Do you understand that?"

I nodded.

"What if you could change that? You could pick a new name, and start afresh. How would you feel about that?"

"A new name?" I repeated.

"A new name. A new start."

I considered it. "For Livvy too?"

"For both of you."

"I'd like that."

"I want to tell you a story, which might help you decide on a name."

I wrapped my hands around the mug of coffee, and breathed in the smell of it. I liked it. It made me feel safe. It made me feel *warm*.

"Do you know the story of Cain and Abel?"

"I guess. One of them killed the other one, right?"

"That's right. Did you know there was a third son? According to the Bible, he was sent to Adam and Eve to heal their heartbreak after the loss of their son."

"I didn't know that."

"He was called Seth. It means 'placed' or 'appointed.' I think that describes you very well. You've appointed yourself as your sister's protector."

"Seth." I said the name out loud. "*Seth*." I liked how it sounded. It sounded strong ... and I really wanted to be strong.

CHAPTER 58

MEMORIES - MAROON 5

Seth

My leg bounced beneath the table, the only outward sign of nerves I displayed, as we sat in the interview room at the police station. Why did I suggest I meet him here? It made sense when I said it. This was the room I'd met him in all those years ago. But now, sitting here, I was rethinking it.

The room didn't look any different from how I remembered. The walls were still a dull gray, the table bolted to the floor, and uncomfortable metal chairs. But I'd wanted to revisit it. To see how my mind reacted to the memory.

My stomach churned when we were shown inside, and my mouth dried up, but I didn't run screaming from the room, so that was something. When I'd told Dr. Santos that I was coming to see the man, the detective who had been the first person to show me how different adults could be, he'd approved of the idea. When I told him my plan was to meet him in the room I'd first laid eyes on him, he hadn't been so enthusiastic. But he understood why I needed to do it, so he spent time preparing me for the possibility of flashbacks or PTSD episodes.

PTSD.

I'd never considered that as something I suffered from. I always thought PTSD was something someone suffered from after being a soldier or a veteran of war. Yet, once Dr. Santos explained it to me, it made perfect sense.

"Are you okay?" Riley's voice was low.

I nodded. "I was standing right over there when he walked in for the first time." I pointed to a corner. "Lexi was behind me, and I had a hard time stopping her from taking the food that had been left on the table. She was hungry, we both were, but I couldn't be sure what would happen if we took it."

I wet my lips, rubbed my hands together, then shoved to my feet.

"Where are you going?" Riley rose beside me.

"Nowhere. I just can't sit still." I prowled the room, wall to wall, door to table. What was taking so long? Had he changed his mind? Maybe he didn't remember me. He'd been a cop for years. Why would I stand out in his memory?

My back was to the door when it opened, then clicked closed. I didn't turn. Footsteps crossed the floor, the sound of a chair being dragged out, then the clink of something metal touching the tabletop.

I turned slowly, feet dragging, and swept my gaze across the room until they landed on the man seated at the table. Riley stood where I'd left her, her eyes darting from me to him and back again.

"I told you names had power, didn't I, Seth?" That crooked smile sent a surge of familiarity through me.

I couldn't move. A lump blocked my throat. I couldn't breathe.

"You were a lot smaller the last time I saw you." He tapped the table. "Are you going to come and sit down or stare at me from over there?" He slid the metal container in front of him across the table. "Do you remember our agreement?"

"Agreement?" Riley asked when I didn't speak.

"Seth had trust issues when he was younger. No one could get him to eat and our medical team was growing concerned. I got him to agree to taste a mouthful of whatever I ordered from the cafeteria menu, in return for toys for Lexi. One mouthful every day for a week."

"You would have given Lexi the toys anyway." I finally found my voice.

"Of course I would, but that wouldn't have got you to eat, would it? You were a challenge, boy."

"What is in the tin?" I jerked my chin at the container.

"Why don't you open it and find out?" He leaned back on the chair. "Of course, that means you'll have to come over here."

"I'm not a scared little boy anymore. You don't have to try and entice me."

"You never were a scared little boy, Seth." His voice was warm. "You were a survivor."

I pulled out the chair opposite him and sat down. My fingers touched the container. It was warm. "What is this?"

He reached into a pocket, pulled out a fork wrapped in a napkin and held it out to me. "One mouthful, Seth."

Riley frowned, puzzlement written across her features. I cocked an eyebrow, took the napkin and unwrapped the fork, then prised the lid off the container. A familiar smell hit me, memories flooded me, and I closed my eyes and took a deep breath, and then lifted my lids to look at him.

"It still looks like vomit."

"Best comfort food on the planet."

"You got that right," I whispered, and ate a mouthful of the mac and cheese. The flavor, like it had all those years ago, exploded on my tongue. "I've never been able to find another that tastes quite like this one."

"That's because my wife makes it. She made every meal you tried until we hit on one you liked."

"Your wife?"

"Jenna. Do you remember her?"

"The woman who looked after Lexi." I nodded. "I didn't know she was your wife." I ate another mouthful, savoring the taste. "I might need to steal her from you."

Detective Mark Peterson chuckled. "She'd let you. All our kids have left the nest. She has no one other than me to cook for anymore." His smile faded. "I heard about Lexi. I'm sorry."

"She's better off now. She never really tried to live. The only reason she hung on was because of me." I could admit that now without breaking apart. It wasn't my fault she had died. None of it was my fault. And the first man to ever tell me that was sitting in front of me.

"We wanted to foster you, you know. That's why you were here for longer than the others we rescued. But eventually, it was decided that because I was too close to the case, it wouldn't be right and you needed a fresh start somewhere else."

I stilled, the fork halfway to my mouth. I considered telling him about the foster families we'd gone through, the good and bad, but decided against it.

When a female officer came in and offered drinks. I declined and suggested I take the detective and his wife out for dinner instead.

"If you want, that is." I couldn't stop myself from adding, just in case he needed an excuse not to.

"Of course, I want to." He reached across the table and covered my hand, where it still gripped the fork. "Seth, you have no idea how many times I've thought about you over the years. Wondered how you were, and what you'd achieved with your life. We'd have conversations, me and the wife, wishing we could figure out a way to find you, just to make sure you were safe. I even considered hiring a PI once, but Jenna told me that you might not want to *be* found, so I never went through with it."

"I wish you had." I blinked away the burning sensation building behind my eyes. "I've been on a quest to find a mac and cheese as good as this one. All those years lost." My quip made him laugh, as intended. "How about we pick you up at seven? I'll book a table somewhere."

CHAPTER 59

FORGIVE - TREVOR HALL

Gabe

I pulled the ball cap low over my forehead and slid on a pair of sunglasses before I climbed out of the car. Dressed in dark jeans and sneakers, I'd left off my rings and wrist wraps in favor of a long-sleeved shirt that covered my tattoos, so from a distance, I wouldn't stand out as unusual.

Remy stayed a short distance away, making it look like he wasn't with me, as I wandered through the cemetery. I *knew* where the grave I wanted was. I just needed to work up the courage to actually get there. I'd never visited, hadn't given it much thought, but Tate's words echoed around my head and I couldn't rest until I paid a long-overdue visit.

I wandered around, pausing to read the different inscriptions, marveling over the dates on some, but eventually, I had to stop stalling and turned my body toward the location I needed to be.

My footsteps slowed the closer I got, until Remy muttered behind me. "If you go any slower, it's going to be obvious I'm following you. At that point, either people will realize I'm a bodyguard, or they'll think I'm a stalker and call the police."

I threw him a frown over my shoulder, not that he could see it from behind my sunglasses, and picked up my pace.

The white marble gleamed in the sunlight, and the area around the grave was neat and tidy. A bouquet of orchids and lilies sat in a crystal vase at the base of the stone. I paid to have them replaced every two weeks. My gaze drifted over the inscription.

Gabriella Mercer
Eternally loved, endlessly missed
Always and Forever

I brushed an imaginary speck of dust off the top of the marble. "Hey, Mom."

I talked for an hour, told her about the band, about Harper, about the foundation for abused kids. I told her about Tate, my eyes turning to the grave beside hers, before shifting back. "I wonder if things would have been different if he'd known he had another son." My attention drifted to the other grave again, the stone dark, contrasting to the white of my mom's. I rested my palm against her name. "I miss you. I always will. I'm sorry I didn't come around. I'll do better."

I turned to the other grave.

Thomas Mercer
Husband. Father.
Finally at peace

"I wish I could say I miss you, but I don't. I sometimes wonder what could have been, but how can you miss what you didn't have? You were an asshole for most of my life, but do you know something? I understand. I get it. When I lost Harper ... for two years I lived your life. I ... I mourned the loss of the only love I'd ever have, and I took it out on the people closest to me. So ... I get it."

I pulled my lighter from a pocket and flicked it open, staring into the flame. "I don't know what happens after we die. Part of me hopes there is a hell and you're burning in it, but the rest of me hopes you're with Mom, and that you've found peace."

Snapping the Zippo closed, I pocketed it and crouched in front of the headstone, then reached out and plucked a lily from my mom's grave and placed it on my da's.

"I forgive you."

CHAPTER 60

ANIMAL - BADFLOWER

Seth

Dinner was ... easy. I wasn't sure what to expect, and I wondered if it would be awkward, but Mark and Jenna were comfortable to be around. They asked questions about my life and the band. We talked about my mom and dad. Riley shared the story of how we met, and teased me with comments about how mean I'd been to her when I brought her on tour with us all those years ago.

The hours passed quickly, and we dropped them back at their home after securing a promise from them that they'd come to L.A. soon to visit and meet my parents. Less than an hour later, we were back in our hotel room.

I lay on the bed, flicking through the television channels until I found something to watch, while Riley did whatever it was she did in the bathroom before coming out to join me. The light was off, and I didn't pay much attention when she slipped beneath the sheets beside me, engrossed in watching the Formula One race playing out on the screen in front of me. It was only when her fingers stroked down my arm, that I dragged my attention away from the screen and turned my head to look at her.

"Did you mean what you said the other day?"

"About what?"

"How if I wanted you naked, all I had to do was say so."

"I meant it. Why? Do you want me naked, Shutterbug?"

Her lips curved up. "I do. But I want to talk to you first, and you being naked distracts me."

"I see. What do you want to talk about?"

She bit her lip, then moved, climbing over my legs so she could straddle my hips and face me. Her hands lifted to rest on my shoulders. My eyes dipped, noting the dark red lacy bra she was wearing. It looked familiar, possibly the same one that had been laid out on the bed when I'd made the naked comment she'd referenced.

"I love you."

I quirked a brow. "But?"

She frowned. "There is no but."

"There's a silent but at the end of that sentence." I hooked a finger into her bra strap and drew it off her shoulder. "I love you, but..."

"There is *no* but," she repeated firmly. "I *love* you."

"But..."

She huffed. "I just wanted to say that over the last few weeks, I've learned a lot more about what you went through." Her fingers stroked over my shoulders. "I understand why sex isn't really that important to you."

My head tilted, and I frowned. "Sex is important to me."

"I know you enjoy it ... at least I hope you do ... with me, I mean." Pink stained her cheeks. "I'm just saying that you don't have to ... you know ... do it all the time ... just when you want to. I won't ever be upset if you don't ... want to ... I mean ..."

I stared at her. The color in her cheeks deepened.

"Let me get this straight. If I tell you I don't want to have sex with you, it won't upset you?" I arched a brow. "Is that what you're telling me?"

"Yes ... no ... I mean ... of course, *I* want to have sex with *you*. But I understand that—" She shrieked when I twisted and dropped her onto her back on the mattress.

My hands landed on either side of her head, and I leaned down above her. "Let me make something very clear to you. I enjoy having sex *with you*. I'm happy to get naked with you any time you want. I'd probably keep you naked all day if it wasn't frowned upon by general society. I *like* seeing you naked. I like burying my face into your pussy. I like making you come. I like having my dick so deep inside you I can feel your heart beating."

She frowned. "Is that even possible?"

I laughed. "No, it's poetic license to get my point across." I lowered my head and nipped at her bottom lip. "That point being having sex isn't an issue. The issue is I don't *think* about making it clear that I want to. I spent so many years *not* having sex, that I need help breaking the habit." I dragged my tongue down her throat. "Anytime you want to give me a hand with that, feel free to instigate things."

Her hands lifted, fingers threading through my hair so she could pull my head back up to hers. "In that case," she whispered, pressing a kiss to my jaw, "do you want to get naked with me?"

Neglected Consequences

AUTHOR NOTE

I know. I *know*.

I said it was over.

I said Broken Halo was the end.

I know!

It wasn't really a lie. When I wrote Broken Halo, it *was* the end. I hadn't planned to write another full length book. You need to blame Claire Marta for it. Go ahead. I'll wait ...

Back? Okay, so Claire was brainstorming ideas with me one day, and everything she brought up I'd already done and then something she said took root, and I slept on it, thought about it, and realised I had to write it.

The result is what you're holding in your hands.

I always knew Seth had more to say, but didn't think he'd ever want to. I always felt that Gabe needed more. And both things evolved into this book. Once I started writing it, I couldn't stop. The words flowed. I had the entire thing done in four weeks.

And then I couldn't tell anyone, because I wanted it to be a surprise. I sat on this book for MONTHS! (To give context, I finished writing it on 17th September 2022, and it didn't release until February 2023.) You have no idea how difficult it was not to tease this book.

Anyway, I hope you forgive me.

PS ... guess what?

There's another book coming ... ;)

There's now a Forgotten Legacy Discussion group where I pop in occasionally so you can yell at me.

https://www.facebook.com/groups/forgottenlegacyrockstarseries

If you're not already a member, you can join me in my
Facebook Group
https://facebook.com/groups/lannsliterati

I also have a **newsletter** where you get a free novella for signing up!

https://lannauthor.com/keep-in-touch

BOOKS BY L. ANN

FORGOTTEN LEGACY SERIES
Tattooed Memories - Book 1
Strawberry Delight - Short Story
Strawberry Lipstick - Short Story
Shattered Expectations - Book 2
Guarded Addiction - Book 3
Exquisite Scars - Book 4
Broken Halo - Book 5
Strawberry Spotlight - Short Story
Neglected Consequences - Book 6

CHAMBERS BROTHERS SERIES
Rook - Book 1
Bishop - Book 2

BLACK ROSARY SERIES
Fractured Angel - Book 1
Hushed Rapture - Book 2

MIDNIGHT PACK SERIES

Midnight Touch - Book 1

Midnight Temptation - Book 2

Midnight Torment - Book 3

Midnight Hunt Book 3.5

Midnight Fury - Book 4

CHURCHILL BRADLEY ACADEMY SERIES

Dare To Break - Book 1

Dare To Take - Book 2

Dare To Fall - Book 3

Dare To Live - Book 4

Printed in Great Britain
by Amazon